DEATH WITH A TWIST

AN EXILED GRIM REAPER URBAN FANTASY NOVEL

RED CITY REAPER
BOOK 3

C. THOMAS LAFOLLETTE

RED CITY REAPER

Book 0 - Dead in Red City*
Book 1 - A Shot For Death - March 26, 2024
Book 1.5 - Death Uncaged - March 21, 2024
Book 2 - Death Orders a Double - July 23, 2024
Book 3 - Death With A Twist - November 7, 2024
Book 4 - Death On The Rocks* - February 25, 2025
Book 5 - A Fifth Of Death*
Book 6 - A Dash Of Death*
Book 7 - A Chaser of Death*
Book 8 - A Nightcap of Death *

*Forthcoming
Titles and release dates may be subject to change.

DEATH WITH A TWIST
C. Thomas Lafollette

A Broken World Publication
13820 NE Airport Way
Suite #K395495
Portland, OR 97251-1158
Death With A Twist
Copyright © 2024 by C. Thomas Lafollette
ISBN 978-1-960766-17-5
(ebook);
ISBN 978-1-960766-18-2
(paperback)

Cover Design: Ravven
Editing & Proofreading: Amy Cissell

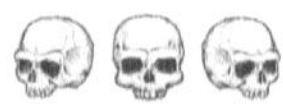

CONTENTS

AUTHOR'S NOTE

This story contains words and phrases in Louisiana Creole and Haitian Kreyòl. They are spelled according to Creole and Kreyòl standards.

ONE

DAX

Morty, his tiny kitten head poking out the door of his litter box, folded his ears back and crouched. Slightly narrowing his eyes, the black and white tuxedo kitten exploded out of the box, a spray of litter following in his wake as he tore across the house.

Dax shook his head and grimaced. "Fuck, dude. I just swept the floor. You do realize you don't need to do a mad dash through the house after you take a dump, right?"

In answer, Morty skidded to a halt in the kitchen, slowing just enough to launch himself at the cupboard door and spring off it like a starting block.

Sighing, Dax grabbed his lightweight denim jacket from the closet but paused instead of putting it on to watch the kitten attempt to slide on the rug near the door. Unfortunately for the rambunctious kitten, his claws got snagged in the rug and he tumbled into a heap against the door.

Dax chuckled and bent over to the scoop up the kitten. "Looks like it's time to trim those again, huh?"

Morty flattened his ears and attacked Dax's nearest finger, chomping on it hard enough to demonstrate his annoyance but not enough to break skin or really hurt. He'd chomped on Dax's denuded bones too many times to try to bite much harder. Sloughing off his mortal flesh, at least on his hands, had turned out to be the most effective way for Dax to keep his hands from being filled with kitten teeth and needle-sharp claws.

Setting the kitten on the floor and aiming him away from the door, Dax gave him a gentle pat on the bottom, which sent the kitten sprinting across the living room and into the apartment's single bedroom. Dax took the opportunity to slip out the door quickly. The kitten delighted in darting out of the apartment and forcing his owner to chase him around their floor of the apartment building.

As soon as the door clicked shut and he locked it, he pulled on the denim jacket. It wasn't cool enough out to need it, but it would keep the sun off his pale white arms. Plus, it was cooler in the underground warrens of Red City where they'd planned to meet The Rat that evening.

After a quick elevator ride to the bottom floor, Dax entered the gated residence's garage. He smiled at the shiny black 1965 Lincoln Continental hardtop parked in his spot. He missed his motorcycle, which had recently been blown up by an assassin, but the car was a balm for his missing bike. And it kept him drier on rainy days, though most of those were behind him as the city careened into summer.

He'd been glad to get the car after his friend Boudreaux and his crew had finished getting it polished up and its origins hidden. One didn't want to be caught driving a car stolen from one of Red City's über-rich and recently deceased corrupt patriarchs.

The ride to Madame Thibodeaux's magic shop was smooth as silk, though finding a parking spot for the land yacht wasn't the easiest task once he arrived. As he approached the door, the open sign dangling on the door flipped over to indicate the shop was now closed.

"Yo, Dax!" Tomi, his tall, fat, Black friend and business partner, jogged up to him from the other long side of the triangular-shaped building. He was dressed in his usual black T-shirt, black jeans, and black Chuck Taylors.

"You got everything?" Dax asked.

Tomi paused to catch his breath. "Yeah. In the car." Dax made to raise an objection but stopped with his mouth open when Tomi raised a hand. "Don't worry. Anything perishable is in a cooler."

Nodding, Dax grabbed the handle of the magic shop's door and opened it, letting Tomi slide in first before he closed it and secured the lock.

At the sound of the bell dangling near the top of the door, a tall, Black trans woman slipped through the bead curtain separating the office and stockroom from the public part of the store. Today, she wore a green and yellow dress with a black turban. Dax wasn't sure if he'd ever seen her hair in the few months he'd known her.

"Right on time as always, Dax."

"Delphine." Dax nodded.

Pulling him into a hug, she kissed first his left cheek, then his right.

He raised an eyebrow at the unexpected gesture.

She winked at him. "I'm feeling European today." She repeated the gesture with Tomi, who replied in kind. "Tomi, always a pleasure."

"Manman Delphine," he said to acknowledge her greeting.

She stepped back, her eyes narrowing as she looked from Tomi to Dax and back again. "Good, you're both still wearing the protection gris-gris I made for you."

Dax raised an eyebrow at the casual comment with its ominous undercurrent. "I doubt the bikers are going to give up after we killed their assassin. They're still going to want blood for what I did to their clubhouse."

"I know. Boudreaux called me a bit ago, wanting to make sure you were meeting him."

"I've never missed one with him before, why is he so antsy about this one?" Dax narrowed his eyes.

This was supposed to be a simple drop off of a bit of thanks for all The Rat and his minions had done to help save Dax. The Rat still didn't feel comfortable contacting anyone else directly, choosing to go through his chosen source — Boudreaux.

"I know, but I don't think it was for Boudreaux himself, so much as him calling on behalf of The Rat. Dreaux implied The Rat has something to tell you."

Tomi groaned. "That can't be good."

Dax was inclined to agree with his friend. "I guess it's a good thing we're scheduled to meet him today."

"Maybe he just wants to add some other fancy cheeses to his list…" Tomi's tone sounded overly optimistic.

"Could be, but I doubt it." Dax sighed. "I'd love to chat for a bit, Delphine, but your news is a bit distracting."

"I understand, cher. Don't worry, I've got the package ready for you. Besides, tonight is card night, and I need to leave so I can pick up a bottle of wine to share with the ladies." She turned, walked to the counter, and picked up a box sitting by the register. "Give this to him with my compliments. I've written the instructions out for him. They're inside."

Taking the box, Dax smiled and nodded at her in thanks.

Tomi winked at Delphine. "Try not to take too much of Mama's money tonight."

Delphine snorted. "If only. If I lose many more games to her, she'll end up owning my shop." She flicked her fingers in a shooing motion. "Now you boys should scoot. The Rat is waiting."

TWO

JAMIE

"I'm going out," Jamie muttered just loud enough for her mother to hear. The late afternoon June weather was too nice to be cooped up in a dank hotel with her cranky mother. "Where—"

Jamie cut off the question by shutting the door firmly—not quite a slam, but harder than a regular close. She knew avoiding her mom was unfair, but she couldn't manage her mother's depression and anger on top of her own.

In the days since Jamie had fled from Ivar into the tunnels of Red City, she hadn't talked much or felt like she had much to say. Well, the latter wasn't exactly true. She had a lot to say to her mom about the road that had led to her father going into hock with a white-supremacist biker gang. She'd even tried to bring it up in those first days when she'd been reunited with her mother after helping Dax and his friends "deal" with the assassin. Jamie had been framed by that assassin for another attempted murder on Dax.

She was tired of being involved in murder attempts on Dax. One of those attempts belonged to her, but she'd made right on it.

There'd been a moment or two of potential progress in her relationship with her mother as they scrambled to pack up their belongings from the long-stay motel to move to their next temporary situation. The mental exhaustion of having to move yet again added to the rest of the weariness dragging her down. The lack of a permanent home joined a long litany of disasters that had plagued her since her father got their family mixed up with a gang of Nazi bikers.

When he'd left, it hadn't been the first time her mom had kicked her dad out of the house, but there was no way he'd be coming home this time. His body was buried under the rubble of the morgue, thanks to the bomb the assassin had set for Dax. But the bit of communication with her mom had only been a passing detente in their ongoing cold war. Jamie had tried to keep the conversation going, but as soon as the door closed on their new temporary lodging, her mother's wall went back up.

Jamie had shot a man—nearly killing him if what they'd told her was true. Then her father had been murdered as another ploy to involve her in an assassin's attempt to kill that same man. Only, Dax wasn't a man, but a cosmic horror who'd nearly killed her and Cory. She still couldn't believe he'd let them live after she confessed she was the one who'd tried to kill him.

Though after saving him from being buried alive in the morgue explosion and helping him track down the assassin, she had probably made it off his shit list…hopefully permanently.

She just wanted to finish high school and get on with her life. Graduation was tomorrow. But somehow that seemed farther away than ever at the moment. She growled low in her throat as she kicked the door leading to the motel's parking lot open, pulled up the hood of her sweatshirt, and stalked away from the building.

She'd been naive and stupid to think she was the only solution to the biker gang's vendetta against Dax. If they'd wanted it done thoroughly, they had plenty of hardened killers in the ranks, including whoever else had shot at him however many times. She'd lost count of how many attempts had been made on his life.

They hadn't set her the task to achieve killing Dax, they'd set it all up to destroy her and her family as punishment for her dad's debts. She cursed herself again, angry and ashamed of her naiveté and actions. She might not be a murderer, but she'd sure as fuck attempted it.

The bikers had won, though maybe not as thoroughly as they'd intended. Her family was falling apart. Her dad was dead, and she and her mother barely spoke to each other. And she'd lost her best and only friend.

After all that had happened to Cory, thanks to her, his mother had forbidden him from seeing Jamie anymore, sold his car, and put the house up for sale. The nice house located in a good neighborhood had sold quickly. Soon, Cory and his mom would leave town. His mother wouldn't even tell him where they were moving.

Cory's mom Linda had been like a second mom to her. Linda had said she felt bad about severing her and Cory's friendship, had even teared up, but when push came to shove, she'd abandoned Jamie. That betrayal probably hurt more than anything.

Jamie kicked at a rock, sending it skittering across the debris-covered ground until it bounced off the trunk of a tree. At least she and Cory still had school, though that was over too. They'd spent every free moment together, trying to avoid the inevitable severing of their friendship while worrying at it constantly.

She'd looked forward to graduating so she would be one step closer to getting out of her parents' place. Now because of everything, Cory's mom was making him to take a year off and reapply to new schools while Jamie would be stuck going to Redemption City Community College, and even that was looking like an increasingly distant possibility. RCCC wasn't the worst place, other than it was still in Red City, but it wasn't a four-year university. She'd gotten into a couple of good schools, but even with scholarships, her family couldn't afford any of them, especially after they had to move to get out of the apartment they'd been kidnapped from.

Unlike Cory and Linda, Jamie and her mom didn't have enough money to even make it to the next town over. Their only solution was to lie low and do everything possible to avoid the bikers' notice. Though Dax had done a good job eliminating the threat against them, thinning out the bikers' numbers drastically.

Sighing, she stopped, checking to see where she was. Her feet had carried her toward Cory's house, like they had so many times before whenever she'd been upset.

Her knees shook, and she sank to the curb, resting her elbows on her knees and placing her head in her hands. At first, the tears started slowly but quickly turned into full sobs. Good thing it wasn't raining. Some jerk would likely have driven by and splashed her. Although rain would've at least hidden her tears, if not the sounds of her crying.

Eventually, her tears dried up, but she kept her head down and stared at the pavement. Nearby, a car screeched to a halt and bumped into the curb.

She looked up to see a tall, familiar form step out of the driver's-side door.

"Jamie?" Cory called. "What are you doing there?"

"I don't know. I just started walking and ended up here. What are you doing?"

"Came looking for you. We're leaving after graduation. I…I wanted to see you before I left." Cory held his hands in front of his stomach, practically wringing them.

Jamie stood up. "Won't you get in trouble with mommy?"

Cory winced at her tone. "Probably." He sighed. "It's our last day to be together. Do you want to go for a run?"

She wanted to say something else biting about him running away but stopped before it could leave her lips. "Alright, one last run."

"We've always got email… Once I'm living on my own, maybe…"

She shook her head. "It's a nice idea. We'll see…" Striding forward, she pulled him into a tight hug.

Cory wrapped his arms around her. "I'm sorry about—"

"Don't say it. I don't want to hear it. Let's just go have a last run and a hamburger. I assume you're going to buy me one last hamburger, right?"

Cory laughed "Two even, if you want."

Her stomach gurgled, though she wasn't sure if it was angst or hunger. "I might take you up on that."

"Well, let's get off this street then." Cory waved at the car and returned to the driver's side.

Jamie climbed in and got settled, staring out the window as Cory pulled away from the curb. They maintained an awkward silence as he wove through neighborhoods toward the outskirts of Red City and through Culver, a nicer suburb. Good thing Cory had borrowed his mother's car. His old, beat-up Hyundai probably would have drawn attention from the overzealous Culver cops looking to keep out the riffraff. A couple of teens from Red City certainly would have qualified.

As they drove up the hills surrounding the valley, her interest piqued. They'd never run up this way before. When he parked in an empty lot of Granville State Park, she became excited, pushing her terrible mood to the background.

"I figured we'd go out with a bang," Cory said, unbuckling his seatbelt.

Granville State Park was one of the last pieces of old-growth forest in the area; the rest had been cut down to fuel the profits of the elite who owned and ran Red City. Cory grabbed a camouflage backpack from the backseat and headed into the tree line. After the car was no longer in sight, they stepped behind the massive trunk of an ancient Douglas fir that reached up into the sky.

Stripping down, they stashed their clothes in the backpack. After zipping it, Cory shoved it under the fronds of a large fern and scooped some fir needles over it to further hide it. He smoothed out the area to make it look natural to any casual observers. Without a word, they blurred into their wolf forms.

It seemed like years since the last time she'd been in her wolf form for a fun run. Lately, it had all been mad dashes to save her life. She shook out her fur, reveling in the feel. She wanted to lift her head and howl but resisted the urge. They were too close to the road.

Nearby, Cory gamboled about, hopping on his back legs, his tongue lolling out. She opened her jaw in a wolfy grin at her friend's goofiness. Narrowing her eyes, she looked deeper into the woods, then bunched her muscles and tore off, skirting the trunks of the giant trees.

Behind her, Cory yipped in surprise. But after only a few seconds, she heard his panting approaching from behind. Putting on a burst of speed, she aimed for a Doug fir even more massive than the one they'd hidden their clothes by, dug her nails into the soft earth, and turned right.

When Cory's body hit the ground with a startled yip, her adrenaline spiked, and she skidded into a sliding stop and spun around. Cory tumbled until he came to rest, his legs akimbo in the air. He rolled to his stomach, his tongue dropping out. He rose to his feet and shook out his fur, sending fir needles and forest debris flying.

He'd only fallen. The big goof probably hadn't slowed enough to take the sharp turn and had lost his footing. As the adrenaline subsided, she shook and panted. If she'd been in her human form, she'd be laughing hysterically. Cory trotted up and licked her face, before taking off at a gentle lope. Once she controlled her laughter, she ran after him, slowing when she drew abreast of him.

In spurts, they sprinted and walked, occasionally jumping at each other in mock play. For a little while, the outside world was forgotten, and she enjoyed the freedom of fresh air and the sounds of nature, letting the dirt and corruption of Red City wash away.

THREE

JAMIE

J amie and Cory sprawled out on the hood of his mother's car, resting their backs on the windshield as they chewed on their hamburgers, and enjoyed dark, evening sky. Cory had driven them all the way across the basin to the hamburger joint they'd last visited when the entire saga of Jamie's foray into hired murder had begun.

The burger joint was close enough to the overlook that their food was still warm when they arrived at the scenic vista. Theirs was the only car in the parking lot. Red City lay stretched out below them. Bright lights, neon signs, and lines of traffic spread out below them, spilling their light pollution into the night sky.

The overlook had always been one of their favorite spots. Few people visited it, because who wanted to look at the festering shithole that was Red City, even if from up here it looked like any other city?

"Will you miss it?" Jamie asked quietly.

"It? Red City, you mean?" Cory took a drink of his soda. "Fuck no. But I'll miss you. Being friends with you was the only thing that made life in this hellhole bearable."

"Hmph." Jamie reached for a few fries.

"I have no idea where we're going. Mom won't tell me. But somehow, I know it won't be worse than Red City." He snorted. "Redemption City. What a fucked-up name. Never has there been a place less likely to be redeemed than Red City." He sighed. "Someone should burn it to the ground."

"Then its smoke would follow the wind, corrupting every place it touched with its filth." The bitterness in her voice no longer surprised her. Though she'd survived crossing the bikers, her sense of hope and optimism—always tempered by the reality of her life—had been killed.

"You'll get out of here eventually." He reached over and squeezed her hand. "You're too smart and talented to not escape."

"No one really escapes Red City," she mumbled.

"You will, believe it."

Not having anything to say that wasn't bitter and angry, she opted for a mouthful of chocolate milkshake.

"I believe in you, Jamie."

She wasn't sure if she believed in anything anymore, least of all herself.

FOUR

DAX

Each time Dax and Tomi had met Boudreaux so he could escort them to The Rat, it was in a different part of town. Even though they'd helped The Rat get revenge on the same assassin that had nearly taken Dax out twice, the odd little man protected his underground lair fiercely.

"How many different routes do you know of down here?" Tomi asked.

Boudreaux, a tall, muscular, bald Black man slowed his steady, ground-eating walk. "Not many more. If he doesn't want to repeat meetup locations, he's going to have to give me a new route soon." He shrugged and stopped, turning in the dimly lit tunnel he was leading them through. "But I imagine by then, he might just trust you enough to meet without me."

"I like him well enough, but I'd rather not have any more meetings out of necessity. It would be nice to meet up with him for no other reason than because I wanted to," Dax said, gradually slowing the large four-wheeled wagon so it didn't tip its contents due to a rapid stop.

"That would be a nice change, but I don't think even you are that naive, Dax." Tomi took some of the sting from his comment with a couple friendly pats to the shoulder.

Sighing, Dax didn't finish the stop, instead keeping the momentum of the wagon moving forward. "No. Even I'm not that stupid, not anymore. Not really. I just wish…"

"I know, buddy," Tomi said. "I'd rather be worrying about getting dates and the state of the bar's books. But we've gotten ourselves mixed up in something bigger than the usual neighborhood crime."

"You ain't kidding," Boudreaux said, resuming his place in the lead. He paused at a junction and shined his large flashlight at the wall just inside the left and center tunnels, then stopped the beam on the right tunnel. "This way."

Dax let Tomi and Boudreaux lead the way and drifted back a few steps to think. As much as he wished it wasn't true, Tomi was right. There was no going back to the time before when he believed he could keep his head down and mind his own business. A small, quiet life stewing in his shame and anger at his exile had been taken from him by the violent incursion of the teen girl and the Nazi biker gang who had forced her to try to kill him.

But despite the danger and several severe wounds he'd received, he wasn't sure he'd want to go back—if he was willing to be honest with himself. Other than Tomi and his family, he hadn't been close with anyone else until recently. Now he had a few more people he trusted and respected and who seemed to consider him a friend.

He'd tried to be alone after the betrayal of trusting someone led to his banishment into a mortal body and exile in Red City. But he was discovering that maybe humans were made of better stuff than the gods they'd created in their need to explain the world. It had been humans who'd given him a home and helped him blend into humanity. More humans had helped him and saved his life over the last few months.

The only two gods he'd seen recently had given him vague warnings, while one of them dropped a burning cigar on his couch and the other had slapped him. No. Three gods. He couldn't figure out what Hel's game was, but she seemed to be enjoying all the dead Nazi bikers he was sending her way. The Valkyries didn't seem interested in making any of that trash into the honored dead.

Dax grunted as he walked into Tomi's back, but the wagon kept rolling, slamming into his calves. Stuck between his large friend and the weight of the wagon, he pushed into Tomi's back before the wagon could trip him.

"Damn, dude!" Tomi staggered forward, barely keeping his footing.

The only thing keeping Dax on his feet was his grip on the wagon's handle, which allowed him to hold himself up and slightly counter his forward momentum until he could regain his balance. "Sorry. Was just thinking."

Tomi's eyes narrowed and he nodded. "No worries, you startled me, that's all."

Dax turned to Boudreaux, who'd propped himself against the wall to wait. "How long do you think until he arrives…" He stopped, the sound of squeaking reverberating down the concrete walls of the tunnels.

"Apparently, not long." Boudreaux pushed himself off the wall to stand with Dax and Tomi.

From the shadows, an initial wave of rats skittered toward them. They lacked the tentativeness of the last meeting Dax and Tomi'd had with The Rat when the first contact with his furry minions had been his scouting party. This time, they just wandered along casually.

As the wall of rats grew denser, a short figure emerged from the shadows, strolling casually with his hands in his pockets. He also lacked the wariness of last time.

The short, white man looked much the same as before in his too-big clothes with his shaggy brown hair and beard. Dax wondered where The Rat went for his haircuts; the idea of The Rat going to a chic salon almost caused him to laugh. Fortunately, he held it in, not wanting to prick the man's sensitive ego.

Once The Rat came within a half dozen paces, he stopped, pulling both his hands from his pockets and waving them both. "Hi, hi, hi."

The high pitch of The Rat's voice still surprised Dax, and he adjusted to pick up the tone.

The rats continued forward, surrounding the three interlopers. A few had crawled up on the wagon, their little ratty noses sniffing aggressively to inspect all the goodies Dax had brought.

"Hello, Mr. The Rat." Dax reached out and offered his hand to shake. The Rat stepped forward and took it. "We have the promised gift basket and maybe a bit more."

"Presents? We love presents!" A wide grin broke through the thatch of The Rat's beard. He looked around Dax and squinted at the wagon. "Now, now, my little friends. Patience. I'll share my presents. Hey!"

A rat that had been trying to get under the cloth covering the basket withdrew its head and looked a bit shamefaced, if it was possible for a rodent to feel such things.

"Don't worry. We brought something for your friends as well," Tomi added cordially. He seemed to be trying hard to overcome the times he'd annoyed The Rat with a few of his comments. Dax was glad. After The Rat and his furry friends had saved Dax's life, he wanted to make sure to keep a good relationship with the man who commanded the rats of Red City's underworld.

The Rat eyed the lumps in the wagon, and his gaze shifted from the wagon to Dax and back again.

Dax stepped out of the way, gesturing toward the wagon.

"No, no. The Rat must listen to his own advice. Patience. Made my little friends wait. So must I." He straightened his spine, looking proud of his decision. "First there must be talk."

"Manman Delphine said you wanted to have a word about something important."

The Rat nodded quickly. "Yes. The manbo is wise. Important things, dangerous things. Bad things."

The Rat had slipped into his unique cadence.

Clenching his jaw briefly, Dax pulled back his shoulders, bracing himself for what The Rat might have to say. The Rat had an army of little ears that could visit every corner of the city and report back to him. He could be a good source of intelligence, if he decided to get more involved, but so far he'd been reluctant. "What news do you have for me?"

"Mmm. News. Bad news. Bad wolves. Wolves on wheels. Lots of them."

"Fuck," Tomi bit out, shaking his head.

Dax wanted to pace but was afraid he'd accidentally step on a rat. "Yeah. You said it."

FIVE

JAMIE

The ride back to Jamie's temporary neighborhood was awkwardly silent. Normally she and Cory enjoyed companionable silences, but this was their last foreseeable time together. He'd drop her off and go home to his mother, who was going to take him who knew where.

Cory pulled onto the street in front of the long-stay motel they'd moved to. It was the latest in the seemingly endless string of shitty motels — barring the brief time they'd crashed at Dax's place — they'd bounced between in an effort to hide. Jamie caught a reflection of light off chrome, which drew her eye toward shadows moving around on the sidewalk by the hotel. "Fuck."

"What? What is it?" Cory asked, his head swiveling around.

"Ahead by the front of the building." She pointed to guide his eye.

He shrank down into his seat. "That looks like bikers."

It was. Maybe three or four.

"Shit, what do I do?" he asked, panic flooding his voice.

"Um…" She looked around franticly. "That house! Pull into the driveway. No one lives there." She'd done a thorough check of the neighborhood while she'd been avoiding her mother and knew there were several abandoned homes nearby.

Unbuckling the seatbelt, she slumped down into the footwell as far as she could go.

Cory, despite his growing panic, smoothly pulled into the driveway and stopped at the gate leading into the backyard.

"Now what?" Cory hissed, looking over his shoulder.

"Quit looking at them. You don't want them to notice you because you're too curious."

He turned his head and stared forward, sitting stiffly.

"Get out. The gate is unlocked. Just reach over and trip the release. It's on the right side. Hold it open for me."

Cory jerked, shaking the car. "You can't open that door. They'll see you for sure!"

"I'm not. Leave your door open. I'll crawl over the console and slip out. Hold the gate open for me. I'll slip along the ground and squeeze through. Got it?"

His eyes wide, he nodded with a wobbly head.

Jamie disentangled herself from the seatbelt and moved closer to the center console. "Now go!"

Inhaling a noisy breath, he grabbed the door handle, fumbling with it. He stepped out of the car and slipped, grasping the door for balance. Jamie held her breath, hoping he wouldn't do something to draw the bikers' attention. He righted himself and stood by the door.

"Come on," Cory hissed between clenched teeth.

Pushing herself up, she slithered around the gear shifter and sank her hand into the crack between the seat and seatback, pulling herself farther along. Once she reached the edge of the seat, she gripped it and tugged her other hand free of the crack. With a mighty pull, she slid along the seat and pushed until she was about to tip out of the car onto her face. Letting go, she pushed her hands out in front of her, willing to risk scraped palms. As her hands hit the concrete of the driveway, she tucked her head, letting her feet follow in a roll.

But instead of landing gently on her back, her left foot snagged on the loose seatbelt that had failed to retract fully, diverting her other foot into the steering wheel. Her heart leapt into her throat as the car's horn beeped, shattering their stealthy silence.

"Dammit," she said under her breath.

"Fuck. Fuck. Fuck." Cory danced around in indecision.

Dragging her right leg around, she forced it under the steering wheel to avoid a repeat of her earlier gaff. "Untangle my foot. Quickly."

Cory stepped over her and reached into the car. Yanking her foot around, he finally freed it from the betraying strap. Her foot flopped out of the car, catching Cory in the gut and he let out a muffled grunt. She rolled to the side, getting out of his way as he shut the door.

"Are they looking?" she whispered, peeking around the tire to see if she could spot the bikers. But all she could see was shrubs.

"Yeah. What do I do?"

"Just do what we planned."

"OK." Cory walked away, but he stopped halfway around the front of the car. "Shit, a couple of them are coming this way. Fuck. What do we do?"

Rolling away from the tire, Jamie found a less obstructed view. Two pairs of motorcycle boots walked toward them, their chains catching glints of light as they moved. The bikers weren't moving quickly nor were they sauntering. She made a snap decision. She had to get Cory out of there.

"Jamie…" Cory whined.

"Get in the car and drive away." She tried to keep her voice low while edging in a note of command.

"What?" he squeaked, panic filling his eyes.

"Drive away. Before they get close enough to see your license plate."

"I can't leave you."

"Shut up, you idiot. *Go.* You have a chance to escape this place." She tried to put as much pleading into her voice as possible. Cory was too good of a person for a place like Red City. She couldn't drag him and his mother back into the mess her father had created. "Go, please."

She rolled over to sit up and pulled her jacket and shirt off. After tossing them into the car, she unbuttoned her pants and shimmied them down her legs. Cory stared at her, his mouth hanging open in terror and indecision. "Cory. Please. For me. Just go."

Something seemed to register in Cory's eyes. He gathered her clothes from the driver's seat and tossed them to the passenger side. "I'll stash them in the usual hiding spot."

"Thank you." Her relief was palpable, though she couldn't focus entirely on her situation until she knew he was safely away.

Popping her shoes off, she removed her pants and handed them to Cory as he slid into the seat. He tossed them with the others and pulled the door shut. "You're the best friend I've ever had. I love you."

"I love you too. Now go, please!" She began the shift to her wolf form as Cory started the engine and slowly backed out. As soon as she shifted, she moved away from the car so Cory could pull out quickly.

Once he saw he was clear, he gassed the engine and flew out of the driveway, the tires screeching when he slammed on the brakes. The tires squealed again as he gunned the engine and flew down the street, back the way they'd come.

The two bikers yelled. She looked over her shoulder—the bikers had broken into a jangly run. Bunching her muscles, she took off, aiming for the lawn so she could use her toenails dig into the soft soil to propel her forward.

Ahead, Cory took a hard right, the tires squealing again. The distant sound of screaming tires marked another sharp, fast turn, then again, but fainter.

With Cory making his escape, she could concentrate on her own. She needed to get to the woods she'd explored after they'd settled into this motel. A motorcycle fired up, followed by a second. Slowing, she risked a glance over her shoulder. Two of the bikers were pulling around and into the middle of the road.

Running the calculations in her head, she broke left and skittered across the pavement just in front of the bikers, who slowed out of instinct. As soon as she hit the lawn on the other side of the road, she dug in and resumed her journey away from the motel and her mother.

The bikers gunned their machines, flying by on her right. But instead of moving to cut her off or splitting left and right to handle both her and Cory, they swung right in the direction Cory had gone. The worry that had slipped away rushed back. She had to hope he'd gotten enough of a head start and made enough turns that they wouldn't be able to catch up with him.

But why weren't they chasing her? She hadn't heard the other bikes fire up their engines…

She skidded to a halt, slipped behind a nearby bush, and peeked around the other side. That was why. Two bikers had stopped to strip and change into their wolf forms. Another had walked out to collect their belongings. She'd have a hard time escaping them. Even if she was faster, and she'd always been very fast, they could follow at a more leisurely pace and sniff out her trail.

Using the temporary refuge of the bush to look around, she spied a gate leading into a side yard. She risked a last look at the two shifting wolves, then dashed across the yard, hoping to escape their notice as they finished their shifts. Digging in deep, she bunched her muscles and leapt, catching the top of the fence under her paws and launching herself over to land gracefully on the mulch covered side yard behind the fence.

She aimed for a spot on the back fence that separated this house from the one backing up to it, ran between two trees, and flew over the fence, propelling off it like she had a moment earlier. Her eyes widened and a small yip escaped her as she spotted where she'd land —a partially filled pool with a layer of leaves and scum on top.

Cringing and hoping the water was deep enough, she closed her eyes and jaw, landing with a loud splash. She struggled to the top and paddled toward the side of the pool. The stench of the rotting debris nearly overwhelmed her. Once she reached the other side of the pool, she tried to propel herself up to grab the edge. But her wolf paws weren't made for gripping against smooth tile and concrete.

She tried again but slipped back into the pool with another splash. As her panic began to rise, she grew angry with herself. She was a human. Though she'd never shifted in deeper water before, she closed her mouth, held her breath, and shifted.

"Blech." The leaves and scum felt disgusting against her skin.

A nearby ladder caught her attention. With a few powerful strokes, she reached it and pulled herself out, quickly shifting back to her wolf form. With a vigorous shake, she sent as much of the debris, scum, and disgusting water flying as she could. Before her fur had even settled, she was off and running again.

Leaping before she looked, she groaned internally. This gate was made of black steel bars. She aimed between the spiked tops and hoped her wet paws wouldn't slip. As they made contact, she flexed her paws and let her pads grip on the top crossbar while her nails wrapped around the front edge. With only a slight jolt of pain along one of her back legs, she cleared the wretched gate, landing with only a bit of a stumble.

She stopped for a moment to assess her situation. She'd only been down this way a time or two, since the road in front of the motel was more convenient to leave the neighborhood or get to the woods. If she remembered correctly, this street went on for a while and intersected with a few side streets that would get her closer to the woods. She thought about heading away from her sanctuary, but the bikers didn't really know her or her haunts, so she opted for comfort and a place where she knew she'd have the advantage.

SIX

JAMIE

Once her paws dug into the loam of the woods, she relaxed and took in a deep breath of air that was only slightly tainted by the pollution of Red City. One couldn't escape it entirely unless they got out of town far enough like she and Cory had earlier that evening. If she hadn't breathed that rarified air, she doubted she'd even notice the slight taint of the clearer air of the woods—the place that had become her sanctuary from the outside world since she'd found them.

She loped into the woods, trying to figure out her next move. A gust of wind swirled around her, dragging the scent of the pool from her fur to her nose. If they found her trail over the fence, they'd be able to follow the stench of the pool scum like a beacon. The stream would have to be her first stop.

The decision made, she broke into a loping run, eating up the ground between her and the stream. She'd work at being more stealthy later, when she didn't stink like hell. Even though she was being pursued by murderous white-supremacist biker wolf shifters, the woods still brought her a modicum of calmness. The bit of space between the terror of being discovered and pursued allowed her to think and strategize.

Shit. Her mother. Hopefully they hadn't found her apartment yet.

She opened up the wolf link she had with her mother. The open link was about the only positive thing to come out of her father's murder. *Hide. Bikers outside. Don't worry about me. I'll contact you when I'm safe. I'm leading them away.*

What? Her mother's reply felt frantic.

Just hide, please. They found the building. Jamie shut down the link before her mother could argue and distract her. They rarely used it. They didn't speak with their human vocal cords much, so why would they use the wolf method?

Jamie had intentionally kept that method of communication shut for a while now, since she'd been forced to try to murder Dax. She didn't want those thoughts filtering to her mother. She hadn't connected with her father in years, though when the link broke after he'd been kicked out, she felt both satisfied and sad at the same time. She'd chosen to ignore the incongruity instead of examining it. There'd be time for that later. If she lived…

She shook herself, throwing a stutter into her run, but quickly recovered. She couldn't let fatalistic thoughts distract her and dull the edge of her instincts. She'd fought too hard and come through too much already to let that happen.

The urge to run and fight pushed her speed up, but she calmly returned to the steady, ground-eating lope. Now that she had a bit of a lead, she needed to preserve her strength and speed for later. Now was the time to be smart. A wolfy grin spread across her snout as her tongue flopped out.

She was grateful for Cory and his burger fixation. The two burgers and fries he'd bought her after their earlier run had done an excellent job of refueling her and replenishing her strength. She'd need every delicious ounce of ground meat and ketchup-soaked starch in order to escape these thugs.

Her grin spread as the faint sound of trickling water drifted on the wind. A few moments later, she slowed and jogged to the edge of the stream. Lowering her nose, she sniffed—cold, clean water. She took a moment to lap some up. Just enough to slake her thirst and hydrate herself for the coming run but not enough to weigh her down.

Licking her chops dry, she shook herself out, but the scum had started to dry and mat her fur. She cringed. Stepping into the stream, she found a patch of rocky bottom and flopped down into it, rolling around on the water-smoothed rocks. After a bit of wriggling, she stood up and shook—still not good enough. After a second thorough splashing around, she felt much better, though a shower would be needed to feel completely clean. A long hot one with lots of scrubbing.

After another good shake, she lifted her nose to the wind. She wanted to go downstream, but the wind would be at her nose, carrying her scent back the way she'd come. Upstream would carry the scent of any pursuers her way, but it seemed like the direction one would go if they were fleeing, if they were smart.

Looking upstream, then downstream, she stood in indecision as the water flowed around her legs, carrying the mud she'd disturbed from the stream's bed away along with the scum she'd shed in her splashing. Upstream. She couldn't take the chance of her scent drifting directly toward her enemies. The wind at her back would give her warning and give her more time to lose them.

That settled, she walked closer to the edge where the water was shallower and started upstream, keeping her feet to the rocks. She didn't want to send a plume of mud downstream to announce a disturbance to anyone smart enough to look down.

Though she regretted the need to go slow, the goal was now stealth and hiding her trail, not speed. Once she felt she'd covered her tracks sufficiently, she could use her speed to open up more distance. Periodically, she stopped and turned an ear downstream, then her nose, checking for pursuit. Nothing.

After several more checks, she decided she'd gone far enough. Finding a place with a rocky shore and plenty of forest debris to cover her tracks, she slipped from the stream and melted into the woods, continuing her flight.

SEVEN

DAX

Neither Tomi nor Dax felt like chatting after they climbed into Tomi's car. No one spoke until they were back in the north part of town.

"Want me to drop you off at your apartment?" Tomi asked.

"No. Take me to the bar. I've got to do inventory and call in the beer and liquor orders, then I'll stay for the late shift if Suzie needs it."

"Sounds good to me. I could use a beer after crawling around the guts of this city."

Dax laughed. "Trading a rat-infested tunnel for a barfly-infested cave?"

Tomi snorted. "The bar may be dark and cave-like, but in there, I decide who gets to stay and who gets kicked out."

"Didn't want to be bounced by a bunch of rats?"

"Fuck no, dude." He shivered. "All those beady eyes and rat teeth still freak me the fuck out."

"The Rat and his minions helped us out a few times now, including saving my life once. I appreciate your added politeness," Dax replied.

"I can appreciate what they did for us, but they're still rats."

"The Rat is certainly a unique character."

Tomi slapped the steering wheel and laughed. "You ain't kidding. But he seemed very happy with the gifts. So did the rats."

"The Rat also seemed to like the big box of voodoo goodies Delphine sent. I think the respect of the gesture might have meant as much if not more than the cheese and rodent food. I'm guessing he isn't hiding in the tunnels of Red City because he's a respected citizen of the world above."

"That's probably true. But he has all those rats to take out anyone who annoys him now." Tomi parked the car and turned it off. "Want me to take you over to your car tomorrow?"

"Nah. I'll take the bus over in the morning."

"Want anything to eat? I'm going to grab something from Mama's."

Dax's stomach chose that moment to growl. Apparently he needed to feed his meat suit. "I guess so. I'll take whatever the special is, or whatever your mama wants to feed me."

Tomi laughed. "If you leave it up to her, she'll try to feed you too much."

"Yeah. She's always insisting on putting more 'meat on my bones.' If nothing else, I'll have leftovers to take home." Dax appreciated her effort. He knew it was a sign of love and affection from the woman who'd raised Tomi. Though he found the phrase she used oddly accurate, given the alternative form he was forced to occasionally take.

"I'll bring it to you in the office." Tomi headed for the small restaurant they'd set up for Tomi's mother after they'd purchased the entire building with the money they'd stolen from the bikers. The restaurant was finally open for both takeout and dining in. Tomi and Dax ate for free, as did Tomi's cousin Suzie.

Heading in the front door of the bar, Dax received a few waves and cries of hello from the evening regulars. Suzie had agreed to come in early and work a longer shift so he and Tomi could make their meeting with The Rat. He wished he could hire another bartender. The current staff were spread a bit thin as was, but business was still a bit down after the chaos of the previous weeks, including the bomb rigged to his motorcycle in the alley.

"Hey, Dax," Little Suzie said. "Need a beer?"

"Not yet. I'm going to do the inventory and place the orders first. I could use a water though."

"I'll bring it back to you after I finish with these customers." She set a pint of Pabst down in front of one of the regulars and made eye contact with the person behind them to indicate she was ready for another order.

After years of doing it, inventory was a simple, grounding task. Simple numbers and pars followed by a few calls and orders left on voicemails. When he was finished, he thought about slipping into the tearoom to make a cup but stopped at the door leading out to the alley instead. Every time he saw that door, a zing of anxiety flooded his system. He'd been shot twice out there and had nearly been blown up.

Swallowing the pool of saliva that had formed in his mouth, he pushed the exit open and stepped out, propping the door against his shoulder to keep it open. He cautiously scanned the shadows to make sure the alley was indeed empty. Then he turned his head toward the street to see if anyone suspicious looking was out there. Nothing. Only then did he feel safe to look around at the space available in the alley.

Nodding to himself, he stepped back inside and let the door close behind him as he headed into the bar. He pulled up a barstool next to Tomi and swung around to face Suzie. "I think I'll take that beer now."

"Righto." She reached into the undercounter cooler and grabbed a cold can of Rainier for him. "Anything else? Whiskey?"

"Not yet." He swiveled around so he was angled toward Tomi. "What do you think about cleaning out the alley and turning it into a patio?"

Tomi quirked an eyebrow. "Are you sure that's the best idea, all things considered?"

"I was considering everything that happened. Right now, it's a dark, shadowy place that's an ideal place to set up an ambush. But if it's lit and filled with customers, there's no place to hide. Plus, our numbers always dip in summer. People don't want to hang out in a dark, dingy bar when it's nice outside. Go figure."

"He's right, cuz." Suzie leaned into the conversation. "A good power wash, some tables, and some string lights, and the alley would make a great patio. Maybe a camera or two so we can keep an eye on it from inside. But we'll definitely have to hire another person. Some overlap on shifts to cover the extra space and traffic would be necessary." She winked at Dax. "And who knows, maybe you can sell some tea during the day."

Tomi snorted. "And use his precious babies? I doubt it."

Suzie leaned closer to Dax, a sly look spreading across her face as she addressed Tomi, "If he gave us a basic setup for up here and some instruction, we could do an easy menu with some rotating tea specials. If we start slow, we can build the tea business." Her eyes slid to Dax. "Think of all the fun new teas you could buy if you freed up some space by moving inventory."

"Damn, cuz! You know how to make a sales pitch." Tomi chuckled. "It would also add more tables for the restaurant."

"I didn't think of that. You know, the more we talk, the more I like this id…" he trailed off as a weird sensation forced its way into his consciousness. His brow furrowed, and he swung around on his stool to look out over the bar.

He recognized most of the people in the place, at least by sight. The sensation kept growing more intense, as if something was growing nearer.

"Hey, Dax, what's up? You got a bad feeling?" Tomi's voice sounded tight with the sudden tension and shift in Dax's demeanor.

"I don't know." Inhaling slowly and deeply, he closed his eyes and reached into the aether.

Everyone in the bar was a mortal human, except for himself. Reaching out farther, he quickly found what he was looking for on the nearly empty sidewalk out front. Something dead approached.

Or perhaps undead might be a better description. He homed in on their life thread. He'd never really looked at a vampire's life thread in detail before, though there was a touch of the familiar about this one.

"Hmm."

"What's going on?" Tomi asked tensely.

Dax held up a hand to forestall his friend as he found the mark on the life thread that denoted it as belonging to a vampire. At the point of conversion, the life thread had been broken and frayed almost to the point of complete separation, leaving only the tiniest of strands keeping the thread together. Then it had been knotted to keep it connected. Over his time harvesting souls on Earth, he'd run into a few vampires and cut their lines, but he had no idea if this one had a soul to harvest or if it had already been collected. Whenever he'd found a vampire in the past, he'd cut the line to finish its completion the rebirth into undeath had halted.

A moment later the door opened, and the familiarity was explained as the owner of the thread walked in. When they'd raided the compound of the man known as "The Collector," they'd freed many captured supernaturals. The vampire had been one of them.

Dax stabbed his finger at the vampire and mentally wrapped the creature's life thread around his finger and tugged. The vamp's eyes shot open wide, and he barely managed to stifle a whimper that tried to escape his lips. Not wanting to make more of a scene, Dax made sure he had eye contact with the creature and tilted his head toward the hall leading to the tearoom.

Tomi leaned over and whispered into Dax's ear, "Anything we need to worry about?"

"I don't think so. Just want to make sure there are no misunderstandings. I don't want our bar becoming a buffet."

"What?"

"I'll explain later." Dax let go of the vampire's thread and headed to the back, unlocking the tearoom.

By the time Dax'd walked into the room, the vampire was waiting patiently at the entrance, clasping his hands in front of himself. Dax didn't know why the vampire hadn't entered.

Though he hadn't seen a lot of vampire movies, he'd seen enough to wonder if the whole threshold thing was true. The main part of the bar was a public business. So was the tearoom, technically. But he viewed it more as his private sanctuary. It didn't matter either way. He wasn't inviting the vamp into his actual home.

"Come in." He pointed to the long communal table that ran down the center of the room, indicating the vampire should sit on the far side, facing the tea bar. Dax always liked to sit with his back to the bar.

The vampire nodded meekly and sat down, keeping his eyes lowered. After shutting the door and locking it, Dax sat down opposite the vampire. "What do you want?"

"I...I wanted to thank you. For freeing me." The words were barely audible.

"You can speak up."

"I'm sorry, my Lord."

"Oh for fuck's sake. I'm not your lord." Dax sighed and leaned forward, resting his elbows on the table. "Do you know who I am?"

The vampire nodded quickly, still keeping his eyes down. Dax took the moment to inspect him. His white skin looked even paler than Dax's. It had been a long time since the vampire had seen the sun. The black jeans and black leather jacket over a black T-shirt felt appropriate both for the venue and for his image as a creature of the night. His carefully mussed brown hair helped too. His cheeks looked slightly sunken, highlighting his sharp cheekbones. Narrowing his eyes, Dax picked up the hint of some makeup and contour work, which looked like it was intended to highlight the vamps' cheekbones.

He chuckled and sat up straight again. He'd never really known any vampires, but this one seemed to have checked all the boxes for the cliche.

"Who am I?"

The vampire lifted his head, his brow furrowing in confusion as he blinked a few times. "I-I'm not sure what you mean..."

"Who do you think I am?"

"You're...the Grim Reaper. Master of death." The vampire sounded more confident now.

Dax snorted. "I'm barely master of this bar. But I get what you're saying." He paused, narrowing his eyes at the vamp. "Well, you've thanked me, not that it was necessary. What do you want?"

"I owe you my existence, such as it is. I-I have news for you. I know of your enemies."

"Enemies?"

The vampire sneered. "The wolf shifters. The Nazi bikers."

Dax raised an eyebrow. "How do you know about them?"

"I keep my ear to the ground. And it's not like your battle with them has been quiet."

Dax blinked rapidly a few times and gathered his thoughts. "I guess not. What's your news?"

"They're back, and I think they've brought some of their friends from other chapters. Dangerous friends by reputation. Beware their leader."

"Ivar?"

The vampire shook his head. "No, as bad as he is, the one who comes with him is worse."

"Great. Just what I needed." The local guys were bad enough. He'd barely survived dealing with them and their assassin. "Can you give me a name?"

"That I don't have. I've heard a few rumors. Nicknames given by those who fear him, which is basically anyone who's heard of him."

Dax nodded a few times, thinking about the implications. First The Rat's warning and now this vamp's. Things were about to get more interesting. Or more likely, worse. He'd have to warn all his friends now that he had some. They deserved to know so they could protect themselves in case they'd been linked to him.

"I'd heard that they were back. But I thank you for the details. Anything else?"

"No, my— No, sir."

"You can let yourself out then."

The vampire stood and headed for the door.

"Hey, what's your name?" Dax asked.

"Vladimir Corvus"

Dax clamped his teeth together to keep the derisive laugh from escaping his lips. *Vladimir Corvus?* He wondered if all vampire names were just as ridiculous. "You can call me Dax. I'd prefer that to 'my Lord' or 'sir.'"

"Nice to meet you, Dax. If I hear anything else of value, I'll let you know. It's the least I can do." The vampire turned and reached for the door.

"Oh. One more thing. No feeding in the area. Not on my customers. Not on my neighbors. I'll know, now that I've felt your essence. You're welcome to come in and have a drink. Talk to the regulars. But feeding is off limits. Understood?"

He gave a half bow. "I understand."

"Good. Close the door behind yourself when you leave." Once the door thumped gently closed, Dax pulled out his phone and sent texts to those who needed to know. Maybe tonight would be a whiskey night after he filled in Suzie and Tomi.

EIGHT

JAMIE

She'd almost relaxed entirely as she loped through the woods toward its northern edge when she heard a rustle of leaves and a branch snap. She froze. Lifting her nose to the wind, she sniffed carefully but smelled nothing. Patience.

A moment later, the night breeze shifted, bringing with it the smell of another wolf. Something familiar about it tugged at her memory. Before analyzing it, she marked the direction. It matched close enough with the earlier snap she'd heard.

Returning to the issue of familiarity, she immediately eliminated Cory, his mother, and her own mother. She knew their scents too well.

Slinking low, she crawled along the forest floor toward a bush, placing each paw carefully. Periodically, she stopped and lifted her nose to sample the air. Though the wind was variable, when it came from the previous direction, she still caught the same familiar but unnamed scent. Inching to the next bit of cover, she froze when another branch snapped, this time closer.

"Fuck," someone whispered.

She raised her nose again. The scent had shifted—still retaining its familiar note—as had its owner.

"I know you're out there, Jamie," a young man called.

Fuck, Travis. Either the bikers were desperate for bodies, so they'd brought a junior wannabe biker like him, or they'd included him because he'd been her classmate through years of school and probably knew her scent.

"You can't escape. We've got this area covered," Travis called.

She raised her nose, sampling the winds as they shifted around, bringing odors from a wide swath of this section of the woods. Narrowing her eyes, she focused on the direction from where his voice had come. She only smelled one wolf and one human, and they were the same entity.

Standing to her full wolfy height, she slowly walked toward where she'd heard his voice come from. After winding around a few bushes and trees, she found him, standing nude in the shadow of a scraggly looking Douglas fir. He had his hands cupped over his crotch to cover his privates.

She waited until he spotted her before stopping. He took a step forward. A low growl and a tensing of her muscles convinced him to stay put.

He raised one hand to signal he'd understood the message. "Fancy meeting you here." He chuckled. "So, you thought you could hide from us?"

She sat down and kept her eyes fixed on him. He shuffled on his feet, wanting to do something with his body, like cross his arms or lean up against something so he could look tough or aloof. But he couldn't, not without uncovering his dick.

She chuffed and shook her head, wondering why he was being so shy. Wolf shifters were used to casual nudity, usually. She was glad he was trying to be more modest and had no desire to see more of the greasy dumb fuck who'd bullied her throughout high school.

"Why don't you change so we can talk properly?" Travis moved his feet nervously.

She stared at him, not twitching a muscle.

"Ugh. You always have to be so difficult. I'm trying to help you, Jamie."

She tilted her head and quirked an ear. He'd never showed any kind of regard for her well-being, beyond trying to destroy it with his bullying. Her curiosity was getting the better of her.

"Good. I can protect you. They want to kill you and your mother because they think you betrayed them to…that monster." He shivered.

She lowered her head and peeled back her lips to show her fangs.

"Look. Help us set him up, help us eliminate him. And"—he visibly swallowed, his Adam's apple bobbing—"go out with me. They won't harm you or your mother if you're my old lady."

Her muscles tensed, but she kept her disgust under wraps, though if a wolf could snort and roll her eyes, they'd have been spinning in her skull like a slot machine. Her mother had married a deadbeat piece of shit. Jamie'd never make the same mistake. Ever.

"I'll treat you real good. If you help me do this, I'll rise up the ranks, and you'll be there with me." A wheedling, pleading note filled his voice. "I can protect you. You're smart. You can help me. Who knows where we can go with you behind me?"

She remained absolutely still, completely blindsided by the proposal. She'd never realized he'd had a crush on her. He'd always been a nasty little shit, harassing her and Cory whenever possible.

He sneered. "Without your dimwitted *friend* around, you and I can get together. Together, we can go places, make things happen. I could be an important man in the club."

She had no doubt he believed it—that her intelligence would help propel him up through the ranks of the club. He'd be sweet at first. They all were. Then he'd own her, and there'd be no escape. She could see the end of the road, see where she'd end up, and it wasn't pretty.

A low, throaty, menacing growl rumbled out of her throat. The kind of growl that couldn't be mistaken for anything but deadly serious. Travis stumbled back a step. Before she knew it, she was on all four feet, her body tensed as she prowled forward, a burning hatred in her eyes.

She refused to be caged in such a manner. Refused to end up like her mother, scrabbling for some deadbeat loser, wishing for release. His honeyed words would harden into chains. The growl deepened and grew more deadly. She'd been pushed and taken advantage of. Used to fulfill the debt of a weak man. Forced to kill. No more.

Her lips pulled back from her brutal teeth as she stalked nearer. Travis appeared frozen, his mouth hanging open and his eyes wide in terror. She prowled closer, gathering her muscles and her determination. A few more steps… He'd stand no chance.

Bunching her muscles, she exploded into motion and leapt at Travis's throat. She missed. He'd collected himself and shifted rapidly into his wolf.

She skidded to a stop and whirled around. He spun, trembling. Stalking toward him, she looked him over—he was only slightly bigger than her. In a Nazi biker gang, a wolf of his size would never climb the ranks. None of his hateful peers would allow it. He was weak and delusional.

They circled. Travis's flicking eyes signaled his desire for escape while she looked for an advantage. She was tired of backing down and complying.

She lunged, her jaws snapping millimeters from his snout. Drool flew from her mouth, landing on his face. He scrambled away. Instead of letting him withdraw or reset, she pursued. Darting in, she snapped her jaws at his face again. As he turned to avoid her teeth, she caught his ear. The coppery taste of blood filled her mouth as Travis yelped and yanked away, tumbling to the ground.

The flop caught her off guard as he rolled away from her, and she stumbled. Pushing back, she regained her balance and swiveled to find the little pipsqueak.

Though he wasn't big, he was nimble, already up on his feet after his desperate roll. He stalked toward her, a growl in his throat— finally. She didn't want to take down a weakling. She wanted to beat the bully.

She answered with a deeper rumble, drawing back her lips to display her long canines. Flecks of drool flew from her mouth on the wings of her snarl. Travis tried to puff up his shoulders to look bigger. Not in the mood to let him think he had a chance, she let her hackles rise.

Feinting to the right, she lunged left. He tried to leap back but was a step too slow. He yelped in pain as she caught his paw in her mouth. Biting down hard, she shook her head, trying to drag him backward. His yelp turned into a scream as he tugged against her.

Somehow, he got the timing right and yanked back at the moment she'd lightened her bite to adjust to a firmer grip. Scrambling back, he whimpered as he limped on a wounded paw.

Blood and spittle dripped from her fangs as she circled him. All he could do was rotate, trying to keep his teeth in her way. Darting in, she nipped him on the snout, raising a line of blood as he yanked his head back. His tail dropped, moving between his legs.

Aiming at his wounded leg, she spun as he planted too heavily on the bad leg and collapsed. She stood over him and grasped his throat in her mouth and snarled hard. He whimpered and tucked his tail fully between his legs, rolling onto his back as best he could with his throat captured.

Her jaw tensed, and she felt her fangs break the barrier of fur and skin. The vibrations of his cry moved through her jaw. One vicious shake and she'd rip his windpipe out, killing him. Even a wolf shifter couldn't heal from that. Travis's strangled yelp cut off as her fangs sank a bit deeper. His entire body relaxed, and the scent of piss filled the air. She gave one last gentle shake and growl, then let go, backing away.

He looked boneless as he lay there bleeding from several wounds. None of them were fatal or even severe. As a wolf shifter, they'd heal quickly. But he didn't move, afraid she'd reengage and finish him.

Once she drew level with a bush, she spun around and dashed away. Her heart thumped harder than the intensity of the fight warranted. She had dominated him. The old Jamie would have diminished herself and diffused the situation until she could get away. But no more. She'd been pushed beyond her ability to endure everyone's abuse.

NINE
DAX

Dax groaned as the door squeaked open, stabbing into his hangover headache. The squeak had almost become a welcoming bell when patrons entered the bar's front door in the months since the shrill sound had developed. Today, it welcomed the consequences of his bad decisions as he entered the bar. He'd been meaning to get out the can of lubricant spray, but just kept getting sidetracked. Now he was paying the price for his procrastination.

"Wow. Sunglasses? I guess you two hit it kind of hard last night." Suzie smirked knowingly at him and held up an empty pint glass. "A little hair of the dog?"

He thought her chipper voice was a bit uncalled for. "No. Just some water."

She scooped some ice into the glass and filled it for him with the soda gun. "Oh, there's a big ass stray dog in the alley. I didn't catch much of a glimpse of it, but it growled at me when I went to throw out some garbage. It's made itself a little nest back there. Might want to call animal control."

"Thanks, Suzie. Best stay out of the alley until it's dealt with." He sighed and took his glass of ice water, setting it on his desk in the office before heading to the restroom. An angry stray wasn't something he wanted to deal with right now. After splashing some cold water on his face, he headed out the side door leading into the alley.

He paused and his heart rate spiked upward. He'd be glad to get this alley turned into something new. Maybe then he wouldn't have to manage this constant anxiety every time he entered the alley. Steeling himself, he stepped through the door.

A low, throaty growl greeted him from near the dumpster before he even cleared the door. Catching himself, he kept ahold of the door, using it as a shield since it stood between him and that part of the alley. Based on the sound and reverberation, it was one big dog. Why it had decided to camp out next to his bar, he had no idea.

He grumbled to himself, shaking his head. He didn't want to have to call animal control. Having to deal with any Red City official could turn a day bad, even the lower-level employees like those at animal control. Obtaining the permits for the new patio was going to be bad enough. Maybe he could encourage the beast to move along. Reaching out, he found its life thread, identifying it quicker than should have been possible for an unknown animal.

Furrowing his brow, he examined it. It was far too strong and long to be a casual street mutt...and it was familiar; his own thread was intertwined throughout its recent history and future. His shoulders slumped.

"Jamie, come out. I know it's you."

The growling stopped, and a large wolf padded out from behind a pile of boxes and a busted pallet one of the beer distributors had left for him to clean up. Stopping about ten feet away, she sat on her haunches and let her tongue loll out.

"I guess you're not here to make another run at killing me, are you?" He crossed his arms and leaned against the door. At this point, he was pretty sure she'd never try it again, not after they'd been forced to team up a few times since then to ensure their own survival.

She shook her head vigorously, an odd look for a wolf. Sliding backward the door, he peeked into the hallway—all clear. He stepped inside, holding the door open as he blocked the view into the hallway from the bar with his back.

"Come on in. Back to the tearoom." He waved her in with his other hand.

She stood and jogged in, crossing the threshold under his outstretched arm. Once she cleared it, he let the heavy door close. Keeping his body between the bar and the back of the hall, he reached over the wolf and slid the pocket door into the tearoom open. She ran in and sat down in the back of the room.

"I don't suppose you have clothes on under your wolf suit, do you?" he asked.

She shook her head again.

Grunting and rubbing his temples, he turned around, shut the door, and fetched the gray jumpsuit he kept in the office for dirty work or construction on the building. He returned to the tearoom and tossed it toward her. It fell across the far end of the long table that ran down the center of the room. He turned around stepped out of the room, sliding the door shut to give her privacy. A minute later, she knocked on the door to let him know he could come in.

He pulled his phone from his pocket and fired off a text to Tomi. *"You here yet?"*

"At the restaurant."

"Good. Bring me whatever and something for a guest. Will explain later."

Tomi replied with an OK.

Strolling around the tea bar, he turned on the water kettle and stared at the wall of teas he'd collected. More potential bad news and a hangover required something robust.. His hand stopped in front of the Amba black tea from Sri Lanka. That would do the trick.

He pulled out a standard pot and scooped loose leaf tea into a basket. "How do you take your tea?"

"From a bag?" she replied, her voice even but quiet.

He snorted, filling the pot with hot water to let it warm up. Dumping the water into the sink, he put the basket into the pot and poured in near-boiling water, setting a timer for four minutes. He reached under the counter and pulled out three mugs, figuring those were the appropriate vessels for the situation. Staring at the timer, it seemed to move too quickly. He wasn't ready for whatever bad news had arrived on Jamie's wings…or paws.

When time was up, he pulled the basket and filled two mugs with tea, taking them to the long table. Pushing one across the smooth wooden surface, he sat in the middle of the table, waiting for the young woman to take her seat across from him.

Jamie ran the mug under her nose. "Mmm, that smells nice."

He nodded once and let the steam drift into his nose. The strong aroma of the tea helped revive his senses a bit. He imagined it was doing the same for Jamie and hopefully clearing the scent of the dumpster she'd hidden next to for who knew how long.

"Um…" Jamie started.

But Dax stopped her, holding up his hand. "Let's wait until Tomi gets here."

"Oh…OK." She returned to the contemplation of her tea.

Trying to seem calm and look cool and collected, he forced his eyes to remain on his tea when what he wanted to do was check the door every few seconds to see if Tomi was opening it. The girl fidgeted, shifting in her seat and looking at the door. A shallow smile played across his lips briefly before he banished it.

A few minutes later, just as the tea was nearly cool enough to sip, he heard the distinct steps of Tomi coming down the hallway. He relaxed imperceptibly, wondering if she could pick up on his shifting anxiety. She was probably aware of the nuances of his tension and the chemicals his body produced in response to it, assuming she was paying attention to her wolf senses. He stood and slid the door open since he knew Tomi's hands would be full with their food.

Tomi stopped before clearing the door. "Oh, I didn't expect to see her so soon."

"Me either, but she was hiding in the alley in her wolf suit. Figured I'd better invite her in before someone realized the mutt in the alley wasn't a dog."

"Ah." Tomi set the food down, then retrieved plates and silverware from behind the counter blocking the wall of tea. He took a seat next to Dax. "If you both would've sat closer to the end, I could have taken the head of the table, and this wouldn't be so awkward."

Dax filled the third mug for Tomi, setting it down near his seat. After Tomi dished up cornbread and chili, splitting it three ways, the two men sat down and all three of them ate Mama Adele's food. Little was said save for noises of appreciation until Dax and Tomi moved the leftovers off the table and refilled the tea mugs.

Dax exhaled loudly through his nose. "What brings you back to my bar, Jamie?"

Halfway through a sip of tea, she choked and coughed. "Sorry." She patted her chest. "Um, the bikers are back."

"Damn, talk about thrice-cursed bad news," Tomi said, his spine stiffening and his eyebrows pinching together in a furrow.

Jamie looked confused as she glanced back and forth between Tomi and Dax.

"As my associate has indicated, this isn't new news." Dax blew over his tea. "But please, go on."

"I mean, we only found out about it yesterday, and only vague warnings," Tomi said. "So, how do you know they're back?"

"A bunch of them found where my mom and me are staying and chased me. Also, I recognized one of them." She looked down at her hands wrapped around the steaming tea mug. "I used to go to school with him. And the others had the same patches on their jackets and vests."

"Not that I doubt you, but that seems pretty definitive. Fuck." Dax pushed back from the table and ran a hand over his stubble covered jaw.

"Yeah, it does, dude." Tomi tore his eyes off the bringer of the bad news. "We're going to have to be on high alert."

"It's inevitable that they'll try to finish the job." Dax shook his head and pursed his lips, the wonderful taste of his dinner fading to ash. "I've already alerted Delphine and Boudreaux."

"You'll have to start wearing that armored vest."

He checked with Tomi to see if his face displayed the telltale smirk of a joke. It didn't.

"Do you think Boudreaux has a vest your size?"

Tomi snorted. "You're kidding, right?"

"Bullets aren't renowned for their sense of humor, buddy."

Tomi shook his head slowly. "Man, a fat-guy bulletproof vest isn't going to contribute to my sexiness."

"Neither will a bullet in the chest."

Jamie sipped loudly.

Dax had nearly forgotten she was there during their bout of attempted banter. "Sorry, Jamie. When was this?"

"Last night. I saw them and shifted and ran away."

"And you've been out on your own since?" Tomi asked, kindness suffusing his voice.

She nodded, the corners of her lips dipping down at the corners.

"Is anyone else in trouble?" Dax asked.

Jamie wilted. "Maybe my mom. They found our apartment building, but I don't know if they found our apartment. I got off a message to her before running."

"How?" Tomi asked, looking confused. "If you're a wolf... Oh, wolf shifter stuff?"

She nodded.

"Can't you reach out to her now?"

"No. I'm too far away, and since I had to abandon my things with Cory—"

"Wait. Your friend is involved too?"

"No, he drove off before they could follow him." She hoped. Until she could visit their hiding spot and see if he'd placed her stuff there and check that the last stage of his move had gone smoothly, she wouldn't really know for sure.

Dax nodded slowly, giving her a bit of side eye. "OK."

"Anyway, since I didn't have my phone, I couldn't call. And because I didn't have clothes, I couldn't find someone to let me borrow a phone."

Tomi pulled his phone out of his pocket, put in his passcode, and set it down in front of her with a *thunk*. "Call your mama, now."

Tomi's tone was firm, and she didn't argue, picking up the phone and dialing.

"Jamie?" the voice on the other side called. "Are you alright? Where are you? Why haven't you called?"

"Mom, I'm OK—"

Dax caught her attention and made a cutting motion across his throat.

Jamie's brow furrowed, but she muted the phone. "What?"

"Don't tell her where you're at, someone could be listening," Dax said.

Jamie's jaw dropped in confusion. "What do I tell her?"

"Ask if she's safe, and then think of some way of finding out where she's at."

Jamie nodded, unmuting the phone. "Mom, listen. I'm safe. Are you?"

Her mother paused for a few moments. "I don't know." The urgency had left her voice, replaced by weariness.

"Did you go to work today?" Jamie asked.

"No. I...I was too afraid to leave."

Tomi pretended to hold a phone in his hand and removed it from the side of his head, pantomiming hanging it up.

"OK, mom, I can't say much else at the moment. I'm safe. I'll be in touch as soon as I know something more."

"Jamie, what do you mean?" The franticness had returned to her voice.

A deep furrow formed in Jamie's forehead as she slowly pulled the phone away from her ear and hung up.

"Sorry to make you hang up on your mama like that, but we can't let anyone trace anything." Tomi said, looking into his empty mug. "Dax, I think we'll need another round of tea."

Nodding, Dax stood up and took the teapot behind the bar and turned on the kettle. A few minutes later, he returned to the table with steeping tea.

"Dax, what are we going to do? She can't go home." Tomi looked worried.

"And she can't lead them here." Dax could tell his friend was slipping into big brother mode. If he chose to adopt Jamie, even temporarily, there'd be nothing Dax could do but work with Tomi to solve the problem.

Tomi folded his arms across his chest. "She can't stay with us.

There's no room for two extra people and I don't want any white-supremacist biker fucks near Mama and my baby sister."

"No. We can't have that." Though Tomi's baby sister was almost as old as Jamie. She wasn't the precocious almost teen that he'd met all those years ago. Now she was an intelligent and talented young woman working to earn scholarships for college.

"The apartments upstairs are a long way from being ready..." Dax said, thinking out loud.

Tomi snorted. "Ready? They're one step above derelict. Studs and wiring aren't acceptable for even a temporary livable space."

"I mean, we'll take whatever is safe if it gets us away from the bikers," Jamie said.

Tomi shook his head. "No, it's not even safe for that." He narrowed his eyes and looked at Dax, a wicked grin spreading across his lips. "Your place is pretty hard to find. And you've got enough space to stash a couple people for a little while."

"What? No!" Dax said. "There's only one bed. Where... What? No!"

TEN

DAX

Dax pulled the key from the lock and pushed the door open. "Well, this is it." He stepped in and out of the way. Jamie and her mom Sharon followed him in, setting down their luggage out of the way.

He shut the door and pointed at the series of locks and other security devices. "When you're here, please lock up fully."

After the attempts on his life, he and Tomi had installed a heavier door. They'd figured it would keep out the more mundane options since it seemed like whoever was looking to end Dax was using both supernaturals and mundane humans to come after him. The reinforced frame and hinges would even protect him some of the weaker supernaturals.

"That won't stop a wolf shifter," Sharon said, her eyes sweeping around the apartment.

"Maybe." Dax moved into the center of the living room. "The apartment is also warded"—he thought back to Baron Samedi's incursion—"mostly."

Sharon's eyebrow quirked up, and she clenched her jaw. "Mostly?"

"It will keep just about anyone who's looking for you from

finding this place. The ward has a decent radius outside the building, but you'll still want to be careful when leaving and returning." He pointed toward the door on the other side of the living room. "Through there is the bedroom. You can share the bed. I'll crash on the couch for now. That door is the bathroom. You can see the kitchen and the dining table."

The head of a black and white tuxedo kitten poked out from the side of the couch, his ears perked up in curiosity. Peeling them back, he hopped out into the open, his back arched, and bounced across the floor hissing and spitting.

Something drew Dax's attention—he thought he heard a word, but nobody had spoken. Shaking his head, he pointed to the kitten. "That's Morty. He's all talk."

Jamie inhaled and bent over and patted her shins to get the kitten's attention. "He's adorable!"

Morty hopped her way but straightened his back and walked the last foot slowly, checking out her offered hand. When he decided she was OK, he headbutted her knuckles and wound around her hand; a raspy purr rose from the little floofball. Soon, Jamie scooped him up and was scratching his chest as he made biscuits in the air.

"It seems we've passed muster with the cat," Sharon said, a bit of bite in her words.

Dax grunted noncommittally. He wasn't exactly happy about having people in his home. With the exception of the time he'd spent on Adele's couch when he first arrived in Red City, he'd never lived with anyone before. He hoped this would be temporary.

While his houseguests focused on the kitten, he went to the closet and pulled out a couple sets of sheets, tossing one on the bed and setting the other on the end table next to the couch. "Towels are in the bathroom. There's not a lot in the fridge, but if you make a list, I can pick up some stuff at the store."

Nodding, Sharon picked up her bags and headed into the bedroom, leaving Jamie with the kitten. Not sure what to do with himself, he stood awkwardly out of the way. He was saved when his phone beeped.

"Can you come to the shop?" The message was from Delphine.

"When?"

"Now, if you can."

Checking the time, he had a few hours to spare before he had to work. *"Be there in twenty minutes."*

"Jamie, I need to run an errand. You and your mom make yourselves comfortable. If you want to text me a shopping list, I can stop on the way back."

"OK." She didn't bother looking up, too enthralled with Morty.

ELEVEN

DAX

When he arrived at Delphine's shop of magical supplies and curios for the second time in two days, he stopped at the closed sign in the window by the door. Tentatively, he pushed on it and found it unlocked. As it swung open, he heard a vaguely familiar voice talking to Delphine.

"Lock the door behind you," Delphine called from somewhere in the back of the shop. The man stopped speaking.

Delphine stepped out of the back room. Today, her brightly colored dress was yellow and covered in green and red shapes of various sizes. She also wore a coordinating wrap on her head, though the dominant color was red.

"Come on back, cher. I've got tea about ready." She waved him toward the beaded curtain leading to the stockroom, then turned and disappeared.

Stepping through, he stopped as soon as the beads fell down his back and clacked against each other as they settled. The masculine voice had belonged to Gunnar, the Nordic runes expert who'd helped translate the runes on the bullet Dax had been shot with.

"Gunnar. I didn't expect to see you here." As far as greetings went, it was accurate, if not as polite as it could have been. Dax still struggled with the courtesies and small talk humans put so much stock in.

"Dax. It's good to see you alive and well." Gunnar rose and offered his hand to shake.

"It's good to be alive and well."

"Haven't run into any trouble lately, have you?" Gunnar raised an eyebrow.

Dax narrowed his eyes, leaning back slightly. "Not in the last week or so…"

Behind Gunnar, a man who'd been unobtrusively standing in the corner pushed off the wall and cleared his throat.

"Sorry," Gunnar said. "Where are my manners? This is my boy, Ragnar. Ragnar, this is Dax, owner of the House of the Rising Sun Pub and Tearoom."

Ragnar was hardly a boy, standing just a bit taller than Dax's six feet but with a far more muscular frame. He had coppery red hair and a matching thick beard. He unfolded his bulging arms and extended his hand in greeting. His hand was calloused and strong.

But beyond his physical strength, the contact sent a tingle up Dax's arm. Ragnar possessed power—untested and at the beginning of its training, but still deep and strong. Dax looked him over and tried to pinpoint what he might be, or be able to do, but looked away before it became awkward. The mystery of Ragnar Gunnarsson would have to wait for another day. With greetings exchanged, Ragnar backed into the corner, folding his arms across his chest.

Dax turned his attention to Delphine. "I take it Gunnar is the reason you've called me down here?"

Delphine nodded, gesturing toward a third unoccupied chair.

Dax took it, and Delphine sat so that he, she, and Gunnar formed a triangle facing each other as equals in the meeting. "You are correct. He's got a bit of news he'd like to pass on."

Gunnar shifted his position on the chair nervously and cleared his throat. "Thanks for meeting me here. I come to Delphine's often enough that it's not out of the ordinary."

"And me showing up in your territory would look out of place. I can understand that," Dax said. Gunnar was a cautious man, wishing to protect his community and keep it from the notice of the dark forces, both mundane and supernatural, that ran through Red City like raging rivers.

"Thank you for understanding." He turned his head just enough to look at his son out of the corner of his eye. "A few days ago, some men approached my son about doing some work for them."

"What kind of work?" Dax asked, leaning forward.

"Rune work. While I'm good with them, Ragnar is a natural." Gunnar didn't elaborate any further on his son's abilities. "He refused."

"Why?" Delphine asked, crossing her legs.

"I choose who I work for and the work I do," Ragnar said, his baritone voice rich. "I don't work for Nazi bikers."

He didn't say anything else. Ragnar appeared to be a man of few words. Dax was glad neither Gunnar nor Ragnar were willing to work for his enemies.

Gunnar nodded. "While the who is important, the what is nearly more troubling. They're seeking runes and a rune worker who can create weapons against"—he rolled his hand, deciding what word he was looking for—"the dead."

Dax snorted and the corner of one side of his mouth quirked up. He wished the bikers all the luck in the world. He wasn't dead—far from it in this place in time. His mortality and aliveness had been part of his defeat and exile. And even though the gods and psychopomps had mocked him by allowing the stereotypical skeletal form of the Grim Reaper, he was still alive. And before his exile into humanity, he'd been a force of nature—neither alive nor dead.

The bullets they'd made to tie him to his human body were a far more effective weapon than something aimed at taking out the dead. A few of those bullets targeted at more vulnerable and mortal spots might have pinned him his mortal form and blocked his access to a majority of his magical abilities.

Dax leaned back in his chair, relaxing some. "Were they looking to do anything else? Make more of those bullets that tie a being to their form?"

"What?" Ragnar asked, focusing on Dax.

"A couple months ago, I was shot with a bullet that didn't allow me to shift forms, which tied me to this weaker human body." He patted his pockets. "Dammit, I wish I'd brought one with me. I have a few unfired shells where the runes aren't marred."

"I have the one you gave me to inspect," Delphine said, standing up and walking to a door that led into a small, dark room. A moment later she reemerged and handed a bullet to Gunnar.

Gunnar looked it over, nodding, and handed it to Ragnar. He stared at it intently, turning it to catch the light.

"I've never seen this combination of runes used like this." He looked up from the bullet to make eye contact with Dax. "What kind of shifter are you?"

"I'm not exactly a shifter, though I can change forms. Would that bullet work on, say, a wolf shifter?"

Ragnar's eyes flicked toward his father and back to Dax. "It's possible, but I'm not sure who'd let us test it on them."

"Would it work if you simply gripped it in your fist?" Delphine asked.

"I'm not sure." Ragnar closed his eyes and concentrated. "It feels…sinister, dark. I think it requires blood to activate." He opened his eyes. "Do you mind if I borrow this? I'd like to see what else I can learn from it."

"Ragnar"—Gunnar stood—"can I have a word with you? Now."

Ragnar nodded and followed Gunnar out to the front of the store.

The two men spoke in low voices, just quiet enough Dax couldn't hear the words, but the tone was unmistakable—they were arguing. He couldn't quite guess about what, though he suspected it had something to do with getting too involved.

Having an established relationship with Delphine and meeting at her shop was one thing, but sticking their necks out for him was something entirely different.

"Damn it, father, how long must we cower?" Ragnar said, raising his voice. "If no one ever does anything, we'll always be subject to the whims of these thugs."

"I'm still your father and head of this family. I have to think about our community. Don't get involved," Gunnar snapped back.

"A community of cowards?"

Dax made eye contact with Delphine. She looked concerned. He didn't know either man enough to do more than sit there awkwardly.

"You judge them harshly because you're young. It takes courage to survive in this city, even if it's through being quiet and meek. I have to look out for them, and you, even if you don't like the way I do it."

A moment later, someone clicked the lock and stormed out the front door.

"Sorry about that, Delphine, but I better go. We've delivered the information we needed to," Gunnar called. He didn't wait for an answer and left more quietly than his son.

Dax'd wanted to ask some more questions to find out if potential customers had provided more parameters. Any hint to whatever their enemy was planning would be a victory, but it looked like that wasn't going to be a possibility.

"Would you mind nipping up front and locking the door, please?" Delphine stood up and headed back to the room where she'd kept the bullet. "I need to make something for you."

"Alright." When he returned to the back room after locking the front door, he found Delphine working in the small side room.

When he approached, she poked her head out of it to address him. "I'm going to make you some Fiery Wall of Protection oil, cher. Use it to anoint the doors and windows of your home and the bar. I'll mix up enough so Adele can renew her protections as well. I can't promise it'll prevent all dangers, but in combination with the protection gris-gris I made you—you're wearing it still, right?"

He reached into his T-shirt and pulled out the leather thong and the red flannel pouch attached to it. "I only take it off at home."

"Good. As long as you wear it, it should tip the fortunes of danger in your favor." She stepped out of the room.

"Do you need anything from me?" He was uncertain.

Though he and Manman Delphine were becoming friends, he didn't want to ask her to divulge too many of her secrets. Secrets were power. And if a person had secrets, keeping them became paramount for self-preservation and survival.

Also, he'd never really participated in humanity. Sure, he'd seen humans and even been called forth by them, at least into the minds of the humans who invoked his name, but only he chose when and where to make an appearance, always based on his own purposes.

A knowing smile spread across her face. "Not much. Only your spirit."

His eyes flew wide, and he leaned back hastily without taking a step.

The manbo laughed. "Your breath, cher. I just want to check to make sure your gris-gris is being maintained."

He took the pouch off and handed it to her. She brought it up to her face, squinting at it. Inhaling lightly, she was careful not to breathe on it.

"Hmm, it's a bit weak. You need to feed it some whiskey weekly. Set a reminder on your phone. It's too important, especially if these assholes keep making runs at you." She took the bag, dropped it into a wooden bowl, and grabbed a bottle of whiskey. She poured two shots, offering one to Dax.

"No, thanks."

She winked at him. "Suit yourself." She tossed one of the shots back and poured the other over the gris-gris. She handed the small bag back to him. "It'll be a bit damp, but it's all charged up and ready to go. Give it a bit more breath while we're at it."

Clasping the red flannel bag in his hands, he brought it up to his mouth and exhaled slowly onto it. When the last of the air left his lungs and was absorbed by the gris-gris, its power pushed out. It felt even more powerful than when she'd first given it to him right before they'd moved against the assassin, as if it was growing to know him.

He knew very little about the magic of voodoo, but he understood the power of forces. Manman Delphine, if she chose to exert herself, could be a true power of the magical world of Red City. He was glad she was becoming his friend. The protection she offered allowed him to reserve his power for when it could best be used. Without knowing the exact boundaries of what he was allowed to do in his exile, he needed the assistance to stretch out the use of his power.

After he was done examining his renewed gris-gris, he dropped it back inside his T-shirt and pulled out his phone to set the reminder. It would be foolhardy to not take care of the gift she'd given him, especially when it was likely to be needed in the near future.

Stepping back, he watched as Delphine, with a practiced hand, grabbed bottles and other ingredients and quickly whipped up a batch of her Fiery Wall of Protection oil. When she finished, she poured it into several prepared bottles, handing him two.

"That should keep you and the Cheneverts safe. If you end up needing more, please let me know."

"Thank you. I appreciate all you've done for me and Tomi's family." Adele was not only Delphine's friend, but also one of her parishioners. Dax appreciated that the manbo took her job of protecting her people so seriously. Adele, Tomi, and his sister were like family to him, such as he understood it. Mama Adele, as she preferred him to call her, doted on him and looked out for him like he was one of her own. Delphine's care for them might have earned her more respect with him than the aid offered to him.

"They've taken care of me when no one else would, despite all the dangers. It means a lot to me to know they're being looked after." He bowed in respect.

Delphine curtsied deeply. "You honor me."

Lifting the bag from his chest, he smiled. "It's even stronger than before."

She laughed. "We'll see how true that is if you actually need its protection."

TWELVE

DAX

Manman Delphine escorted him from the back room and stopped on the way to the door to grab something from under the counter near the register. "I have a little gift for you."

"The gris-gris and oil are more than enough." He took the small black wooden box she offered him. "But I appreciate the sentiment."

"It's more a desire for you to quit messing with my tarot decks." She winked at him.

He opened the box and turned it over into his other hand. A deck of elaborately decorated black and gold cards came out of the box. On each card were beautifully drawn skeletons, forming the major and minor arcana of a tarot deck.

"Skeletons, really?" He shook his head, a smile on his face. While he didn't care for the form he'd been forced to use by his betrayers, he could appreciate the gift and humor with which it was given.

"Just bring those if you wish to have your cards read. I can do it, or I can provide the name of someone *trustworthy*"—she quirked her head to the side and looked at him significantly to emphasize his special needs—"who can give you a proper reading."

"Thanks again. When I'm ready, I'll reach out to you, and we can sort out the details then."

Delphine followed him through the store, and taking the earlier hint, he carved a wide path around where she'd stacked her tarot cards for sale. He didn't want to accidentally taint any of her decks. They were valuable merchandise that didn't need to show the Death card on the first draw every time. Unlocking the door, she followed him outside.

Stretching out her back, she stood to her full height, her spine popping as she brought her arms back. "Too much hunching over today."

"Thank you for everything—the information, the gris-gris, the oil, and the thoughtful gift. I appreciate it."

"Those of us of good conscience have to look out for each other in this city. And I hope you won't think too badly of Gunnar and Ragnar. They're good men, though they have different approaches to how to keep their own people safe."

"I'm glad Gunnar decided..."

A beat-up old pickup flew around the corner. The glint of a gun barrel from the back was his first hint of trouble. Men popped up from the bed, while two more stood on the wooden sideboards attached to the metal top railing. In a flash, he counted at least four guns pointed at him and Delphine. A scream barely had time to fall from Delphine's lips.

He shifted into skeleton form and grabbed his cloak, spinning to present his back to the shooters and protect the manbo. A blitz of bullets exploded the relative quiet of the neighborhood.

Nearby, the glass of a car window exploded—he hoped it wasn't his 1965 Lincoln Continental. Brick fragments sprayed at him, bouncing off his skull. Bullets tugged at his ragged cloak. He even felt the heat of one pass through the aether where his kidney would have been. Delphine grunted, then released a squawk of pain. Behind her, a window shattered, spraying them both with shards.

Almost as soon as it started, the hail of automatic gunfire ended and the pickup screamed away, swerving to make the turn and sideswiping a parked car. With a shake of his cloak to shed any debris, he returned to his human form, catching Delphine before she could fall to the ground.

"Are you OK?"

"Yeah. I think it just grazed my leg." She panted, shaking.

Looking back over his shoulder, he heard the truck screech and hit another car.

"Go. I'll be fine. Find out who they are." Her breaths still came in short gasps.

He swung his head around to her.

"Go! I'll call Boudreaux." Her command was firm.

He nodded, then spun around and dashed to the black Lincoln. Thinking about sliding across the hood on his ass to shorten the distance, he decided against it to avoid scratching his new ride. As soon as his butt hit the seat, the engine roared to life and he flew forward, the momentum shutting the door for him.

Checking his surroundings, he took the corner sharply but kept control. Ahead of him, he saw the car that had been hit. The truck had smacked it with enough force to knock the car up onto the curb. A small crowd was descending on the scene.

He mashed the horn and put on his blinkers. People scattered as he dodged them and the car partially in the roadway. In the distance, he saw a tailgate that matched the rusty, Bondo-spattered body of the truck and the pack of assholes that had opened fire on him and Delphine.

Pushing the gas pedal down, he tried to make up some distance while he had a straightaway. At least he was close enough that if they turned, he'd be able to see onto which road and in what direction. So far, they hadn't noticed him or at least figured out someone was following them.

Up ahead, they took a left, this time slowing enough to do so without committing vehicular destruction. Using the long, straight road and the fact they couldn't see him, he coaxed out as much speed from the big engine as he could. Though the sinister-looking land yacht would never be agile or quick, it did have power.

Slowing just enough to keep control, he gritted his teeth, and his tires let out a squeal of protest as he made the turn to follow them.

He'd managed to make up a little ground. They must've thought they'd made a clean getaway and were now trying to blend in more. He couldn't see the men riding illegally in the bed of the truck.

"Fuck!" He slapped the steering wheel and slowed down as a car pulled onto the road in front of him.

Checking his mirrors and the oncoming traffic, he gunned the engine and slammed the car into the oncoming lane, roaring by the small compact car struggling to get up to the residential speed limit. They honked and flipped him off as he passed. He hoped the commotion wouldn't draw the attention of the truck and anyone behind them who might be observing to what was happening. So far, so good.

As he passed the next intersection, he caught the names on the street sign to see where exactly he was and what lay in front of him. Soon they'd hit Arbuckle Avenue, one of the major diagonal roads that cut through the city and sliced weird angles into the ninety-degree grid.

On his motorcycle, he'd used the big avenue to evade pursuit a few times. He wished he had his motorcycle at the moment. It would've been easier to slip through traffic in a pursuit situation like this. Too bad it was now scrap.

Ahead, the truck's brake lights flashed red momentarily—far shorter than was needed when approaching a stop sign—and banked right, choosing the easier obtuse angle as they merged into traffic.

Growling in annoyance and trusting his luck—maybe he should see if the manbo could make a luck gris-gris—he pushed the gas pedal down and blasted through a stop sign, then another a few blocks later. When it came to his turn to merge onto Arbuckle, he went for more of a rolling stop than the full-on disregarding of the sign.

As soon as he straightened out, he began the task of reacquiring his target…but couldn't see it. A quick *bwoop-bwoop* of a siren and a sudden assault of red and blue lights in his rearview mirror ruined his last shot of catching the bikers. He held out hope that the police were interested in someone else, but after the black and white cop car tucked in directly behind him, he gave up that delusion.

"Fuck!"

In this kind of traffic, there would be no evading them, nor would he attempt to in a boat like this, though he hadn't tested the car to its full capacity yet. Looking for a place stop, he opted for a right turn off the big five-lane avenue onto a quieter side street. As soon as he found a safe place, he pulled over and put the car in park, leaving his hands on the steering wheel. He had no desire to be shot for annoying a gun-happy cop. He'd had enough bullets in his body the last few months.

While he waited, he quickly pulled out the counterfeit registration—fake papers were part of the service Boudreaux provided when he fixed up the stolen car—from the glove box and pried the license from his wallet, holding the items in his hands while he rested them on the steering wheel in plain view.

As the cop approached the side of his Lincoln, Dax rolled the window down.

"Do you know why I stopped you?" the cop asked, a bored tone dominating her demeanor.

He didn't answer, not wishing to incriminate himself by ratting out his driving infractions or by speaking a lie the cop could use against him. Out of the corner of his eye, he caught the cop's eyebrow quirk up.

"Very well. License and registration, please."

Dax slowly reached out, handing her the paper and laminated card in his hand.

She grabbed them quickly, pulling them from his grasp before he could fully release them. "Wait here and keep your hands where they can be seen."

He nodded and complied. She walked back to the car to run him and the car through the system. His index fingers bounced nervously on the steering wheel while he waited. The license was a forgery as well or rather, a real license acquired fraudulently like the rest of his papers which proved he could live in a modern society. He hoped they passed muster, or he'd be truly fucked.

A couple minutes later, she reemerged from the driver's side and a second uniformed cop exited from the other side of the car. She approached the Lincoln on the driver's side while the other cop came up from the passenger side. Both rested their hands on their holstered guns.

Dax sighed, his shoulders slumping slightly. He didn't need this. He'd nearly been gunned down, yet the cops were harassing him.

"We're going to need you to step out of the vehicle," the female cop said, giving him space. Her body was coiled and ready in case things didn't go as expected.

"Nice and slow," the male cop on the other side of the car added.

Dax lifted his hands from the wheel, leaving one in the air while he slowly reached for the door handle. Pushing it out, he stood, keeping his hands in the air.

"Put your hands on the hood of the car." The female cop's fingers ran back and forth over the handle of her gun.

He stepped around the door and bent over, placing his hands on the shiny black hood of his Lincoln. Behind him, the cop stepped up and shoved a booted foot between his legs, bumping his feet out wider.

"Got anything sharp in your pockets? Needles or other drug paraphernalia?" she asked.

Again, he remained silent.

"If I find something, this will go a lot harder on you." The cop's tone had become more aggressive, the threat growing more intense.

"Be careful, Johnson," the male cop said, pulling his gun but keeping it at his side.

Officer Johnson started a slow, careful pat down, working from his head down to his feet. He knew the only thing she'd find was the gris-gris around his neck and his wallet in his pocket. The keys were in the ignition, and he wasn't armed. He didn't need to be, not when he could bring forth a blade from out of the aether.

"Anything?" the male cop asked.

Johnson scoffed. "Nothing yet. Not even pocket lint. Though he kind of smells like alcohol. You been drinking?"

As before, he said nothing.

"Hmm, we'll have to test him down at the station." When she

finished her last bit of the pat down, she stood up straight. "Put your right hand behind your back."

Sighing, he moved it slowly. In a rush, she grabbed it before he'd brought it all the way around and slapped on some handcuffs.

"Now the left." As soon as his left arm was in range, she yanked it within range of the right and cuffed them together. Pulling him up to full standing by the wrist, she shoved him forward and around the car. "Sit on the curb."

He complied, hating every moment of this indignity. The rolling stop should have just necessitated a ticket, not this treatment. To be fair, he'd committed a few very illegal activities during his time in Red City. But as far as he knew, none of them had been documented by any authority figures.

With him sitting cuffed on the curb, the cops stepped back and took up station behind him, one on each side, and proceeded to pick up a conversation they must've paused earlier. The flashing red and blue lights of their police cruiser spun lazily, providing a visual annoyance that kept drawing his attention.

Time dragged on interminably until an unmarked car stopped alongside his pulled-over Lincoln. A hand reached out and slapped a single dome light onto the roof of the car. When it fired up, it spun around, rotating between red and blue. Another fucking cop.

"Detective," Officer Johnson said.

"Sergeant. Thanks for holding him," a familiar voice said. A pair of scuffed shoes stopped in front of him.

"No problem."

As Dax looked up, Detective Randall Ryan squatted down until they were looking at each other eye to eye. Dax wanted to slam his head forward to wipe the smug smirk from the detective's face.

"A car matching this one was seen fleeing from the scene of a drive-by shooting a little bit ago. You wouldn't know anything about that would you, Dax?"

Trying to keep his anger in check, he forced himself to breathe evenly and look straight ahead. He blinked slowly, letting his eyes stare past the corrupt detective who always took delight in harassing Dax. He wondered what would have happened if he'd paid the young Patrolman Ryan when he'd asked for a contribution to the neighborhood protection fund all those years ago.

"He's a quiet one," the male officer said.

Ryan looked over Dax's shoulder. "Has he said anything?"

"Not a word," Sergeant Johnson replied.

Shaking his head, Ryan returned his gaze to Dax, a gleefully smug smile spreading across his lips. "Let's see if a night downtown will loosen up his tongue. Read him his rights and take him down to county."

THIRTEEN

DAX

Dax had seen it enough in movies, but when the heavy metal door slammed home on the cell, he felt it. He'd been locked up inside this human form, and now he was locked up in a human jail.

In the blink of an eye, he could have reached out and cut the life threads of Johnson and her partner and been on his way. But he wasn't sure what information had been radioed in. If he were linked, even circumstantially, to the death of two cops, the Redemption City Police Department would make his life miserable, assuming they just didn't hunt him and assassinate him outright. So, now he was stuck in a jail cell with a handful of others who'd run afoul of Red City's law enforcement. He had no idea if they belonged here. As corrupt as the cops were, he might be the only one in the cell who'd actually committed several crimes.

Turning around, he looked for a bench to sit on and found one currently unoccupied. Sagging back against the cinder block wall, he extended his legs and exhaled noisily.

"Those are some nice boots you got there," a man with a deep raspy voice said. A man had stood up and walked over to stand in front of Dax. He appeared to be a few inches taller than Dax and probably had an extra hundred pounds of muscle and fat on him compared to Dax.

Dax would be generously described as skinny, though he had reasonably broad shoulders, which allowed him the illusion of body mass as long as he wore a heavier jacket like the leather coat he preferred.

"I think I like your jacket too." The behemoth crossed his arms, flexing his pecs and biceps under his tight, dirty T-shirt and black leather vest. "It's a bit warm in here. You might be more comfortable If I took them for you."

Dax rolled his eyes. The man had chosen the wrong words and meant "from" him. Forcing his jaw to not clench in annoyance, he tried to remain neutral, raising his eyes just enough that the man trying to shake him down could see them clearly. Careful to control the intensity so as not to go over the top, he let the cold blue flames of death flicker into his eyes.

When the man took a step forward and opened his mouth, Dax poured more fuel on the flames until the very edges of his facade released faintly to the point his gaunt face became one step away from revealing his bleached white skull beneath. The man swallowed and uncrossed his arms, holding them out in supplication as he backed away.

The would-be thief turned around once he neared the opposite wall and flexed at a man sitting on the bench there. The smaller man scrambled off the bench, giving it up to the man who needed to make a point after being so quickly cowed by Dax.

Returning his gaze to the tips of his leather boots, Dax put out the fire and let his human form resume its dominance. He probably should have kept his cool, but he was in no mood to be fucked with after being arrested and thrown into jail.

After the big guy retreated, the other four men in the cell chose to pretend the entire side of the cell where Dax sat didn't exist. That was fine by him. He could focus on his brooding while he waited for his phone call.

He hadn't gotten a truly good look at the men who'd shot at him from the back of the beat-up pickup, but they had all the markers of bikers, with their patch-covered leather vests and unruly beards. Though it could just as easily have been someone else trying to run a Trojan horse operation on him to throw suspicion on the bikers, since they'd been gunning for him a few months before.

Without knowing the why or who, there were too many directions to look in. He knew the bikers were back in town. They weren't known as forgive-and-forget types. The bikers would be the logical place to start. Find them and turn them upside down to see what fell from their pockets.

But how to find them was the question.

There'd only been one direct contact—Jamie.

FOURTEEN
DAX

Now that he had a few thoughts on how to track down the assholes that kept trying to kill him, every second stuck in jail prickled at him. Each time he asked for a phone call whenever a cop strolled by the cell, they chuckled and kept walking. They seemed in no hurry to stop violating his rights.

It was fortunate he was a light sleeper, because his cellmates made another attempt to invade his space a few hours later. He sent them scattering again, and they let him be until morning.

After he relieved himself in the cell's filthy toilet, he turned around to find Detective Ryan leaning up against the bars. "Have a pleasant sleep?"

Ignoring him, Dax returned to his bench and kicked out his legs, crossing them at the ankles. "I believe you owe me a phone call."

"Oh, did they not give you your phone call?" Ryan chuckled. "I'll have to look into it for you."

A uniformed cop strode down the hall.

Ryan held out a hand to stop him. "Sergeant, did our guest get his phone call?"

"We would have let him if he'd asked."

Ryan turned back at Dax. "All you had to do was ask. Now we

just have to see if there's a working phone in the building." He laughed as he strolled away, patting the other cop on the back.

"Fuckin' pigs," one of the prisoners muttered. The others nodded, acknowledging the point.

"What did you do to get on the bad side of that detective?" another asked.

Dax made eye contact with the man who'd spoken to him—a small, shifty-looking white man with patchy hair—and shrugged. Then he looked significantly at the corners of the cell at the ceiling and tapped his ear. Hopefully the man figured out that saying anything in this cell was a stupid idea.

"Wha—"

One of the other men in the cell interrupted the speaker with an elbow to the ribs. A couple mumbled words he didn't quite catch, and they all nodded knowingly. The combination of their shared distaste for Red City's cops and the fear Dax had inspired finally had taken the fight out of the other men. Dax relaxed a little but kept up his alertness just in case.

Despite asking Ryan for his call, no one came by to retrieve him and take him to a phone. So far, he hadn't been charged with anything, and he had to be approaching the point where they'd have to do so or let him go.

None of his friends knew where he was. The last person to see him, besides the cops and the bikers, was Delphine, and she had no idea where he'd gone after taking off in his car. He hoped the cops had locked his car, though likely they impounded it—another hassle to deal with. The only connection he had to the manbo was the gris-gris she'd made him.

The gris-gris the cops had somehow missed and left around his neck.

He wondered if it was just mistake, or if the gris-gris bag had already given him a bit of luck and protection since renewing it. Reaching a finger from each hand into his T-shirt, he snagged the leather thong and pulled the gris-gris out. A couple of the other prisoners looked shocked that he'd been left with a possession. Placing a finger across his lips, he requested their silence.

He didn't wait for a response before closing his eyes and gripping the red flannel bag in his right hand. Letting his awareness sink into the bag of magic, he searched all the currents of power swirling around it and found a faint but familiar thread leading away from him. It disappeared into the distance.

Reaching out in the aether, he plucked it a few times and sent a bit of his consciousness along the line. He had no idea how long it took for the piece of essence to find Delphine, but her awareness blossomed in his mind. Whatever she was doing, she stopped and focused inward. It only took her a moment to recognize his presence.

She placed a little more of herself into the connection and allowed him to drag it back with him. When it returned, he only felt confusion and darkness from her. His eyes, which were closed, shot open and he looked around, focusing on anything that screamed "JAIL." Dawning and recognition occurred on her end, and he let go of her borrowed piece of awareness and sent it zipping back to her.

If the cops refused to give him his call, he'd make it however he could.

FIFTEEN

DAX

Throughout the rest of the day, the cops pulled the other prisoners from the cell, either releasing them or moving them elsewhere in the jail. They must have thrown him in with what they viewed as the "hard cases," hoping they'd beat the shit out of him. Now he sat by himself in the large holding cell.

Though he wasn't entirely alone. Periodically, Delphine would ping him with her presence. He appreciated the gesture and the general sense of *searching* and *frustration* she sent along with the awareness. Since the cops were determined to leave him to rot for the moment, he decided a nap would be the perfect way to fight back.

The clanking of a Maglite on the bars roused him from his sleep. "Get up," a uniformed cop said, annoyance dripping from his tone.

Dax sat up, swinging his feet onto the ground. "Can I have my phone call?"

The cop answered by opening the cell door and stepping in. "Hands against the wall."

Sighing, Dax turned around and followed the cop's instructions. A moment later, his hand was grabbed and pulled aggressively behind his back and cuffed too tightly followed by the other. Smiling smugly, Detective Ryan leaned against the frame of the open cell door.

The cop shoved him roughly toward the door. Stumbling, Dax regained his balance and tried to stand as straight as possible as the cop steered him out of the cell and into a long hallway. After a few more turns, they emerged in a busier part of the jail. They stopped by a door and the cop opened it, shoving Dax into an interrogation room. The cop didn't bother removing the cuffs or loosening them, before forcing him into a hard chair.

Casting his eyes about the room, Dax found the usual accoutrements—a one-way mirror, recording equipment, and a camera placed near the ceiling in a corner. He chuckled to himself when he saw that its cable had been detached.

Dax leveled his gaze on Detective Ryan, who sat opposite him. "I don't see a phone here."

A pleasant smile spread across Ryan's face. "Your powers of observation are unmatched."

Standing up, he strolled back and forth along the other side of the table that sat between them. As Ryan passed by the recording equipment, he reached down and pulled the plug from the recorder. Dax rolled his eyes. He knew what was coming next as Ryan strode around the room to walk behind him.

His nose cracked in pain and stars exploded in his eyes as Ryan slammed his face into the metal table.

Ryan tsked. "You've got to be more careful. It's a dangerous world out there."

Blood dripped down Dax's face when he lifted it from the tabletop. Waiting until the detective moved back to the other side of table and faced him, he blew out between his pursed lips and sprayed blood across the metal table and onto the detective's crisp white shirt. It was petty, and he'd pay—

Ryan kicked out, slamming the table into Dax's chest, and his face smacked into the hard surface again. Blinking to clear his vision, he licked his lips to remove the blood from them, then spat a glob onto the floor.

"I waht my phow cawl." He was glad there wasn't actually a

phone in the room. No doubt the detective would've used the opportunity to slam him in the face with it. Ryan would have likely brought one of those old heavy rotatory numbers to make sure it actually hurt extra.

Dax longed to shed his flesh and blood and snap the cuffs. Then he'd reach into the aether and pull out his scythe and slowly shove it into Randall Ryan's gut just below his belly button, gradually sinking it in as the detective bleated his pathetic human mewlings of pain until he was entirely impaled on the blade. At the last moment Dax might shift the angle so he missed the heart to prolong the agony for a few seconds more before the cop bled out on his blade. There was no camera or recorder to document it. He doubted there was anyone on the other side of the glass either. Red City cops didn't like other cops to see them doing naughty shit that could be used to blackmail each other. They no doubt called it professional courtesy.

"Oh, you're angry." The detective chuckled, though Dax noticed a hint of fear laced through it.

Perhaps Ryan remembered the last time he'd pushed Dax and had seen the burning pits of Dax's eyes. The cop had broken one of his teapots as a petty retaliation for letting someone frighten him.

Instead of indulging himself, Dax sat up straight and let an evil smile lift the corners of his lips as he stared at Ryan through half-lidded eyes. Ryan shivered.

Someone knocked on the door. When Ryan didn't turn to open it, they knocked harder. Finally, Ryan shook himself free of Dax's gaze and turned around, yanking the door open a sliver.

"What do you want?"

"Detective Ryan, there's a lawyer here looking for him," said a voice on the other side.

"How the fuck… Which ambulance chaser did his deadbeat friends find?"

"Um, it's not an ambulance chaser. Um, it's the head of the local chapter of the ACLU."

"What?" Ryan barked.

"It's the head of the ACLU—"

"I fucking heard you." Ryan's eyes darted around, and he mumbled something to himself. "I'll send him out in a few minutes."

Ryan didn't wait for the cop on the other side of the door to acknowledge him and shut the door hard. Grumbling to himself, he paced across the far side of the room for a minute, then slipped out. He came back a minute later with a damp cloth.

He strode across the room and snatched Dax's hair and held him still as he roughly wiped the blood from Dax's face. After he was satisfied, he folded the towel and wiped around the collar of Dax's black T-shirt.

Grabbing Dax under the armpit, Ryan dragged him to his feet. "Stand up. If you know what's good for you, you'll keep your mouth shut."

Dax ignored him, letting himself be yanked and pushed toward the door and through it. Ryan left the cuffs in place as he steered Dax down the halls to the main part of the station.

Leaning in close, Ryan hissed into Dax's ear, "Remember, keep your mouth shut."

As the detective reached out and grabbed the door handle, Dax scrunched his face up and exhaled hard through his nose, sending a gush of thick, nearly coagulated blood blasting out of his nostrils and over his own face. Before Ryan knew what was going on, they'd emerged into the room where the lawyer waited, camera aimed at the door and recording.

"My client appears to have been beaten bloody. Detective Randall Ryan is escorting him. Please remove the cuffs." The lawyer backed up and kept his phone pointed at them.

Randall yanked Dax around, pushed him against the wall, and planted a shoulder into his back as he reached down to remove cuffs. Dax huffed as the detective's shoulder dug into his back, exaggerating the sound. The years-long cold war between the detective and Dax appeared to be over.

"That was unnecessary, Detective," the lawyer said, his voice deep and authoritative but annoyed.

With his hand free, Dax rubbed his wrists, trying to get some feeling back into his hands.

"Let me document those, Mr. Smith."

Letting his sleeves slip down, Dax held up his wrists for the lawyer to inspect. The cuffs had left nice red marks on his skin where they'd dug in. Once the lawyer was satisfied and nodded, Dax resumed his earlier attempt to get the blood flowing again.

"We were just about to start questioning him," Detective Ryan said, petulance slipping into his voice.

"My client will be answering no questions at this time." The lawyer swung his gaze over to Dax. "Have you said anything?"

Shaking his head, he smirked at Ryan. "No. The only words I've spoken were requests for my phone call, multiple times, which were never granted."

"According to what I've been told, you haven't charged my client with anything, and you're past the point where you can continue to detain him. So, unless you're going to charge him, I will be leaving with my client, and we'll be preparing a suit against Redemption City Police Department for police brutality and denying my client's constitutional rights."

Detective Ryan sputtered, caught off guard by someone who didn't cow to his badge and position. Before he could collect himself and respond, someone poked their head into the room and waved Ryan over. Whoever it was whispered harshly at Ryan, who nodded a couple times.

When they were done, Ryan shoved his way out the door, grumbling. Another man stepped in, this one wearing a suit that didn't come off a rack.

"There's no need for that camera," the new man said.

"Based on my client's appearance, there's a very good need for recording. Have you come to charge my client?" the lawyer asked.

"Not at this time. But as a person of interest, I would suggest you advise your client not to leave town."

"Very good." The lawyer kept the phone up and pointed at the man in the nice suit.

"Good day." The man turned and left the room.

Nodding at the door, the lawyer kept the camera rolling as Dax crossed the room and pushed out into a busy, more public-facing portion of the jail. When they emerged from the building, Dax squinted at the bright afternoon sun, blinking until his eyes adjusted.

"Don't say anything, Mr. Smith. Not until we're safely away." The lawyer put his phone away once they made it down the block and across the street.

They turned down another street. After they cleared that block, Dax thought he recognized the black Lincoln they were walking toward.

"It was easier to find your car and get it back than it was to find you. But don't say anything yet." The lawyer waved to the car.

Tomi popped out of the driver's seat and walked to the trunk to open it. Reaching in, he pulled out a black wand and pantomimed to Dax "to spread them." Dax spread his feet and held his arms out to the side as Tomi ran the wand over him, stopping when it went off near his left jacket pocket.

Dax was drawn by the sound of a latex glove snapping on as the lawyer approached, his hand now gloved. Taking hold of the jacket, the lawyer reached into the pocket and fished around until he found something, though he seemed to have trouble getting a grip on it.

Finally, he stepped back and held up a tiny, shiny object that wasn't much bigger than coffee bean, and a broad grin spread across his face. He set the object down on the concrete of the sidewalk in front of Dax, then stood and backed up, pointing at it.

Dax smiled and raised his boot, then smashed it down on the device and ground his heel in. The feel and sound of the device being pulverized warmed the cockles of his heart. He was about to speak when the lawyer raised his hand to stop him and waved Tomi forward again. After another pass without the wand being set off, they collectively breathed a sigh of relief.

"Tomi, do you have anything in the car that Mr. Smith can use to clean off his face?" the lawyer drawled.

Now that the lawyer wasn't in the middle of a tense stand-off with one of the most corrupt police departments in the country, a slight southern twang had slipped into his speech. He was a tall, Black man, a little overweight, and he wore an impeccably tailored suit. His natural afro was a bit on the longer side, reminiscent of an earlier generation. It matched the thick mustache.

Tomi emerged from the car with some wet wipes and handed them to Dax. It felt good to get the crusty blood off his face, though he imagined he still looked a mess.

"Fuck, Dax. You're going to have some nasty shiners." Tomi cringed. "And your nose is kind of jutting off to the side. What the fuck happened? We need to get Boudreaux down here to fix ya up?"

"That would probably be a good idea."

"I'm afraid we're going to have to get you to a proper doctor, Mr. Smith," the lawyer said.

"Please, call me Dax, Mister…" Dax stuck out his hand.

"Abernathy, but you can call me Frank."

"Not to be rude—"

Tomi snorted. He was always chiding Dax about not being more personable.

"But how did Tomi get ahold of you?" Dax asked.

"You'll have to ask Manman Delphine," Tomi supplied.

Shaking his head, Dax ran his hand through his sweaty hair. "Does she know half this city?"

Tomi shrugged. "She's a well-connected woman in a few different circles. And you're lucky she's taken a liking to you. She's bailed your ass out of trouble more than once."

"For that, I'm grateful." He owed the manbo much at this point. He'd have to find a way to pay her back, though more than likely she'd use any favors to help her community, as she had before.

"If Delphine Thibideaux doesn't know you, you're probably not worth knowing," Frank said. "I don't think a street corner is the place for this conversation. We need to get you to an urgent care to have your injuries cataloged and your nose straightened."

Dax sighed—more of his week ruined.

SIXTEEN

JAMIE

Morty the kitten screamed shrilly as he sat by an empty food bowl.

"Will you feed that damned cat?" Sharon called from the bedroom. "I'm trying to take a nap."

"Right now, he's more enjoyable to talk to than you," Jamie barked back, pushing herself off the couch.

"Don't sass me, young lady."

Rolling her eyes, Jamie headed into the kitchen to see if she could find food. Dax hadn't returned yesterday after saying he was only leaving for an errand. She tried to keep her cool, but what if the bikers had got him?

Jamie bent over, placing her hands on her knees. "Well, little buddy, where's your food at?"

Morty made one last shrill mew at the empty bowl and wandered over to rub her legs. Then he marched across the kitchen to a cabinet. Standing on his back feet, he propped his front paws on one of the doors.

"Is that the place?" She hated to rifle through a virtual stranger's cabinets, but the kitten hadn't had anything to eat since he'd run out of food the previous evening.

Inside, she found a few stacks of soft kitten food in cans. Grabbing one, she peeled the top and found the silverware drawer, pulling out a spoon. The entire can was too much for the pudgy little kitten, at least at a single sitting or on a hungry belly. She had no desire to clean up cat vomit, which would necessitate digging through more of Dax's sparse apartment.

The kitten shoved his head into the bowl almost before she could finish mashing the chunk of food into smaller pieces. He growled and almost pounced on the bowl, attacking the chunks of stinky, soft food. Jamie spun the can around in her hand, checking out the label. It wasn't the cheap stuff, but a high-end brand that wasn't sold in grocery stores.

Most of the things Dax had in his fridge were store brands or other bargain brands, but he splurged on the little black and white kitten.

He was supposed to have been back with groceries hours ago. Too afraid to leave the apartment, they'd been forced to raid what little food he had in his fridge and cupboards when he hadn't returned. She'd tried calling him but hadn't heard back, and she didn't have any other contacts.

So she called the bar after feeding Morty, asking for Dax. A woman told her he wasn't working. So Jamie asked for Tomi. Again, not working. It was nearly dark, and she wondered if she could sneak out for a quick grocery run.

She settled back on the couch to watch TV to wait for full dark but whipped her head around when metal scraped in the locks. After a couple more locks tumbled, the door swung open and Dax and his friend Tomi strolled in, carrying grocery bags.

"Where did you go?" She tried to temper her fear and annoyance. "I thought you'd gone to the corner store for cigarettes."

Dax's brow furrowed. "I don't smoke." His voice sounded weird, like he had a stuffy nose.

Tomi laughed. "It means she thought you made up an errand so you could skip town."

He grumbled low in his throat. "If only. Something else came up." He turned into the light.

"Holy shit, what happened to your face?"

The white gauze over his nose and the pair of black eyes spoke of a badly broken nose. She'd seen a few in high school, when hormonal, testosterone-fueled boys had gotten into fights to prove they were jackasses.

"Hey, kid, mind helping with the groceries?" Tomi said, lifting one of the three bags he carried awkwardly.

She leapt up from the couch and grabbed a bag from Tomi. Following them into the kitchen, she stopped abruptly when Dax stopped and blocked the way in. He stared at the kitten, who'd raised his front paws and pounced on his bowl, snapping up the last bit of mush before giving his head a little shake.

"Dude, you're holding up traffic," Tomi said, giving Dax a gentle nudge in the back.

"Right, sorry." He headed in and set his bags on the counter.

Jamie and Tomi followed, dropping their bags next to his. Tomi stepped out of the kitchen, but she stayed to help Dax and learn where everything went. If she was going to be a guest in his home for a while, she'd like to make sure things stayed clean and tidy. She didn't want to be a bad guest.

When they finished putting everything away, Dax picked up three generic colas, handing one to Tomi and one to her. They leaned against the counters and cracked open their cans.

After a few sips, Dax shifted his feet, looking down at the linoleum between the three of them. "Jamie, I hate to ask this of you, but I don't think there's much of a choice. Not if we're going to get out from under the threat of violence."

She didn't respond immediately after she realized he was pausing for a response. Fiddling with the tab on top of her cola, she finally looked up. "I'll do what I can, though I'm not sure what I can do that would be useful."

"You have a unique skill set we could use this evening," Tomi said.

"OK," she replied, sounding uncertain.

"Do you remember where you had that fight with that biker?"

"Biker?" She was confused momentarily. "You mean Travis? That pipsqueak wishes he were a biker. He's just their errand boy."

"Today." Tomi folded his arms across his chest. "If he doesn't find a way out, he'll be a full member someday. And after you kicked his ass, he'll have a grudge against you."

She'd left out the part of her story where he'd tried to get her to be his girlfriend for protection. She still felt gross about the whole thing. At no point in time had she ever wanted to be a biker's "old lady," nor would she consider it even for her own safety.

"Well, it sounds like you spilled his blood. That leaves a powerful scent trail." Dax's gaze intensified.

"What? Oh… Wait, what? I'm not a bloodhound." She shook her head to emphasize the point.

"Do you know a bloodhound shifter?" Tomi asked.

"No? Is that a thing?"

"How the fuck would I know?" He shrugged. "I figured you might know one. Isn't there some kind of pack in Red City?"

"No. Not that I know of. We're not part of one. All the shifters I know are unattached. Except for the bikers. I guess that might count." She wasn't sure she wanted to be used as a tracker, but she didn't want to be hunted by the bikers either. Most of all, she didn't want to be out in the open where they could make yet another attempt to hurt her.

"How many have you known?" Dax asked.

"Cory and his mom. Travis, and the bikers I've interacted with."

"That's weird." Tomi scratched his chin. "Wolves are pack animals. I'm surprised there's not one here, especially if there are several shifters in the city."

Dax smirked. "Alright, David Attenborough."

Tomi looked sheepishly at his friend. "What? I like nature documentaries. Though I doubt we'll see one anytime soon on the urban werewolf."

"Ugh." Jamie rolled her eyes. "We prefer the term 'wolf shifter.' We're nothing like movie werewolves."

The corner of Tomi's lip quirked up as he looked at Dax. "Guess you learn something new every day." He looked back to Jamie. "Are there other kinds of shifters?"

"Not that I'm aware of, but I don't have a big social circle. Plus it's not like we go around announcing we're paranormal humans. Do you know any?"

"Just the ones we've met through you," Dax said.

"We know a few magic users," Tomi added.

"Really?" She looked back and forth between them. "What kind?"

"A powerful voodoo practitioner and a couple of guys who work with Nordic runes. The non-white-supremacist kind. But they don't seem interested in getting involved in what's happening other than agreeing to the occasional clandestine consultation." Dax shifted his gaze to Tomi. "Do you know any others?"

"Besides you and Delphine?" He shrugged. "I don't get around as much as you do."

"You met Gunnar, briefly. And all the werewolves I have, almost."

Tomi chuckled. "I guess that's true."

Jamie was glad the conversation had taken a turn. She didn't want to go back out to the woods and track someone by their blood. She didn't know if she could even do it. She'd never tried before. Also, she didn't want to admit she was afraid to leave this supposedly safe and magically warded—whatever that meant—apartment. Even the illusion of safety helped her feel more comfortable for a rare change.

She lifted her eyes from the floor and looked at Dax. She'd seen what he was capable of when he'd chased her and Cory down after she'd shot him and they'd fled in Cory's car. And again when he'd beat wholesale ass in the bikers' clubhouse. Then there was what he'd done to the assassin… She shivered.

Taking a deep breath, she let it settle in her chest and filter through her body. If she didn't do what she had to do to help eliminate the threat against her, she'd always live in fear as long as she lived in Red City. And at the rate things were going, she'd never be able to escape this hell hole. That didn't mean she had to volunteer her services as a bloodhound, though…

"Let's return to the point we were discussing earlier," Dax said, steering the conversation back.

Damn, she thought.

She sighed heavily. "I'll do it. But on one condition. No, two conditions."

Dax narrowed his eyes. "What?"

"We need to stop by my hiding place to pick up my phone and wallet. Cory stashed them for me when I made a run for it. I need to get them and make sure he got away safely," she replied.

"And?"

"We bring a bathrobe."

A furrow of confusion split Dax's brow.

"You're not wolf shifters, so I won't be able to communicate with you when I'm in that form. And I'm not going to go butt naked at night in the woods in front of two old men I don't know." She crossed her arms and placed the most obstinate expression on her face she could.

Tomi laughed.

Dax nodded. "Fair enough. Do you have a robe, or do you need to borrow one?"

"I have one. Oh, and we'll need a backpack to stash my clothes in when I shift. Also, I can't make any guarantees about my abilities to track someone after two days. Or at all, really. I've never tried it before."

Dax nodded slowly a couple times. "Do your best. That's all we can ask, right, Tomi?"

"Yup. That's always the way of it. Do what ya can and hope it works out."

"When do you want to go?" she asked.

"No time like the present." Dax pushed off the counter. "Do you need anything else? Should we wake your mom?"

Jamie rolled her eyes, thinking about the argument that would ensue if she tried to talk her mom into letting her disappear into the woods with two strangers. "No. I'll leave a note. Let me grab my robe out of my bag."

"I'll get a backpack out of the closet." Dax strode into the living room while Tomi pulled out a notepad and a pen from a drawer and handed it to her.

In five minutes, they were out the door and rolling away in Dax's big black car.

SEVENTEEN

JAMIE

Jamie did her best to guide them as close as she could to where she'd emerged from the woods after her fight. Tomi, who had driven, found a nearby pullout and parked, then he got out and opened the back door for her, the door swinging backward instead of the normal forward.

"I don't know if I've ever seen a door open like that before," she said, watching Tomi close it as she pulled the robe out of the backpack.

"They're called suicide doors. I don't know why though," Dax said.

"Since they swing back, if they open while you're moving, whoever has to reach out to grab it and close it is likely to be pulled out and dumped onto the road," Tomi said.

Dax looked impressed with his friend's trivia. "Hmm, you're a veritable font of knowledge."

"Nah, I was just curious when you first showed them to me, so I looked it up."

Dax chuckled, then turned to Jamie. "Which direction do we go?"

"I think back a bit. I'm going to need to shift so I can find my trail." She took the robe and walked around to the other side of the car so it blocked her from being seen from the road. "Turn away, please."

She waited until they had, then waited until a car passed before taking her shirt off quickly and draping the robe over her shoulders to cover herself as she stripped down to nothing. Before she shifted, she folded her clothes neatly and shoved them into the backpack, tossing it over the trunk to land with a soft *thud* on the ground by Tomi's feet.

Taking a deep breath, she shifted quickly, wiggling out of the robe. She caught it in her mouth and dragged it around the car for Tomi to add to the bag. She'd have to wash it after dragging it on the ground.

Once they appeared ready, she looked both ways, then bolted across the road and into the woods, stopping just behind the line of shrubs.

She didn't look like a dog, even if she walked next to two humans —or one human and one…comic horror. Yipping to indicate her location and readiness, she snuffled along the ground, hoping they'd parked close enough. Unfortunately, they weren't that lucky.

She would have to try to the south instead. Keeping her nose low, she wound her way through the underbrush, periodically popping out to show herself to Tomi and Dax. She hated that this was where her life had led her—snuffling through the dirt looking for her own scent. But at least she was doing something.

The day and a half she'd spent locked in the small apartment with her mom with nowhere to go had ground on her faster than the fear of being hunted by violent bikers. It felt good to be outside and in the woods, even if this wasn't a leisurely trip.

"I hope she doesn't take too long to find something," Dax grumbled. "These boots are not made for hiking through the forest."

Tomi laughed. "That's your own dumbass fault for not making a better footwear choice."

If she could have laughed, she'd have joined Tomi in his assessment. Or maybe not. Dax intimidated her, maybe because he'd left The Rat's furry friends to finish killing the assassin. Fuck. Scared the shit out of her might be more accurate. After what she'd seen him do and who she guessed he was… She felt grateful she'd made the decision of turning against the bikers who'd extorted her. She'd half expected to sell her life for the lives of her parents and Cory and Linda, but Dax had been gracious enough to forgive her in favor of going after the real perpetrators.

She slowed and stopped. A shift in the breeze brought a familiar scent. Circling back around, she methodically sniffed back and forth until she found her own trail.

Excited, she turned and ran out of the bushes toward the road.

Tomi yelped and skidded to a halt, clutching his chest. "Damn! You nearly gave me a heart attack."

Dax snorted. "Don't make such a big fuss about it. Your life thread is perfectly strong."

"Dude, I told you not to tell me about shit like that. I don't want to know. I have to live a mortal life, I ain't got time to fixate on things I shouldn't know." Tomi shook his head and stood up straight, looking down at Jamie. "What's the matter, did Timmy fall down the well?"

Stepping forward, she peeled back her lips and growled.

Tomi held up both hands and backpedaled. "Sorry, Jamie. No more Lassie jokes."

Nearby, Dax chuckled. "Did you find something?"

Satisfied with the apology, she stopped the growl and hid her teeth. Nodding at Dax, she turned around and walked back into the woods, finding her trail again. Once she was sure she had it and that her companions were behind her, she advanced, her nose low as she followed her own scent trail back to the scene of her fight.

She wasn't sure she really wanted to visit the location of her victory. She'd killed a man a few months ago to save Dax from being shot. And though it had been necessary and the man she'd killed had been a truly bad man, she still struggled with the fact it had been her hand that had taken a life. But here, she'd savagely ripped into a boy she'd known for years and who'd just turned eighteen, like her. His destiny still wasn't entirely written. She'd done it with her teeth and tasted his blood on her tongue.

She gagged, backing up.

Forcing her mind to go blank, she stopped herself before she could go too far down that road. Keep her mind on the task, that was what she needed to do, even if it was proving increasingly difficult.

It didn't help that she didn't have anyone to talk with. Cory had been taken away from her and she couldn't tell a therapist, even if her mother's insurance covered one. Murder was murder, even when it involved the head of a criminal gang of violent bikers.

Shaking out her fur, she tucked her worries in the vault she hid such things in so she didn't lose the trail. Unfortunately the vault was getting full, so she had to cram the door shut. She wasn't experienced enough with her nose to split her attention. It was as good an excuse as any.

She stopped. The scent of blood, even after two days, smacked her in the face. The reflex to gag nearly overwhelmed her. She opened her jaws wide and dry heaved before getting herself under control.

Tomi squatted down nearby, his forearms resting on his thighs. "You OK? You need your robe?"

That slapped her out of her growing nausea. She shook her head vigorously, not wanting to shift here. She didn't know why being naked, even under a robe, felt so dirty in this place where she'd maybe killed someone with her own teeth.

No. He didn't die. Shifters could heal from almost anything, and she'd left him alive. He should have recovered. She stopped herself from thinking about it. She moved away to find a place to take a clean breath and inhaled deeply a few times. After noisily huffing out several deep breaths, she returned her nose to the ground.

Be professional. Be strong. Get it done. She sniffed around the clearing where Travis had confronted her. His scent was still strong. A lot of his blood had been spilt. Finding the spot where they'd tangled, she looked for a trail leading away that didn't contain her scent.

Once she found one, she moved along it. Travis had crawled off to the south, so she followed the strong scent of his blood. The crunch of leaves and the occasional snap of twigs let her know Dax and Tomi were following.

But when the trail of blood changed, she was forced to stop. It still smelled like Travis, but also different. She sniffed back down the trail, then returned to the transition point. Shifting… He must have shifted.

She swallowed hard. Was it *the last shift*? Had she hurt him worse than she thought?

Sensing something was up, Dax and Tomi stopped by a tree out of the way and talked quietly. If she wanted to, she could easily pick up what they were saying. Her ears were both wolf and supernatural, but she was too focused on figuring out what was going on with Travis's trail to care.

Sweeping widely over the trail, hoping to see if maybe Travis's biker buddies had maybe found him and helped him away, she stopped when she found a second scent.

The new scent trail had come from the north. It smelled human and dirty—rank body odor, marijuana, tobacco, and alcohol. It also had a mechanical aspect, like motorcycle exhaust. It must have been one of the other bikers, coming to see what was wrong with Travis, or at least to find out what had happened, though she hoped they'd at least shown enough care for one of their own to help the young asshole out of the woods and to some sort of medical care.

She'd have to change and talk over the next move with Dax and Tomi. She'd found the trail and followed it, and now they were at a decision point. She jogged back to Tomi and yipped at him.

"Ready for your robe?"

She nodded.

He pulled out the robe, then looked at her. She turned around so her tail was to him. Once he'd draped the robe across her back so the top came to just below her head, he backed away. She looked over her shoulder to make sure they had their backs to her—just in case.

In a flash, she shifted, shoved her arms into the sleeves of the robe, and tied the belt tightly, shivering a bit from the transition out of a warm fur coat and into her birthday suit.

"So, I found where I had the fight. And this is the first new scent I've picked up that isn't me or…Travis."

"The guy whose ass you kicked?" Tomi asked.

She grimaced. "Yeah. Him. There's a third scent."

"And you're sure it's human?" Dax asked.

"I don't know any deer that smoke or drink. I also got the distinct scent of human body odor and gasoline fumes. It smelled like one of the bikers." She held up a hand to forestall the question she could see forming on their lips. "Not one I know, but I've smelled the combo enough to place it. It was one of them. Anyway, what do you want to do now?"

Tomi and Dax looked at each other, but it was Dax who spoke. "Which way does the trail go?"

She pointed to the south. "That way."

EIGHTEEN

DAX

The ride back to Dax's house was filled with silence and frustration. They'd followed the trail to its end—an abandoned stretch of highway that led away from Red City, if they kept heading south. It seemed unlikely after spending so much time going south, they'd change directions and head back towards Red City.

The walk back to the car took a long time, and by the time they returned to Dax's apartment, it was closer to morning than midnight.

Trying to be courteous of Jamie's sleeping mother, Dax tried to unlock all the door's locks quietly. A small squeak when he opened it felt entirely too loud. He'd need to bring home a can of door hinge lube from the bar to resolve that problem. After letting the others in first, he backed in and shut the door quietly, releasing a held breath.

When he turned around, Tomi and Jamie had frozen in place and were staring at the couch. He saw why. Jamie's mother Sharon sat on the couch, stroking Morty like a cartoonish supervillain, her face a mask of anger.

Jamie swallowed, then licked her lips. "Mom—"

"What the fuck did you think you were doing, sneaking out after dark?" Her tone was low but laser sharp.

"Mo—"

"Leaving a note? No context? While I slept? With bikers trying to hunt us down?" Sharon's voice rose with each question until she was only a bit below yelling. "And now it's the wee hours of the morning. Is this what I have to look forward to? You staying out to all hours doing who knows what with who knows who? I was worried sick."

Next to him, Jamie had slumped, staring down at the ground until the last line, when her spine stiffened. "Worried? About me?" She scoffed. "Since when have you worried about me? I got good grades, so you ignored me and focused on fixing the fuckups committed by your deadbeat husband—"

"You watch your tone with me, young lady. Whatever he may have done, he's passed on now and you owe—"

Jamie's eyes bugged out. "Owe him what? What do I owe him? Just because you slept with him and got pregnant, doesn't mean I owe him anything. He didn't do anything for me. Or you, but you kept him around as he dragged us down. And look where it got us! Kidnapped by bikers. They were going to make me… They threatened to prostitute me to pay dad's debt. Where was your worry then? At least *daddy dearest* can't cause us any more harm, if we live through what he's already caused."

Sharon looked like she'd been slapped in the face and her arms relaxed in her lap. Morty rolled with the movement and crawled away, hopping down to the floor to wind between Jamie's legs, who scooped him up to pet him.

It took a few moments for Sharon to recover, but she'd lost some of her steam. "I'm still your mother, and you owe me the courtesy of at least discussing your plans with me."

"Do I? I'm the only one in this"—she made air quotes—"'family' who has been trying to keep us safe and get us out from under the shadow your husband created. And stop calling me a young lady. I'm an adult now. I'm making my own decisions, and if I fuck up, I'll own it and try to do better. That's more than you can say you've done."

Sharon stared at Jamie, her mouth open and tears threatening to spill from the corners of her eyes.

"You know what, *Mom*? I'm tired. I was out trying do something about our *family's* safety tonight. I'm going to bed." She stalked off to the bedroom, Morty still in her arms, and shut the door calmly behind her.

Tomi took a step backward, the movement drawing Sharon's attention.

"And you two? Grown-ass men—"

Tomi held his hand up. "I'm going to stop you right there, Mrs. Rodriguez. You're not my mama, so you don't get to yell at me like you are. Your daughter is a strong woman. And as long as she makes it out of this situation, she's probably going to do alright in life. Now I'm going to go home and get a few hours of sleep before I have to get up. I'll hug my mama and thank her for all she's done for me and my baby sis, then I'll go to work." Tomi turned to Dax. "You can crash on the couch at my place and let them have a little time to get their house in order."

Dax nodded, mouthing "Thanks" to Tomi.

"Please feed the man's kitten, and it wouldn't do you wrong to scoop a little shit, too." Tomi pursed his lips and shook his head, then grabbed the door and pulled it open. "Let's roll, Dax."

"Um, there's food in the refrigerator." Unsure what to say after that, Dax followed Tomi and locked the door from the outside.

NINETEEN

DAX

The sound of voices murmuring in the background brought Dax out of a dream featuring a pale-faced woman who disappeared like mist through his fingers when the light of day touched his eyes. Sitting up, he stretched and yawned, then grabbed his bag and headed to the bathroom to freshen up and change.

Peeling off his shirt, he cringed at his own body odor. The night in jail followed by a busy night trekking through the woods hadn't done much for his fragrance. Pulling a towel and a washrag from the cabinet, he turned the water on and took a quick shower, glad he had clean clothes to put on.

The shower went a long way toward waking him up, but what he really needed was a full night's rest, maybe two or three, to make up for the two nights of short and bad sleep. When he emerged from the bathroom, he caught a whiff of coffee and floated along into the kitchen on its tantalizing aromas.

When Dax walked into the kitchen, Tomi stuck out his hand and passed a freshly filled mug into Dax's grip. "Good morning, sunshine."

Dax grunted, running the cup under his nose. Coffee might be one of the finest of human inventions. Since he'd upgraded the bar's coffee, per the request of their patrons, he'd come to enjoy the dark elixir almost as much as his beloved tea. Tomi, always a fan of the finer things when he could afford them, used the bar's wholesale price break to stock the beans at home.

"Got anything to eat?" Dax asked, pulling out a kitchen chair.

"Yes, but mama said to come see her first thing. She's running her Louisiana red beans and rice as the special today, and she'll have some set aside for us. Said it was a good way to start a day after a short night."

A smile tugged the corners of Dax's tired lips up. He'd had her red beans and rice many times, but only as a guest in their home. She'd always complained she couldn't find proper Andouille sausage in Red City. Now that she had a little buying power as a restauranteur, she'd found a sausage maker who'd work with her for a custom job. She got the sausage she wanted, and the meat company got a new product to sell—Mama Adele's Louisiana-style Andouille, for which they paid her a small percentage of the sales.

"That sounds amazing."

Tomi set a travel mug down on the table. After Dax transferred the coffee into it, Tomi topped it off before putting on the lid.

"I like the way you think, Tomi. Let's not keep your mama waiting. That'd be rude." He smiled the first genuine smile he'd worn in a few days.

Tomi chuckled, picked up his own mug, and headed to the door.

Without discussing it, they skipped taking Dax back to his house to get his car. Neither of them wanted to walk in on another familial storm. Jamie would make sure Morty was fed. The little fuzzball seemed to have taken a liking to the young werew—wolf shifter.

He had to admit, he was growing to appreciate her presence. She'd done well taking them through the woods and had saved his life on a few occasions now. He didn't know what her future held, but he hoped Tomi was right and she'd find her place on a positive path.

Sharon… He had no idea what he thought of the woman. If he went by what Jamie had said, he wasn't certain he could form a positive impression of her mother. But that was a deeper story than he had the time or desire to dig into.

Tomi waited until they were on the road to attempt conversation. "So what we going to do? Wait until the bikers take another crack at you?"

"I'd prefer not to have that be our main plan. I'm reluctant to rely on the protection gris-gris and the protection oil"—he couldn't remember what kind of oil it was—"Delphine gave us."

"The manbo made oil? We'll put some of it around the bar. And Mama will want some for the restaurant. I'm glad you've still been wearing the gris-gris. I thought you were lucky not to take a bullet in that drive by. Even those biker fuckwads can't be that incompetent. Shit, it's Friday. You better give it some whiskey. I'll pick something good when we get to the bar."

Dax snorted. "Does the quality of the booze matter?"

"Bro, do you want to take the chance? Whiskey is cheap in the scheme of things, and it already sounds like it's done good work for you. Reward it with top shelf. We pay wholesale anyways. Don't cheap out on top-rate protection."

Dax stared out the window as Tomi wound his way through the surface streets of Red City. The shooters had been awfully close, and they'd missed him. Though some of the bullets might have penetrated flesh if he'd been wearing any at the time. It wouldn't hurt to give the gris-gris top shelf. The manbo hadn't steered him wrong yet, and Tomi certainly had kept him on the right path since they'd met.

"Do gris-gris work for locations?" Dax asked, looking around, his brow furrowing.

"Sure. We should probably have the manbo come down and bless the bar and set us up with some additional protection. The oil is a good start though. I'm surprised Mama hasn't had Delphine down to take care of the restaurant."

"Um, where are we going? This doesn't look like the normal way we take from your place."

"Sorry, the app is taking us this way. Something must be going on to block traffic on the boulevard." Tomi reached for his travel mug and tested his coffee, then gasped and noisily sucked in air. "Fuck, too hot still."

Now Dax recognized where they were. He'd been near here a couple weeks ago. He shivered, a nauseous pit opening in his stomach. The morgue. He'd been buried alive there after the assassin's bomb had nearly defeated him. The spirits still lingered, angrier than ever.

His breath grew shallower, and a sheen of sweat broke out on his forehead.

"Shit, you OK?" Tomi asked when he noticed his friend's discomfort. "Oh, shit…I'm sorry. I didn't think about the directions."

Dax could feel the rage and torment of the spirits tethered to the bodies. The city was busy trying to clean up the mess the assassin had made. He couldn't get anywhere near the building because of the tight quarantine the city had set up to investigate the building's destruction, nor was he sure he should. As pissed off as the spirits were, he wasn't confident he'd be able to resist their attempts to get to him. They saw him as an outlet, as a way to end their suffering.

He didn't know if he had the power to deal with them and free them, nor was he sure he'd be able to do it and stay under the radar of the death gods and psychopomps who'd teamed up to exile him. Ending the pain of the tethered ghosts might violate his agreement and the restraints they'd placed on him.

As saliva pooled in his mouth and stomach acid burned at the back of his throat, he swallowed roughly.

"Fuck," Tomi mumbled, and yanked the wheel to make a sharp turn. He followed it with another one that aimed them away from the morgue.

As the distance opened up, the anxiety and pressure in Dax's head lessened. "Thanks, Tomi."

"I'm sorry I didn't think of it in advance. Is it…you know… worse than before?"

"Yeah. Way worse. It's like their torment and anger have doubled. It's bad enough they were murdered and forced to stay tethered to their corpses, but someone set off a bomb and caused even more damage to the meat shells they'd once inhabited. Couple that with the time that's gone by…" Dax shook his head and shivered.

"That's not good. You're going to have to do something about it eventually."

"If we survive this. Though I'm not sure I want to jump from the pan into the raging inferno."

TWENTY

JAMIE

Dax's apartment was too small. She couldn't avoid her mother, though they spoke no words to each other, existing in the small space as if they were two ghosts from different eras.

The only solace Jamie got was petting and playing with the strange kitten, but Morty couldn't shield her from the icy glares of her mother. She'd lingered in the kitchen long after feeding time to watch him eat and play with one of his toys. At least in the kitchen, she couldn't see her mother's storm-darkened glare.

Finally, Jamie had enough. Snagging her keys and her wallet, she unlocked the door and pulled it open.

"Jamie—"

She interrupted her mother's admonition by shutting the door crisply. Her mother could take care of the locks herself. If she lingered to do it herself, it would only lead to a fight in the hallway.

Instead of hoping the elevator was on their floor, she pushed the bar on the door leading to the stairwell and flew down the concrete steps until she popped out of the back of the building. Only then did she slow down and look around, making sure she didn't see anyone suspicious lurking about.

She knew she was within the border, if she stayed close to the building, of the wards Dax had described, whatever those were. There was so much she didn't know about magic and all its varieties. She knew what she was, but not what anything else really was or what others could do, including the strange man who'd at first been her mark and was now her protector and ally.

Dax frightened her. More than a whole gang of Nazi werewolf bikers. She understood them, at least what they were and what they represented. Dax, though. He was the thing horror writers tried to capture but couldn't. At best, they danced around the edges. But she'd seen him. Seen what he could do. She had no doubt he could do far more scary things than what he'd shown to her.

Normally, she'd find a quiet piece of nature and shift. Running on four paws helped her think and find some semblance of calm, but she didn't know this part of town or if there were any safe parks or nature preserves nearby. Sighing, she walked toward the front of the building but stopped at the corner and leaned up against the wall.

She needed to do something more than sit around, hiding in an apartment. She and her mother couldn't stay in a borrowed place for much longer, not with the way their relationship was going. The cold anger burning between them felt worse than the hot grip of fear she felt being out in the world at large. She had to act if she wanted to reclaim her life.

Pushing off the wall, she took a step forward, then slumped back against the hard brick building. The will to act wasn't much good without a plan. A frown on her face, she stood in the shade as people walked by and tried to come up with an idea. It wasn't until a woman holding hands with a man strolled by that the first inkling of a plan took root.

If she was going to pull it off, she'd need help. With an idea in her head and purpose in her stride, she headed to the bus stop.

TWENTY-ONE

JAMIE

Jamie stood across the street from Dax's bar, staring at it. She was only eighteen, three years shy of the legal drinking age. Finally, she took a deep breath, waited for a car to pass, and jogged across the street. Before she could talk herself out of it, she confidently pulled the door open and stepped in. Blinking to adjust to the dim interior, she strode past the tables and chairs to address a short Black woman behind the bar.

The Black woman raised an eyebrow and opened her mouth, but before she could speak, Jamie cut her off. "I need to speak to Dax or Tomi, please."

"OK… Who should I say is asking?" she replied.

Jamie cut off a chuckle with a snort. "Tell them Dax's houseguest."

She wasn't sure why she didn't use her name, but when she cast her gaze into the mirror on the back bar, she caught a few curious eyes looking her way. She didn't know who was drinking here at noon in the middle of the week, but she thought caution was better than bravado.

"Alright, you wait here. I'll see if one of them is available." The woman paused to look around the bar to make sure the patrons would be fine for a minute, then headed down the hallway leading to the tearoom. A few moments later, she reappeared and waved Jamie over. "Come with me."

Jamie followed her back and waited for her to pull the sliding door open.

"Come in," Dax said. "Thanks, Suzie. I'll take it from here."

Suzie gave Jamie a faint nod and a neutral smile before returning to her post behind the bar. Dax and Tomi sat at the large table, bowls of steaming food in front of them. It smelled deliciously spicy. When her stomach growled, she realized she hadn't made herself breakfast or lunch before leaving the apartment.

Both men stared at her midsection. Her stomach must have been louder than she realized.

"Always seems like you show up at mealtime." Tomi chuckled and shook his head. "Go around the corner to the pickup window and tell Mama to hook you up with a bowl of beans and rice. Tell her you're a friend of the bar's."

"But...I can't—"

He raised his hands and made a "scoot" motion. Rolling her eyes, she turned around and headed out of the bar. Once she was outside, she followed her nose to the pickup window and rang the bell.

A moment later, an older Black woman wearing a green and black head wrap slid the window open and poked her head out. "What can I do for you, honey?"

"Um, Tomi said to ask for a bowl of beans and rice and to say I'm a friend of the bar." She gripped her hands, squeezing them nervously.

"You must be Jamie. No worries, dear. I'll be right back." She closed the window and reappeared a couple minutes later with a brown bag. "Here you go, honey. You enjoy that." She smiled warmly with what Jamie imagined was a motherly expression of encouragement.

"Thank you, ma'am." She fished around in her pocket for a few crumpled dollar bills and flung them into the tip jar before Tomi's mother could close the window, then walked away briskly before she could ask Jamie to take the money back.

Jamie appreciated the free food, but tipping felt like the least she could do. This time when she walked into the bar, she felt slightly more confident as she wound her way to the back. The conversation Dax and Tomi were having stopped once she opened the door. She hadn't caught anything distinguishable, though she could have if she'd wanted to. Dax gestured to a spot at the table where they'd set out silverware and a napkin, along with a soda. They must have done it while she'd been procuring her lunch.

Once she got out her sausage-laden red beans and rice, along with a nice chunk of cornbread, she tore into the food, eating silently as the two older men finished their lunch. Once Tomi cleaned up the empty to-go tin bowls and wiped the table down, he put on hot water, probably for Dax's tea, which he always seemed to drink whenever they met in this room.

She waited, growing more impatient to explain her idea with each moment Dax took to fiddle with his tea while humming some melody she'd never heard before.

Once a cup of green tea steamed in front of each of them, Dax leaned forward, making eye contact with her. "What brings you out today, Jamie?"

She looked down, fidgeting with her fingers. "Um, I think I have an idea, but I'm not sure I can pull it off by myself."

"How so?" Tomi asked.

"Well…" She swallowed and picked up her tea, taking a hasty stip. "Ah!" She fanned her scalded tongue as Tomi chuckled and Dax smiled indulgently. "Sorry about that." At least her tongue would heal quickly. There were benefits to being a shifter.

"I appreciate your enthusiasm for my tea but do give it a bit more time. You were saying?" Dax prompted.

"To pull off my idea, I'm going to need a bit of money and maybe some magical help, but I'm not sure where to start with either." When they indicated she should continue, she sketched in the basics of her idea.

Dax and Tomi glanced at each other, exchanging a look of some sort, before returning their attention to her.

"It sounds pretty dangerous. Are you sure you want to go

through with it?" Dax asked. "I mean, I'm not your family, but someone should bring it up."

Jamie nodded. "I want to get out from under this…whatever it is we're living under. I'll never be able to live a real life without seeing this through and making sure there's no one coming up behind me to stab me."

Dax let her statement stand for a moment, taking a sip of tea while keeping eye contact. "Alright. We've got a bit of money we can give you, though it probably won't take much for what you have in mind."

Tomi chuckled. "I love the irony of using the bikers' money to turn the tables on them. I think Suz can help her out."

"Then the manbo?" Dax asked.

"She's our go-to for magic. Or she'll know who can help us."

Dax shook his head. "If she'll even want to help after I got her shot at."

Tomi shrugged. "We're from New Orleans. A little gunfire isn't going to scare away the manbo. Besides, she's already in deep. She likes you and respects you. Having her in your community is a good thing, and she's invested in your continued survival. She knows a lot of people, and they all seem to owe her favors."

"I know. She's helped me out too many times already, but still…"

Jamie narrowed her eyes thoughtfully as she listened to their debate. She had no idea who "the manbo" was, or why she'd cause Dax concern. If someone like him had a healthy respect for the manbo, she wondered if it was a good idea to get involved with some mysterious power broker with magic that worried the likes of Dax. But it was either take some chances or live in fear forever…if she made it that long.

"Tomi, would you mind asking Suzie if she'll help out? It'll be on the clock with a bit of bonus to cover any missed tips." Dax finished his cup of tea, tipping the cup up dramatically.

"Sure thing, dude. I'll send her back and cover the bar." Tomi stood and headed toward the door but stopped. "But if we're going to be sending Suzie on a task outside the bar, we're going to need someone else to bartend. Even with Becky, we're running ragged as it is."

Dax sighed. "I hear you. If either you or Suzie know someone who's trustworthy, let me know." He looked down at his phone briefly after it buzzed, a furrow wrinkling his brow. "Hell, just get them hired. I don't have time to sit for interviews. I trust you both to get the right person."

"You got it, Dax." Tomi left.

A moment later, the short, curvy, Black woman from behind the bar stepped into the room, sliding the door shut behind her. She had awesome natural hair, which was arranged in an afro. "What's up, Dax? Tomi said you have a favor to ask."

"Suzie, this is Jamie. She needs a little help, and you're probably the best person suited to provide it. Jamie, this is Little Suzie. She's punk as fuck." He winked at his bartender and smiled.

Suzie snorted, then eyed Jamie up and down, a mask of neutrality spread over her face. "OK. What is it?"

"I'll let her explain so it's not twisted through a middle person. Do you know Manman Delphine, the manbo?"

"I don't think I've ever met her, but I know of her," Suzie replied.

"Good. When you're done with the first part of Jamie's plan, take her to the manbo for the second part. I'll let Delphine know you're coming. Oh, and I don't know if Tomi mentioned it, but if you know of someone who's reliable and *trustworthy*"—he emphasized the word again—"we need to hire some more help behind the bar."

"I might know a person or two, but I'll want to think it over and talk with Tomi before reaching out to them. Becky was my top-of-mind good suggestion, and I haven't been in town long enough to have a deep list to pull from."

"I understand. Go wrap up anything you need to do behind the bar. Tomi will take over for the rest of your shift. Jamie, you stay here until she's ready." Dax stood up and left the tearoom.

A couple minutes later he reappeared and pulled out his phone, checking a message before typing out a couple while Jamie fidgeted with her hands under the table.

Fifteen minutes later, Suzie came in wearing a light jacket and holding a big, black leather shoulder bag. "I'm ready to go."

Reaching into his pocket, he pulled out a rolled-up wad of cash and handed it to Suzie. "Expenses."

She winked at him. "I'll be careful with it." She turned to Jamie. "Ready to go?"

Jamie nodded and followed her out, saying nothing. She couldn't tell what the woman thought of her so far; she'd been less than revealing in her reactions. Nor did Jamie know if she was normally reserved or just holding judgement for the moment.

A few minutes later, they stopped at a small, immaculately clean and cared-for black Honda Civic.

"This is us. You can tell me what I can do to help you as we roll. OK?"

"Sure."

Suzie laughed. "You're a quiet one. I'll need more details than that."

TWENTY-TWO

JAMIE

Once Jamie told Suzie the sketches of her plan, the young Black woman got excited for the chance to help Jamie with her makeover, taking her to a few thrift and boutique stores where they could find the gear Jamie would need.

Suzie turned out to be a fun, vivacious person once the ice was broken. Jamie hadn't had a female friend since Rachel had moved away after seventh grade. After that, it had just been Cory.

As Suzie loosened up, so did Jamie. It felt good to talk to someone near her own age. Suzie was twenty-five. With the exception of the brief outing with Cory, she'd only had her mom to talk to recently, and they hardly spoke, not lately anyway. It helped to ease her anxiety, but the closer they got to finishing their shopping, the more nervous she got about meeting the mysterious Manman Delphine.

"Um, so, Suzie, who or what is Manman Delphine?"

"The manbo? She's a powerful voodoo priestess. Auntie Adele is good friends with her—you met her when you picked up food today. We're all from New Orleans originally, though they both moved away after Hurricane Katrina."

"Voodoo?"

Suzie nodded.

"If your auntie is her good friend, how come you haven't met her?"

"My mama didn't want me getting involved with voodoo. It can be dangerous stuff." She smirked.

"And Dax thinks she can help me?"

Suzie shrugged. "Maybe? I don't know. I don't know much about voodoo, really. Only what ran through the zeitgeist in New Orleans." She paused for a moment. "I've never met her, but I've heard a few stories. She's not a good person to get on the bad side of. Be respectful. Refer to her as Manman Delphine."

"Is she scary?"

Suzie laughed. "If you're her enemy, I hear she can really fuck you up."

Jamie's nerves flared up again as her stomach twisted and grumbled, and her brow furrowed.

Seeing her expression, Suzie reached over and patted her knee. "Don't worry. Delphine and Adele are good friends, and Delphine has taken an interest in Dax. I'm sure you'll be fine."

Nodding nervously, she stared ahead, not seeing where they were going. *"I'm sure you'll be fine"* didn't have much of a ring of certainty to it. She sighed, shaking her head and slumping deeper into her seat.

She'd spent all her life protecting herself by not trusting anyone except for a select few. Her parents weren't even in that number. Cory had been. She'd thought his mother could be trusted, but there'd been a line beyond which that trust had faded. Now she'd put herself in a place where she had to trust strangers for her future well-being. Not just one, but several. And they weren't just some random humans—except for Tomi and now Suzie—but scary, powerful supernaturals. The Grim Reaper and a voodoo priestess.

It wasn't a comfortable place to arrive at in such a short period of time. Not only was she relying on new people but relying on them to put her in contact with others she had to trust in some limited fashion.

"Welp, we're here." Suzie turned off her Civic and pulled the parking brake lever.

Taking a deep breath, Jamie opened the door and practically threw herself out of the car to overcome the inertia of fear. She caught herself after a brief stumble and exhaled noisily, straightening to her full height. "I'm ready."

Chuckling, Suzie placed her hand in the small of Jamie's back and pushed her gently toward a door at the corner of an odd, triangular shaped building. The small wooden sign above the door said, *Madame Thibodeaux's*.

Suzie held the door open and guided Jamie in. The smell of spices, herbs, and carved wood assailed her as soon as she crossed the threshold. Bright colors, unique objects, and bins of mysterious supplies filled the shelves. As someone who'd only shopped at soulless chain discount stores, this small shop screamed exciting and forbidden. She didn't know if it was magic she felt, but there was something here that touched her in a way that was entirely new to her experience.

"Wow…" she mumbled under her breath.

"Right?" Suzie said, catching what her new friend had said. She cleared her throat and stepped past Jamie, deeper into the store. "Manman Thibodeaux? Hello?"

"Welcome to my shop." A rich voice with a New Orleans accent drifted from the back of the store as a tall, Black woman stepped from a door behind the counter. "Ah, you must be Suzie and Jamie. Dax let me know you'd be by. How can I help you?"

"I'm just the wheels. Jamie is the one who needs some help." Suzie marched forward, dodged down an aisle, and offered her hand to Manman Delphine, who took it.

The manbo stood up straighter, her eyes flashing wider before narrowing as she fixed her gaze onto Suzie's face. "You're Adele's niece?"

"Yes, ma'am," Suzie replied with a bit of a quaver in her voice, her hand still gripped in Manman Delphine's.

Something important was happening, but Jamie didn't know what or think it was her place to ask.

"Child, we need to talk in detail when we have time and privacy. But now you have a mission, and when it's finished, I have to close up and get ready for cards with the gals tonight." The manbo let go of Suzie's hand, then placed hers on the girl's shoulder. "Don't worry. I don't think it's anything bad. At least I don't think so..." She winked at Suzie and turned to Jamie. "What can I do for you? Dax gave me the outline of what you're looking for."

"Yes, Madam Thibodeaux..."

"Please, call me Delphine. Or Manman Delphine if you insist."

Jamie held her hands in front of herself, gripping her fingers tightly. "Yes, Manman Delphine. I need a way to disguise myself... magically...from wolf shifters."

Suzie stepped back, quirking her head to one side, her gaze flicking from Jamie to the manbo.

"I see. Just scent?"

"I mean, if you can disguise my appearance too, that would be amazing..."

Manman Delphine narrowed her eyes. "Hmm, from wolf shifters? I'm guessing they already know you?"

"One definitely does. A few others also, probably by sight and maybe scent."

"Let me think... Let me think..." She rolled her eyes up slightly, staring toward the ceiling at nothing. Lowering her gaze, she leaned her head forward and squinted at Jamie.

The scrutiny of the manbo made Jamie want to step back and hide, but she steeled her spine and stood still, though her heart beat faster.

"Come here, child." The command was inescapable.

First one step, then another, then before she knew it, she stood in front of the manbo.

Lifting her hands to both sides of Jamie's head, Manman Delphine paused before laying her hands on the young woman standing before her. "May I place my hands on your temples? There's something about you... If I can make this work, I need to ensure it's tailored to you. And for that, I need to know you better."

Jamie, unable to get her mouth to form words, simply nodded. When Manman Delphine's palms covered Jamie's temples, her body went rigid, and her eyes rolled up into the back of her head. Doors she didn't know she kept closed tightly suddenly opened, though they weren't kicked down violently. The touch felt gentle and soothing. Then the manbo's presence disappeared as quickly as it had entered.

Drawing in a deep, gasping breath, Jamie's knees wobbled but two sets of hands caught her upper arms and held her upright.

"Let's get her to the back room, Suzie." The manbo's voice sounded distant, yet strong.

Together, the two women navigated Jamie through the confines of the store's aisles, around the corner behind the counter, and into the back room and onto a chair. Finally taking back control of her legs, she propped herself up before she could slide off the end of the seat onto the floor.

"My apologies, child. I didn't expect that to happen, at least not quite like that." Manman Delphine pulled out two chairs and set them opposite Jamie.

"What did you see?" Suzie asked. The words floated out airily, though Jamie couldn't tell if it was due to something about her ears or Suzie's voice.

Manman Delphine narrowed one eye and quirked the eyebrow of the other up. "Would you like to see for yourself?"

"What? No? Why?" Panic tainted Suzie's voice.

A rich laugh erupted from the manbo. "Perhaps we'll leave that discussion for later. I'll see if Dax will let me borrow his tearoom. It can't be a proper discussion without tea."

"Wha…what happened?" Jamie squeaked out.

"You have many doors shut against the outside world, child. When I entered your mind, those doors opened quicker than I expected, all of them nearly at once. Or almost all of them, anyway."

"How?" Jamie kept her emotions and memories tightly walled inside to protect them from the world she'd been forced to grow up in, both in her home and the larger world of Red City. It didn't feel like the manbo had broken in. Her touch had been gentle…understanding.

"Kindness, child." Sympathy and empathy poured from Manman Delphine's eyes and face. "You protect yourself from the harshness of your world. If I'd tried to force my way in, it would have taken a lot of strength to break your doors down. Which I wouldn't have done, even after your initial consent."

"Then how did you get in?"

"Deep down, you crave kindness, friendship, community. In protecting yourself from those who would take advantage or abuse, you've also cut yourself off from those who would nurture and care. Without those who would help you grow, you won't be able to develop and defeat those who seek to use and dominate."

Jamie blinked erratically, trying to keep the burn in her eyes from spilling over into tears. "How do I tell the difference?"

"Use what you've learned and experienced in your life. You've got a pretty good idea of what bad people and even indifferent people look like. Have you known good, kind people?"

She swallowed and thought about the manbo's question. "Cory… But he was basically a big dumb puppy dog. Not everyone is that open."

Manman Delphine laughed. "How very true. But it's still useful information. You've experienced both sides of the spectrum; use that to figure out where people fall on it and be open to adjusting your initial impressions as you learn more about them. Sometimes first impressions are incorrect, but trust your instincts."

Jamie dashed the tears from her eyes. "That doesn't sound easy."

Manman Delphine reached out and squeezed Jamie's shoulder. "It isn't, but it's worth it." She sat back and took a deep breath. "Now. Onto business. You are a wolf shifter yourself, aren't you?"

"Yes."

"Really?" Suzie said. "That's so cool!"

"Indeed. But it does make things a little more difficult. Shifters, in my experience, are fairly impervious to most magic."

Jamie slumped in disappointment.

"Don't fret, child. Difficult does not mean impossible. I believe I can create a gris-gris bag that can filter your scent, even from an experienced shifter. I think I'll mix it with a fast luck gris-gris. Give it a little boost." Her finger tapped her thigh. "Let's focus on your main target. How strong of a mind does he have?"

Jamie scoffed. "Not very. He's not bright, and he's easily controlled."

Suzie leaned closer, interested. "What about her appearance? We're giving her a new wardrobe and a new hairdo, but…"

Manman Delphine smiled knowingly at Suzie. "If what I have in mind works, the gris-gris will also obfuscate her appearance somewhat. Maybe. I'm not a Hollywood visual effects master. But I think I have some other things we can do in combination."

"What do you mean?" Jamie asked.

"I think I'll send you home with some blue bath for protection or maybe white bath for purification. That might be the better option. It'll cleanse your aura and revitalize your spirit. And I think it'll provide a cleaner slate for the gris-gris to work its magic. If I boost the gris-gris with some Dragon's blood oil, it'll kick it up a notch."

The manbo stood up and turned around, picking up bottles and setting them back down. "I think a bit of confusion oil as a backup is a good idea. It works by inhaling the scent. If you get desperate, you can put some on your target. Hmm." She tapped her chin as she looked at her shelves. "I think, though, we'll do a spell to create confusion."

"Will it work? On a wolf shifter, I mean?" Jamie asked.

"On a weak one? Yes. At least partially." She turned and grinned. "But without a bit of gambling, life isn't as fun."

Jamie's stomach grumbled nervously. Her life was exciting enough, and not in the good way. But it was her plan, and it was the best they had at the moment.

Manman Delphine pulled down a black skull candle from the shelf. "I'll need you to carve the name of your target into this candle. Be sure to hold that person in your mind as firmly as you can and pour your intent into the candle. If you let me touch your mind while you do it, I can finish the spell when you're ready and give it a boost that should make it more effective."

"Will it work to change her appearance?" Suzie asked.

"It'll confuse the mind of the target so any signals that get around the gris-gris which might identify her will fall on a dull mind and be missed."

"Whoa, that sounds so cool," Suzie whispered. "Will they notice it?"

The manbo shook her head. "No. Most people aren't terribly observant, especially with the spell in effect. Only a serious magic user would be able to notice something was off. With the confusion spell, even people who know what she looks like and know about the gris-gris will have trouble working out what's going on. People's minds are wonderful at filling in the gaps and turning confusing stimuli into recognizable patterns, even if they're not the correct ones." She narrowed her eyes at Suzie, the corners of her mouth tipping up a bit. "Though maybe not with you."

Suzie's eyes flashed wide as she sat back, drawing away from Manman Delphine.

The manbo returned her focus to Jamie. "So, what do you think, Jamie? Are you interested in trying something new with me? I will need a bit of your person for the gris-gris."

"Of my person?"

"Something as simple as a lock of hair will work. The gris-gris needs to know you so it can take what it's given and modify it."

Suzie chuckled. "We can take a bit of hair off the end somewhere. I'm thinking something a bit more radical than just a trim will be needed for the makeover."

Jamie reached up and touched some hair protectively. Then her eyes narrowed, and she pulled a lock free. "Do it."

TWENTY-THREE

DAX

Dax pulled up to the roadhouse dive located thirty minutes outside Red City. The exterior wood of the building had been weathered by rain, snow, and time, making it look like a prairie derelict, except it was still fully standing and the disrepair appeared more from intentional cosmetic choices than poor maintenance.

The parking lot was filled with pickups, cars of all varieties, and a fair few motorcycles, gathered in small packs. Neon beer signs for domestic brands belched their light from shadow boxes spread about the covered porch running along the entire front of the building. A few smokers sat at the two top tables situated down the length of the porch as a pretty server in a tight shirt and short shorts buzzed about, dropping beers and collecting more orders. Old-school "outlaw" country music, dulled a bit by the walls, drifted into the night.

As Dax rolled around the parking lot, he looked for anything suspicious, but it was hard to tell if something was or not, since he'd never been out to The Honky Tonk Woman. He'd always been curious about the bar named after the famous Rolling Stones song, though he didn't know if it was in fact named after it. But it was a long drive to drink cheap beer and listen to country music, which was why he hadn't bothered to visit until he got an invite.

After finishing a circuit of the lot, he slid into a spot that pointed out to the road, so he couldn't be blocked in from the front if he needed to make a quick exit. He normally didn't live his life planning to be…bushwhacked—as the denizens of a country bar might say—but with the bikers back in town potentially looking for trouble and this new meeting place, he let caution dictate his actions.

Taking one more glance at his mirrors, he decided everything looked like a dive bar having a busy night.

Stepping out, he shut the door and shoved his hands into the pockets of his black leather jacket. With a glance back at his 1965 Lincoln Continental, he decided he'd have to get it washed tomorrow to knock off the dust from the road and the parking lot.

As Dax approached the entrance, a thick, tall bouncer stood by the set of double doors, his muscular arms folded menacingly over his bulging chest. With a shaved head and a scruffy, medium-length beard, a black T-shirt, and black leather vest, he looked the part. The mean mug he gave people as they entered served as punctuation.

Walking in like he belonged, Dax nodded politely to him as he passed. When he pushed through the doors, the wall of sound nearly knocked him back out the door. They had the jukebox cranked up tonight.

He stepped out of the way of the door and looked around until he saw the thatch of red hair and beard that belonged to Ragnar Gunnarsson, who sat in a booth in the left front corner of the bar. As Dax strode toward the booth, eyes swung his way, checking out the new guy.

"Ragnar," Dax said, stopping at the edge of the table.

Ragnar gestured to the open booth seat opposite him. "Dax."

As soon as his butt hit the vinyl seat, a server in a tight T-shirt and short shorts sauntered up to the table. "What can I get for ya, hon?"

He caught sight of the can of PBR sitting in front of Ragnar. "I'll take a Pabst tallboy and one for my friend, if he wants one."

Ragnar nodded, and the server smiled at him and departed.

"Thanks for the beer, Dax." Ragnar leaned back, stretching an arm down the back of the seat's top. "And thank you for driving out here to meet me."

"It's a bit out of my range, but I was curious. After what happened at Delphine's, I figured I wouldn't see either you or your father, though I figured the same when last your father's path crossed mine."

"The bullet?"

Dax nodded. Ragnar seemed a man of few words, which might make this difficult, since he was too. But instead of pressing, he decided on patience. Ragnar had made the effort to invite him out; he'd get to the point eventually. And if he'd invited Dax just to scope him out, it still would be worthwhile use of his time. In the present circumstances, a relationship with a man who had knowledge of Nordic rune magic would be worth cultivating.

He'd hoped Ragnar's father would be that man, but he, like so many people in Red City, was afraid to get involved. Dax wasn't interested in getting involved either, but for different reasons. Gunnar had a community to protect, which Dax assumed included Ragnar. Dax had considered refusing the meeting to honor Gunnar's wishes to not involve his son any deeper than his father could control, but Ragnar was a grown man who could make his own decisions.

Ragnar looked around the bar, then fixed his gaze on Dax and lifted a coppery eyebrow. "So what do you think of the Woman?"

"The Woman"? He must mean the bar. "I like it so far. Definitely gives classic roadhouse from the outside and doesn't disappoint when you walk in."

Ragnar quirked the corner of a lip up and nodded. Apparently, that was all the acknowledgment he was going to give Dax. When the server returned, Dax gave her a ten-dollar bill and put the change back in his wallet, save for two bucks for the tip. Pabst wasn't his favorite cheap beer, but he didn't know if they had Rainier and he didn't want to make a fuss over which cheap beer to order.

Taking his cue from Ragnar, he relaxed into the back of the booth with his can of beer, taking a sip. Some old Kris Kristofferson song was blaring over the jukebox. Dax had always enjoyed the bit of outlaw country he'd heard. He felt it was the flip side of the coin to punk. Both were antiauthoritarian and made by outsiders for outsiders. He didn't get much of a chance to listen to it since Tomi wasn't a fan, preferring hip-hop and rap when they weren't listening to punk or metal.

He caught himself bobbing his head along after a couple songs. The only thing that tipped him off that he was being watched was the appreciative smile on Ragnar's face.

"Didn't think you'd be into country and western. Dad said you owned a punk and metal bar." Though Ragnar didn't speak loudly, his smooth voice carried over the music just enough to land in Dax's ears.

"It's good." Dax smirked. "It's just punk with a pedal steel guitar."

Ragnar narrowed his eyes and leaned forward, staring at Dax. At first he snorted, then shook his head as a chuckle bubbled into a laugh. "That's a good point." He lifted his can of PBR, tipping the top slightly toward Dax. "Fuck the man."

Dax raised his can. "Fuck the man."

Leaning forward, Ragnar adjusted his seat, resting his elbows on the table in front of him. "How much do you know about…the magic community in Red City?"

Tapping his forefinger on his can, he tried to order a list in his head. "Not much, really. I've lived here for a few years, but until recently, I've minded my own business and kept to myself. I didn't know of anyone else specifically, nor did I go looking."

"Nor?" Ragnar smirked.

Giving half a shrug and an eye roll, Dax continued. "But beyond Delphine and I guess your father and you, I only know a few wolf shifters. Besides the white-supremacist bikers. that is."

Nodding, Ragnar slid his fingers into his beard and scratched his jaw before smoothing the wiry hair out. "I'll sketch some basics in for you. My grandparents emigrated from Norway before my father was born. They thought Redemption City sounded like a good place, mostly based on the name."

He scoffed derisively, shaking his head. "That was a mistake, but by the time they figured it out, they were here and too broke to move anywhere else. Having my father kind of cemented their fate. It wouldn't have been so bad if they could have found a community. Sure, they stayed in the neighborhoods where other Scandinavian immigrants tended to gather, but what they were looking for was a new wolf pack to join."

He paused and raised an eyebrow, and Dax gave him a slight nod to acknowledge that he understood the information he was being given. Apparently, he knew at least two more wolf shifters.

Ragnar continued. "When he couldn't find a pack, even though there were other wolf shifters in town, he tried to form one, in spite of being warned not to by some of his new friends. He never could get a firm answer from them as to why he shouldn't try.

"However, he did get an answer when a group of men showed up at his door. They were Norse like my grandfather, and they informed him that only one pack was allowed to exist and only those of pure Scandinavian heritage could join. They offered to let my grandfather and his family join under the condition he quit associating with shifters of other cultures."

"I'm guessing these fine gentlemen who accosted your grandfather were the same bikers I'm stuck dealing with now?"

Ragnar nodded but didn't continue his story. A moment later, the reason why sidled up to the table to see if they needed another round. Ragnar ordered a couple more beers, putting it on his tab. He kept silent until after the server returned and dropped off their next round of tallboy cans.

"Back to your question. You are correct. One and the same. Anyway, my grandfather told them to go fuck themselves, though probably in a more polite tone. But he didn't quit. Behind the scenes, he tried to bring together the disparate wolf shifters of Red City. But every time he tried, the Norse gang would intimidate those who considered throwing in with my grandfather."

"Why didn't they get tougher with your grandfather?" Dax asked.

"I think they were still hoping to get him to join. People liked him and he'd gotten further than anyone else in uniting everyone, so they thought he'd be a good asset. But the old man wasn't into that racist bullshit. Once the bikers realized he wouldn't join, they did get more aggressive with him." Ragnar looked down, his shoulders tightening. "They eventually murdered him."

Dax scowled. "Let me guess. The police couldn't find a suspect, and no one was arrested?"

Ragnar tapped his nose. "Yup. Even back then, the cops and bikers were in bed together. The bikers make for cheap hired muscle when you need dirty work done that you don't want laid on your doorstep. I guess his killing is officially a cold case, like a lot of other murders the cops either performed or sanctioned through one of their cronies."

Dax had assumed a link between the cops and the bikers existed, but having it confirmed, even if it was still opinion and conjecture, helped him solidify some fuzzy lines in the chart of suspects who were trying kill him he had running in his head. "Is that why your father is into keeping a lower profile?"

"Yeah. Don't get me wrong, I love and respect my dad, but losing his father that way scarred him. He's a good leader and looks out for the unaffiliated wolf shifters of Red City, as quietly as he can. But without being able to form a real pack, he's limited to community organizing, like any other activist. He's a smart man and keeps things on the downlow."

Dax narrowed his eyes. "But you don't exactly agree with his methods?"

"I'm sure our little argument spelled out some of our differences for you. But—"

A short, brown man wearing a black cowboy hat with the sides folded up sharply and a rattlesnake head affixed to the front of the band stopped by their table. "Ragnar, it's time for soundcheck. You ready? Or are you going to flap your gums all night?"

"Yeah. I'll be up shortly."

Seeing Dax, the man lifted his hat slightly and tipped his head down. "Sorry for interrupting."

"No problem," Dax replied.

"Well, I have to go onstage for a bit. I figured we'd be done talking before they called soundcheck." Ragnar slid out of the booth and strolled across the busy barroom floor toward the stage. On his way to center stage, he picked up a guitar and plugged it in once he stood in front of his band and behind the mic.

After a brief soundcheck, Ragnar and the rest of the band stepped offstage and through a door leading to what was probably a greenroom.

TWENTY-FOUR

DAX

A white woman in worn jeans, a plaid shirt, and a brown cowboy hat stepped on stage. "Welcome to music night at the Honky Tonk Woman! We're proud to welcome back local favorites Ragnar and the Desert Rattlers. Put them hands together and give 'em a warm Honky Tonk Woman welcome!" She demonstrated by backing up and clapping.

The crowd clapped and stomped, some even whistled. They kept up the noise until the band reemerged and plugged in.

"Thank you, Honky Tonk Woman! I'm Ragnar and these are the Desert Rattlers…" He swept his hand back to indicate the others on stage with him—a tall, muscular white woman on standup bass, a skinny Black man wearing a bolo tie on pedal steel guitar, the brown man who'd interrupted their conversation on guitar and, judging by the instrument on a nearby stand, banjo, and an Asian woman on drums.

Counting down from four, Ragnar launched them into a hard-driving tune reminiscent of the old-school outlaw country that had been playing on the jukebox. He couldn't tell if it was a cover or an original, since his knowledge of the genre was just above basic. The band, anchored by Ragnar's rich baritone, kept the audience happy.

As the set continued, more people drifted in, and the latecomers had trouble finding decent seats.

Several eyed Dax sitting alone in his booth. The only thing that kept them from haranguing him was the sign on the end of the table that said, *Reserved for the Band*. Ragnar kept the audience hopping as he led his band through a set driving tunes with an occasional down tempo song interspersed. The lyrics focused on topics ranging from poverty to crime and racism, as well as classic themes like bootlegging and evading the law. Once the first set ended, the crowd stood, clapping and whistling, and stomped their boot-clad feet, making the wood floor shake.

The band took their bows and quickly set their instruments aside, weaving their way through the crowd toward Dax's table. For a moment he panicked on the proper protocol. He had no idea if he was supposed to find his own spot with the whole band on the move, or what.

"Scoot over, Slim," the bass player said, nodding at Dax.

Relieved to have the decision made for him, he edged over until he was against the wall. The bass player slid in next to him as the rest of the band packed themselves into the booth. With hips pressed to hips, Dax felt like a sardine in a can in the tight confines of the booth.

Chucking his chin toward Dax, Ragnar placed an arm around the drummer's shoulders. "Everyone, this is Dax. Dax, this is my band. You're sitting next to my bass player Melinda. Next to her is Mississippi Pete, who also plays a mean harmonica when he's not on the pedal steel, but we just call him Sippi. You kind of met Jose earlier. And this"—he squeezed the drummer's shoulders—"is Constance; the band calls her Crash."

She stuck out a hand across the table for Dax to shake. "You can call me Connie; only Ragnar and my parents call me Constance. So how do you know Ragnar?"

"I guess you could say I'm an acquaintance of his father, Gunnar."

Melinda nodded. "Ah. What brings you out this way? Big fan of country western music?"

Ragnar smirked, jumping in before Dax could answer. "What is it the Irish always say? Oh yeah, we were just talking treason."

Before they could continue the conversation, the server dropped off a round of drinks that must have been the standing order for the band on their set breaks, and she included another can of PBR for Dax. Once she left, the conversation turned toward music and discussion of how the first set had gone. Since Dax had little to offer other than a few affirmations of enjoyment, he sat back and tried not to feel too squished into the corner. Though the company was pleasant, he felt distinctly like an outsider.

Ragnar wasn't his friend, but he was being friendly. Dax still had no idea why he'd been invited out here. The bit of Red City wolf shifter history Ragnar had relayed was interesting and helped him form a bit more of a complete picture of Red City, but the man couldn't have invited him all the way out to the bar just for that.

Without Tomi here to guide him through the new social situation, he felt uncomfortable and even more awkward than he normally felt. The band's camaraderie did splash over onto him, even if he wasn't one of them.

Checking his watch, Ragnar grabbed his can of beer and drained it. "Let's wrap it up, next set starts in a couple minutes."

After the band slammed down their drinks, not one of them leaving a partial, they vacated the booth, though Ragnar lingered.

Once the band reached the stage, Ragnar leaned over the table. "Sorry for keeping you. If you need to go, we can do this some other time."

"No, I'm enjoying the music. Plus, you've piqued my interest."

"If you need to, the roadhouse keeps a bunkhouse out back to put up traveling musicians. Those of us who live in the city use it when we play here. There'll be a spare bunk for you, so you don't have to drive all the way back into Red City after drinking."

Dax nodded, unsure if he would take the offer. If he needed to, he could find a bit of solitude, shift over, and purge the alcohol from his system. But an alliance would be a good thing to cement, and a strange bed and a night of shared comradery might be exactly what was needed. As an added bonus, he wouldn't have to venture into his own apartment and see where Jamie and her mother were in their ongoing fight.

After a quick tuning check, the band launched into their first song, this one a more introspective, medium-tempo song, which they followed up with a slower one that drew a few couples into the open space in front of the stage to dance.

Now that Dax was by himself, he relaxed and enjoyed the music. Ragnar and his band were quite good, maybe better than quite good.

Halfway through the set, something drifted in through the bar's doors that dislodged him from the calm place he'd found in his little bubble—danger and ill intentions had entered The Honkey Tonk Woman.

Swinging his gaze to the door, every muscle in his body tensed as a dozen bikers strolled into the bar. Each of them wore the paraphernalia of the biker gang that had been trying to kill him.

Dax looked for an alternative exit, but the only one he saw was on the far side of the room. The bikers stood between him and the restroom, so that direction wasn't an option. When he couldn't locate an exit not blocked by the bikers, he checked for windows but found none. As panic set in, he tried to think of a solution. He'd seen windows when he walked in. The bar must have some sort of facade to cover them on the inside, but they had to have them for egress purposes, right?

The woman who'd announced the band strode purposely across the floor toward the bikers. Dax focused on her as she spoke. "You fellas are going to need to mind your manners if you're going to be here. Buy a beer, enjoy the music, and be respectful of my patrons, and we'll all get along fine."

The lead biker mumbled something and nodded. Whatever it was must have satisfied the woman because she gave them one last look, then walked back to bar.

The bikers flared out, circulating through the room. One of them, spying Dax, tapped the elbow of the one next to him, who seemed to be in charge of their little gang, and chucked his chin at corner where Dax sat.

"Fuck," Dax mumbled under his breath, easing toward the end of the booth so he could get out.

The pair of bikers strode quickly over, the underling sliding into the booth and shoving Dax back into the corner while the leader sat on the opposite side. Dax didn't recognize them. Either he hadn't cataloged their faces during the fight at the biker's bar, they'd run away early, or they hadn't been there. It didn't matter though. It wasn't like they were compiling an airtight prosecution to be presented in court.

Dax knew he'd already been tried, convicted, and sentenced to death by the bikers. The initial threats against his life had likely been commercially motivated. But after killing the head of the chapter and a bunch of their goon brothers and burning down their bar, it had become personal.

"Lookie who we have here," the leader said. The goon blocking Dax in tried for a sinister chuckle, but it only managed to sound like a weak wheeze.

Dax reached out and grabbed the folded tent of card stock off the table, pointing the face toward the leader. "Sorry, fellas. This table is reserved for the band and their guests."

The leader grabbed the sign form Dax's hand and crumpled it up, tossing it on the floor next to the booth.

"Hey, what—" The server stopped, scooped up the sign, and walked briskly back to the bar.

"Ah, she didn't get our drink orders," the goon said, his voice nasal and falsely jocular.

A minute later, the woman who'd confronted them at the door stood in front of the booth, her fists resting on her hips. "Now, gentlemen, this table is for the band"—her eyes flicked to Dax—"and friends of the band."

The leader plastered an unctuous smile on his face. "Oh, we're dear friends of the band." He turned his head to Dax. "Aren't we, Dax?"

Not in the mood to play along, Dax pursed his lips and blinked slowly at the leader. "I have never met these two before in my life, and I doubt they're friends with a band made up of people of different ethnicities who sing songs about punching Nazis."

Out of the corner of his eye, Dax caught Ragnar staring daggers at the table as he sang a song about fighting fascists. Dax wasn't sure if the song was scheduled for the set or if it had been slipped in to fit the occasion, but he appreciated Ragnar's bravado.

Now that they were paying attention to the music, the two bikers' fake smiles slid off their faces. The leader clenched his jaw.

Ignoring the change in mood, the manager continued, "I'll let Ragnar sort that out, but if you aren't his friends, you'll need to vamoose. And if you cause any trouble, I'll eighty-six you faster than grass goes through a goose." She turned around and made her way to the bar, taking up a post where she had a clear view of the booth.

"You think you're funny?" The goon slid closer, and something made a metallic click. The sharp point poking into his side told him it was a switchblade knife.

"Switchblades are illegal to have in this state," Dax said, staring at the stage. Now the rest of the band had shifted their focus to the table, though it didn't seem to detract from their playing.

"The idiot thinks he's a comedian," the leader said.

The goon pushed the knife a bit harder. Dax was glad he'd worn his leather jacket. At least it would delay the blade for a moment and keep the incidental poking from drawing blood.

"I guess they can add it to the charges if they ever catch us for doing you," snarled the goon.

Throwing caution to the wind, Dax turned his head slowly until he made eye contact with the goon and smiled pleasantly. "How'd that work out for your brothers? If you come in here making threats, you better make sure you can handle the heat."

A low growl rumbled up from the goon's throat.

"Chains, mind your manners. He's just trying to rile you." The leader leaned forward as far as he could and stared at Dax. "You see, Chains here has some plans for you. Leisurely plans. But if you don't watch your mouth, I'll let him ventilate your guts a bit. He's almost as good with a blade as he is with his namesake. That'll be slow in a different way. And you won't recover from it neither. We got us some weapons with a little extra juice—the kind to make sure you don't cause more problems."

A wave of tension tightened his muscles. If the blade had dark runes carved into it, he might be in trouble. The ones carved into the bullets they'd used on him had nearly done him in. He tamped the anxiety down as quickly as he could, instead focusing on the words the leader had used. They could have been cut from a B-level gangster flick. He wanted to laugh but thought better of it. He'd save it for when he told Tomi later.

"Why don't you fellas just mind your business and listen to the fine music being played. Then I'll let you depart so you can warn your pals about messing with me. After what happened a few months ago, I figured you'd have learned your lesson by now."

The goon shoved the knife a bit harder.

Dax hissed in a breath.

"I suggest you shut your fuckin' beer hole," the goon hissed.

"I think he gets the picture," the leader said. "You're going to go with us quietly, and we'll leave your friends alone. Your friends on stage and your friends at your bar."

All Dax had to do was shift into the reaper, then there wouldn't be any flesh to pierce. He could reach into the aether and bring out his scythe and end these two in a couple of quick slashes. It would be so easy. But the crowd would panic and create bedlam at the sight of a supernatural creature whose job it was to collect the dead. Innocent people would be hurt. It would also send the other bikers into a frenzy. They'd draw weapons and things would devolve from there.

It took Dax a few moments to realize that the music was still playing but there hadn't been any vocals for a while.

TWENTY-FIVE

DAX

"You're sitting in my booth," Ragnar said, standing at the end of the table with his arms crossed.

"Go sing your songs, Lone Wolf McDouche." The leader made a shooing motion with both hands. "It would be a shame if you couldn't pluck any strings for a long time."

In ones and twos, the other bikers assembled around the room — four blocked the stage and six formed a barrier behind Ragnar, penning him in. A couple guys cracked their knuckles and tried to look menacing, while another couple of the bikers kept an eye on the crowd, who was suddenly aware something was going on.

The manager, who seemed to be missing as the situation escalated, finally appeared, shoving her way through with the bulky bouncer following in her wake. "What the hell is going on here? I told you, you could only stay if you didn't cause any trouble."

"And do you think a woman and one bouncer is going to stop us?" the leader said. "Red over there looks gym tough, but I doubt he's ever thrown a punch in his life."

Several customers flagged down their servers and paid up. Those with folding money dropped bills on their tables and exited the bar, post haste. Impressively, The Desert Rattlers kept up their instrumental break from the stage.

"This bar has always been neutral ground. Leave your conflicts at the door. It's always been honored in the past." The manager drew herself up to her full height, which wasn't much physically, yet it somehow managed to be impressive on a level Dax couldn't quite comprehend.

"Well, sister, things are changing. The old management failed, and now we're under new management. You better decide where you want to land—inside our protection or on your own, and all that implies." The leader rotated and kicked up his legs onto the booth, crossing them at the ankles.

Ragnar reached out and settled his hand on the manager's shoulder. "Tallulah, if you need us to leave, we'll go, but if you'd rather we stay, we have your back."

"Ragnar, honey, you've been playing this dive for years and packing them in. You're staying right where you are."

Ragnar nodded, a sinister grin spreading across his face as he shifted his focus back to the leader. "Show some respect and get your boots off the seat."

"Or what?" the leader asked, raising an eyebrow.

Ragnar flicked his eyes to Dax, the hint of a question in the gaze. The young man was perceptive. He probably knew the goon was holding some sort of weapon against Dax. He and the biker weren't getting cozy. Ragnar shifted his stance and bounced slightly on his knees.

Drawing in a breath, Dax nodded. Shifting in a blink of the eye, he brought his bony elbow up in a blur of tatty black cloak and slammed it into the goon's temple just as the biker thrust with the switchblade. But instead of rune-magicked steel sinking into Dax's flesh, the blade clicked and retracted into the handle. The goon collapsed like a sack of potatoes and twitched lightly where he fell.

Ragnar, pivoting, smashed a fist into the face of the leftmost biker, dropping him. The biker flopped to the side, crashing onto a table and banging his head on the way down.

Screams erupted as people scattered and made for the exits. The band kept playing, though they'd shifted songs to something upbeat and punchy.

The bikers near the stage seemed undecided on whether they should stay there and keep an eye on the band or help their brethren. As one of them turned his back to the stage, Melinda used her bass as a pole and spun around, her leg arcing out. The shiny tip of her cowboy boot cracked into the head of the biker who'd looked away, knocking him into his pal.

Sippi, still working his slide with one hand, reached under his pedal guitar and emerged with a sawed-off double barrel with a pistol grip in his other hand, leveling it at the two bikers staring back at him with open mouths.

Using the distraction to his advantage, Dax surged forward into the table and slammed it into the leader, sending his head smashing into the corner of the wooden booth. Though he didn't go down fully, he groaned groggily. Kicking the goon's legs out of the way, Dax squeezed out of the booth and returned to his human form.

Ragnar had put down another of the bikers while the bouncer squared off with two others, who seemed to be giving him trouble by darting in and out of his reach.

Not above a sucker punch, Dax mashed his fist into the side of the head of the nearest biker, who was more concerned about Ragnar and the bouncer.

"Fuck!" Dax yelped. He'd never hit anyone with his human fist before. It hurt like hell.

The biker staggered back, and Ragnar pounced, catching the biker with a wicked uppercut that launched the biker into the air and backward against the wall, blood flying from his face in a red arc. Sliding to the ground, the biker settled there with a *whoosh* of air. Shaking his head, he planted his hands and shakily tried to push himself off the ground.

Drawing back his foot, Dax kicked the biker in the same side of the head where he'd hit him seconds earlier. His aim was true, and the hard edge of his boot's sole protected his foot and knocked the biker out.

The screams died down as the last of the innocent bystanders flooded out the exits. Adrenaline coursed through Dax's veins. While the last fight he'd gotten in with the bikers was in a bar, he'd never been in a good old fashioned bar fight before.

With the odds turning in their favor, Ragnar and the bouncer quickly handled the last couple of bikers. While they did that, Dax looked to make sure Tallulah was alright. He couldn't find her. She wasn't on the ground or under the table.

Sweeping his eyes over the rest of the bar, he found her, standing on top of the bar, a bright, natural glow in her eyes. She held her hands at her side, her fingers curled into claws. He wasn't sure if it was the blood pumping through his head, but he thought he saw strange lights arcing between her fingertips.

He shook his head and looked to the stage. The two bikers left standing reached for the sky, since Sippi had them covered with both barrels. If they were wolf shifters, they'd heal—most likely—but taking a blast of buckshot to the face wouldn't be fun for anyone, no matter how magically gifted they were at healing.

In a matter of a few seconds, Dax, the bouncer, and Ragnar and his band had handled the dozen bikers. Dax sighed in relief. But Ragnar groaned. Dax figured out why a second later as a bunch more bikers burst through the doors. Some carried baseball bats while others had guns.

Moving quickly, Ragnar slipped the toe of his boot into the jacket of the nearest biker and flipped the jacket open, revealing a holstered handgun. He dropped to his knee and snatched it up, tossing it to Dax.

Dax grabbed at the gun but fumbled it a couple times before getting hold of the barrel. By the time he had it under control, Ragnar had secured a gun of his own from one of the other downed bikers. Likewise, the bouncer had come up with a pistol from somewhere.

With the exception of Sippi, the rest of the Rattlers had somehow maintained their melody, which was impressive as fuck.

"Now, boys," Tallulah called out, an odd, multi-harmonic tone to her voice, "I'm giving y'all a chance to walk away clean and take your friends with you. They made a mistake and have paid for it. Don't add to it with mistakes of your own."

"Bitch, shut the fuck up." The leader, having regained most of his senses, stood up in the booth, wobbling either from the hit he'd taken to the head or the softness of the cushion, Dax wasn't sure which.

Since he was the nearest and behind Ragnar and the bouncer, Dax swung his gun around to point it at the leader.

"We came here to get someone who did far more than make a mistake." He peered at Dax.

"I don't care. This is my place. You can take your disputes elsewhere." Tallulah's eyes lit up with a green glow as greenish energy bolts arced between her fingers and vibrated in her palms and around her forearms.

The leader snorted. "Do you think we give a shit about your little light show?"

A series of guns were cocked. Several more bikers had come in the back door quietly. Six of them had guns pointed at Tallulah.

"See, we have magic wands of our own. I do believe lead trumps all." The leader wobbled to the end of the booth, trying to look smooth but only succeeding at looking goofy, and dropped to the floor. The wood creaked under his weight.

Dax kept his gun pointed at the leader as the man walked over to Tallulah. She kept her power coursing around her hands, but her eyes flicked around the bar, finally settling on Ragnar. They exchanged something in their glance. The music stopped.

Tallulah withdrew her power and her hands blinked out. The glow in her eyes faded last. Slowly, she lowered her hands all the way to her sides and clenched them into fists. Then she spread her fingers wide and thrust them up above her head.

Shutters flew up all around the bar, revealing the windows a split second before they exploded outward, showering the porch and whoever might have been out there in glass shards.

"Now!" Ragnar shouted.

Dax didn't know what exactly the big redhead had in mind, but since he had his finger on the trigger and the bikers' leader in his sights, he squeezed the trigger. A mist of blood exploded from the side of the biker's head, and he dropped to the ground.

Around him, guns erupted. In the flashes and shouts, he saw Ragnar firing and darting toward the nearest open window. Sippi unleashed both barrels, then hurled the sawed-off at the nearest head. The band, instruments in hand, dashed toward the nearest exit, be it door or window in all the confusion. Green surges of light flashed in the back of the bar as the bar's lights exploded into shards of glass and sparks.

Dax, using the flashes of green light as a guide, unloaded the rest of the gun's magazine, aiming wherever he saw movement that he knew wasn't Ragnar, Tallulah, or the band as he backed up. Once his back bumped up against the wall, he fired his last shot and threw the gun. It was useless to him without more magazines.

"Whoa!" he screamed.

Strong arms reached through the window and wrapped around his chest, tugging him backward over the windowsill. Pain flared up his leg as they were dragged across glass. In a flash, he switched to his skeletal from to lighten the load and start the healing process. Once he cleared the window and was set down, he returned to his flesh suit, but nearly fell when the injured leg didn't want to work for a second.

"I gotcha, buddy," Ragnar said. "Can you stand?"

His wounded leg took the weight, though he kept most of his balance on the good leg. "Yeah."

"Good, now run!"

Turning, Dax nearly lost it when he pivoted on the non-working leg but managed to get around and shift his weight to his good foot. Taking two hops for every one on the bad leg, he hobbled across the dusty parking lot. As the bystanders had fled, they'd done so in a hurry, kicking up a ton of dust. Breathing it in wasn't fun. He squinted and coughed.

Doors slammed on a nearby beat-up old van as Melinda stood next to it and slapped her hand on the back door. "Go!"

Before the single syllable was even all the way out of her mouth, the tires peeled out, throwing dirt, dust, and rocks. Melinda coughed as she spun around. She spied Ragnar and ran toward him.

"My car's on the other side of the lot," Ragnar shouted.

"Shit," Melinda barked out, sliding to a stop in her boots.

"I'm…closer…" Dax panted, slipping between a couple cars on the way to his Lincoln. "Black…Lincoln."

Reaching into his pocket, he searched for his keys and his hand bumped something before he found the familiar crenelations of his keys. He yanked them out of his pocket and fumbled with them until he had the one to the car ready to go. Careful to put his weight on the strong leg, he slid to a halt and unlocked the door, collapsing into the driver's seat. In another second, the engine purred to life as Melinda dove into the passenger seat and Ragnar yanked the back door open.

"Go!" Ragnar yelled, slapping the back of Dax's seat, still not all the way into the car.

Dax spared a look in the mirror. Bikers streamed out of the bar. Mashing the gas pedal, the tires spit dirt and rocks, sending up a din as it hit the cars parked behind him.

"Go, go, go," Melinda muttered, bracing herself against the dash.

The car surged forward and bounced off the curb and onto the highway as he straightened out. The door Ragnar hadn't closed earlier stood open, held in place by the wind. Ragnar gripped the top of the backseat and started to reach out for the suicide door.

"Don't!" Dax barked. "Everyone brace yourself."

He gave Melinda and Ragnar a moment to prepare, then he slammed on the brakes. The car fishtailed some, its tires screeching. But the shift in momentum flung the suicide door shut. As soon as the door closed, Dax put the gas pedal to the floor.

Behind him, green light surged, and he looked over his shoulder.

Tallulah floated out of the bar, green light surrounding her as she held her hands flat and pointed down at the ground. Bikers cleared a path around her and headed for their bikes.

"Stop!" Ragnar shouted. "Back up."

Smashing his foot on the brakes, the Lincoln screeched to a halt. He looked over his shoulder, slipped the car in reverse, and gunned it. The tires threw smoke as they gripped and rocketed backward. Tallulah shifted her glide toward them. Gauging where they'd intersect, Dax braked hard again. Ragnar threw the back door open and slid across the car to the other side.

Dax expected Tallulah to float all the way into the car, but as soon as she broached the border between dirt and concrete, she dropped to the ground. Her legs seemed to already be churning as she dashed the last few feet, diving headfirst into the back of his Lincoln.

"Smash it, Slim! Get us out of here," Melinda called.

He didn't have to be told twice. As the car grabbed pavement and moved forward, Ragnar and Tallulah wrestled to get disentangled from each other, the back suicide door stuck open again, momentum and the car's slipstream keeping it that way.

Finally, Ragnar righted himself. Resorting to just moving Tallulah by bulk force, he lifted her over his lap and set her down on the right side, then shimmied over, grabbed onto the back of Dax's headrest, and reached out.

It took him several fumbling grasps to reach the handle and pull the door closed. After he pulled it shut, he sagged into his seat, panting heavily. "I guess that's why they call them 'suicide doors.'"

TWENTY-SIX

DAX

Now that all the passengers were in the car and the doors were shut, Dax flicked his eyes around to the mirrors. Bikers trickled out of the parking lot in ones and twos, pointing their bikes in the direction Dax drove.

"Did you see which way the boys went, Melinda?" Ragnar asked, leaning over the middle of the front seat.

"They're probably only a minute or two ahead of us. If Slim here can show some love to the gas pedal, we'll probably catch up to them," she replied.

Tallulah sat on her knees, facing out the back window, and watched her bar disappear in the distance as they rounded a gentle corner. Sighing, she turned around and sat, her head sagging into her hands.

Dax focused ahead, trying to catch up to the van, with only occasional check-ins with the mirrors.

"Why didn't you get in the van, Melinda?" Ragnar asked.

"Sippi trapped his scrawny ass behind his pedal steel guitar and my bass. There was no way I was fitting into that mess, and I knew you had your ride. So, I slammed the doors and got them moving."

"Quick thinking."

Tallulah seemed to have recovered. She sat up and stared out the window. "What kind of trouble did you bring into my bar tonight, Ragnar?"

"I'm sorry, Tallulah." He sighed, sagging in on himself a little. "I'm not entirely sure."

Dax caught a wary and almost frightened glance tossed his way by Ragnar.

"Who were those guys?" she asked, shifting tracks. "I've never welcomed that gang into my place, but when they've showed up, they've always behaved."

"I don't think they're the local thugs, Lue." Ragnar ran a hand through his sweaty hair.

"That's my fault," Dax said, finally speaking up. "I kind of… well…" He looked in the mirrors. "I kind of reduced the membership of the locals a few months back."

"'Reduced the membership'? What the hell does that mean?" Tallulah asked.

"They kidnapped some acquaintances of mine, and I wanted to retrieve them. The bikers objected, and things got violent." Dax shrugged, glancing into the rearview mirror when several flashes of light caught his attention. The bikers had formed up and were behind him, slowly gaining.

Ragnar snorted, turning his head toward Tallulah. "If rumors are true, he killed them all and burned down their bar."

"And you brought this asshole into my bar? I thought you were my friend, Ragnar."

He groaned. "I am your friend, Lue. I just wanted to invite him out to get to know him a bit since some fairly sophisticated rune magic is being used against him. I figured—"

"That this was far enough away so your father wouldn't get word of it?" Tallulah finished the sentence for him. "I wish you'd found some other bar to meet at. Preferably one where the owner wasn't your friend."

Ragnar made a contrite-sounding grunt. "I know. I'm sorry, Lue. I'll figure out how to make it up to you. I'll get some folks out there and we'll help you clean up the place and get it back in good shape."

"That's the least you can offer." She raised an eyebrow. "How about some free shows?"

"I love you like a sister, Lue, but I can't promise my band's time for free. You know I'm handy with a hammer and a good woodworker. The place will be better than ever when I'm done."

"Yup. If I'm swinging my bass, I'm getting paid," Melinda said. "But I'll be there to help with any work that needs doing."

Dax cleared his throat. "I don't mean to be the asshole twice in one night…"

"I'm sure that's a light night for you, hon." Tallulah shook her head. "Sorry. I'm being peevish."

"No worries, I did piss off the bikers pretty badly. I just didn't expect them to show up right then and there. That seems like a coincidence I'll need to investigate later. But a more pressing matter is the bikers currently gaining on us."

"Can't you make this old hotrod go any faster, Slim?" Melinda asked.

"I haven't had it that long, and I'm not sure what all it can do. Though my friend gave it a tune-up before he delivered it."

"A sweet old ride like this?" Melinda lovingly rubbed her hand over the dash. "I'd love to get my hands on this baby's ample carburetor, if you know what I mean." She waggled her eyebrows at him. "Tell ya what, Slim. You get your little foot to push the pedal down to the carpet, and we'll talk about it in more detail."

He wasn't sure why she kept calling him "Slim," but it seemed to amuse her, and right now, he didn't need more enemies. He complied with her request, and they picked up a bit more speed, the engine smoothly accelerating.

"Not bad," Melinda said.

"I think I see the van up ahead." Ragnar pointed between Dax and Melinda.

Dax saw three taillights. One on each side of a vehicle, and one at the top. Behind him, he heard the rumble of a bunch of motorcycles. They didn't seem to be in a big hurry, but they were still gaining.

"Uh, the plan we never talked about. It would be good right

about now." Dax tried to force his eyes forward but couldn't stop himself from checking the rearview mirror and the left-side wing mirror. The bikers had flared out into the oncoming lane.

"Get up behind the van, then you'll want to get around it. Sippi will have a surprise or two," Ragnar said.

"Shit!" Melinda fished in her pocket for something and pulled out a phone. "We better let them know it's us behind them, or we're just as likely to get the surprise. That skinny son of a bitch is way too eager to play with his toys." She sent off a message. "We're good."

As they neared the van, a set of lights coming at them sent the bikes scurrying out of the oncoming lane. When the car passed, the bikers resumed their hogging of the road.

"Alright, we're almost behind the van. Now what?" Dax asked.

"If it's clear, swing around and pass them," Ragnar said.

The van's two back doors popped open and were wedged open, presumably by Sippi—it was hard to see precisely with the headlights blaring—so they stuck out straight behind the vehicle to prevent the wind from throwing them closed. It would've been a disaster if one swung shut at the wrong time. Sippi appeared in the opening and lit a cigarette, the cherry glowing bright, and flipped them off. Melinda rolled down her window and returned the gesture with a chuckle.

As far as Dax could tell, the oncoming lane was empty, so he eased the car over, then pulled back as a car came around the bend. Tapping his finger on the steering wheel, he waited until it passed, swinging over, and mashed the pedal to the floor. The car surged forward slowly.

Seeing movement ahead of them, the bikers sped up and closed the last of the distance.

A tap or two on the brakes from the van helped Dax get past them, and he pulled into the correct lane just in time.

Ragnar rolled down his window, stuck out his arm, and gave the van a thumbs up. "Now, I want you to open up some more space so we can make sure Sippi has some room to work with. No sense having someone interrupt his party."

Nodding, Dax pulled forward and the van drifted behind them, either from tapping on the brakes or letting off the gas. To prepare for whatever they were going to unleash on the bikers, the van drifted over the center line. A moment later, a huge explosion sent a fireball into the air. The bikers scattered or crashed, and headlights that had been pointed straight ahead shot off in multiple directions, creating light patterns like a disco ball.

Unducking his head, Dax looked over his shoulder. "What the fuck was that?"

"That would be the pipe bomb." Melinda cringed as another ball of fire rose into the sky, accompanied by another explosion. "And another…"

By now, Dax couldn't tell if there were any bikers left following them. The Lincoln was far enough head and enough bikers had scattered that the grim wall of headlights wasn't there anymore.

In the backseat, Ragnar lifted his phone to his ear. "Jose, we all clear? Almost?"

A third fireball punctuated the night.

"All clear. Keep an eye on things. We'll update you if we see anything coming our way from up here." Ragnar lowered the phone. "Dax, let's get off the highway and see if we can find another route in case they try to rally and come back."

"You got any ideas where? I don't come out this way often."

Melinda pulled out her phone. "I'll find something."

A minute later, she fed him directions that would take them onto some smaller roads. The first turn put them on a narrow, paved street with sizable trees lining it. The trees would hide their lights, at least mostly. He didn't trust turning his headlights off on a dark country road.

It was nervous work winding along small country lanes and keeping an eye out behind them in case the bikers found their trail. The only headlights he saw belonged to the band's van. But after a couple hours of turns and exploring the rural roads around Red City, the two vehicles descended into the glowing valley that contained the city and its 'burbs. Thirty minutes later, Dax parked around the corner from the bar, followed closely by the van.

"Our gear going to be safe here?" Melinda asked, looking around warily.

"Probably not," Dax replied. "Better bring it with you. You can stash it all in the back of the tearoom."

For the first time since just after leaving the roadhouse, Tallulah perked up. "I could really use a cup of tea right now."

"I can take care of that need." He stepped out of the car and locked it after everyone else had vacated the vehicle.

"Sippi, grab the gear, we're bringing everything inside."

"Walk past the bar and up the alley. I'll let you in the side door," said Dax.

Sippi raised an eyebrow. "What's the matter? Musicians can't come in the front?"

"If you do, everyone is going to think you're there to play, and there isn't room for that." He hated to do it, but the financials weren't in too bad a shape, especially since he still had some money left over from the score they'd made when he'd burned down the bikers' bar. "Drinks are on the house while you're here; least I can do after messing up your gig tonight."

Tallulah sighed. "It's not really your fault. I shouldn't have let those fucks in. The locals have left me alone, so I thought keeping the peace was worth it."

Looking around nervously, Ragnar shoved his hands into his pockets. "We can talk about that later. When we have some privacy."

TWENTY-SEVEN

DAX

"It's me. Open the door, please." Dax stood outside the tearoom, putting his body between the opening door and the loaded drinks tray he carried.

As Ragnar stepped back, Dax spun around and the Rattlers cheered. Moving around the long central table of the tearoom, he distributed the drinks to the band and set the empty tray on the bar in the corner.

In the back corner at one of the two-tops, Tallulah stared at the table, holding her teacup in both hands as she rested her elbows on the table. Retrieving his own tea, Dax dodged by the raucous table as the band excitedly recapped their narrow escape from the bikers. The only one who didn't participate was Ragnar, though he did listen and smile at their antics. Somewhere in between raucous and reserved was Connie, who seemed to want to be part of the gang but looked like she felt a little awkward.

"Mind if I join you?" Dax asked Tallulah.

She shoved the other chair out with her foot, still staring at the table. In front of her, she'd dealt three Tarot cards—four of cups upright, the tower reversed, and the moon reversed.

"What do they tell you?" Dax took a sip of his tea.

"Uncertainty."

"Not speaking, then?"

"No, they're speaking clearly, but what they're saying is we've gone from stagnation to sudden upheaval, and now face an obscured future." Sighing, she scooped up the three cards and moved them to the bottom of her deck. He had no idea how she'd brought a deck out with her, but figured it was rude to ask a woman he'd just met such a probing question. Especially after starting a barfight with Nazi werewolves in her establishment.

After she shuffled them thoroughly, she dealt the first card—the tower.

Her brow furrowed. "Unexpected changes and sudden catastrophe." The next card she added to the top left corner of the first card. "Six of swords in the reverse—fear of the unknown or unplanned or forced change to thinking."

Already two cards in and she didn't like what she saw. He'd never seen somebody read cards. Delphine's suggestion that he get his read had inspired him to look up the process on the Internet. He thought he'd seen this type of spread but couldn't remember its meanings.

"Next, the knight of pentacles." An eyebrow lifted. "Driven and reliable."

The card seemed to soften the wrinkle in her brow.

The next card, she placed below and to the right of the first. "Two of wands in the reverse. Fear and indecision. And now, the fifth…" She turned over a card and placed it at the bottom left corner. Both her eyebrows lifted, and she blinked at the card a few times. "The magician. Upright."

"And that means?" He leaned a little closer.

"To find solutions, I need diverse knowledge and cleverness." She picked up her teacup for another sip.

"What do you need solutions for?" Dax asked, staring at the cards.

She chuckled bitterly and smirked. "Take your pick. What to do about the Nazi bikers. They aren't going to let me be after I drove off with you." She pointed to the six of swords. "Do I even bother trying to get my bar back? Or do the unthinkable and pack up?" She ran a finger under the fourth card. "I can't let fear and indecision be the choice. But what choices do I make?"

Dax pointed to the fifth card, careful not to touch it, then cast his glance toward the people drinking at the table. "A cast of diverse people with a variety of knowledge."

"Perhaps. Perhaps not." She shook her head and scooped the cards up, returning them to the deck with an exasperated sigh. "They often ask more questions than they answer." She looked up and smiled at him. "Perhaps a question for you."

"And that is?"

She pointed to her empty teacup with her chin. "Another cup of this fine tea?"

He nodded and stood, fetching the pot from the warmer to refill her cup and top his off. After he returned the pot to the counter, he rejoined her.

"And now a question for you"—she slid her deck toward him— "if you wouldn't mind me asking."

He gave a half shrug.

"Who are you?" She cast her glance down at the deck.

He removed his hands from the table and dropped them in his lap. "I was informed by a trusted acquaintance that I should not touch another person's deck."

"That may be their bit of personal etiquette, but I'm offering."

He chuckled. "No. You misunderstand me. If I touch your deck, it will cease to function as your deck."

Tallulah narrowed her eyes and mouthed, "Who are you?" She leaned closer, staring at him, a faint greenish glow appearing in her eyes.

He felt like she was trying to peel back his layers, like he was an onion. Sitting up straight, he solidified his aura as gently as he could to keep her out without hurting her. Shaking her head, she squeezed her eyes together tightly, then blinked hard several times.

Hoping to distract her from trying to peer into his being, he reached into an inner pocket of his jacket and pulled out the deck

Delphine had given him. He placed it across from Tallulah's deck on his side of the table.

Nearly quicker than he could see, she scooped up her cards and stashed them away. "Have you used them yet?"

"No. They've been in my pocket." He patted his jacket just over his heart. They'd been there since the lawyer rescued him from the jail and gave him back the few things the cops had taken off him.

"May I?"

He nodded.

"Shuffle, please." She took her teacup and ran it under her nose to enjoy the aroma on the rising steam.

Taking the cards and splitting them in half, he shuffled them like playing cards several times, then returned them to the center of the table. She set her cup aside and smeared the cards over the table, shifting them around, adding her own more chaotic shuffle to the deck. After about a minute of moving them around, she carefully gathered them back into a well-organized stack.

She looked him up and down, leaning across the table a little. "I think I'll explore one card at a time."

"You're the expert."

She flipped the first card. "Death…" She blinked hard a few times. "In the reverse—profound grief and hopelessness."

He stared at the Death card. He'd read enough to know it didn't exactly mean literal death or the persona of death—him. But its appearance first, twice over the last few weeks, was unsettling.

"Temperance." She shook her head. "Again, in the reverse. Imbalance. Pettiness. Frustration." She stared the cards. "My, these are not happy cards."

His breath shortened and shallowed as he stared at them too. He didn't want to see the next card, but he couldn't look away or speak the words to stop her from pulling it.

"The lovers." She poked her tongue out to wet her lips. "Reversed. Betrayal. Unfaithfulness. Jealousy." She quickly added a fourth to the line of cards, her shoulders slumping. "The magician. Reversed." She cursed under her breath. "Mistakes, deception, failure. Brokenness."

As she reached for the deck another time, her hand shook. She paused, then looked up at him. His eyes were plastered to the line of cards—paper and ink—telling deep stories he didn't wish to have told.

"The hermit reversed." Her voice came out in a barely audible whisper. "Loneliness. Depression. Exile."

Dax's heart thumped hard in his chest as pain burned in his eyes. It was all laid bare before her—his fall, his exile, the betrayal, the loneliness, the emptiness. He couldn't take his gaze off them as he blinked erratically.

"No, you can't go in there… Stop!"

The door slid open and slammed in its frame.

"What have you done?"

Forcing his gaze away from the cards, he dashed the back of his hand across his eyes and focused on a disheveled middle-aged-looking man in wrinkly clothes. His hair was clearly suffering from bedhead. Dax had never seen Gunnar this emotional. Usually he maintained a pleasant meekness, but in his loss of control, there was an underlying power coursing beneath the surface.

Suzie poked her head around Gunnar. "Sorry, I tried to stop him."

"No…" It came out a garbled rasp. Clearing his throat, Dax tried again. "No worries, Suzie. Please bring our new guest the drink of his choice."

"I don't want a fucking drink, now quit bothering me," Gunnar snapped at Suzie.

His jaw clenching, Dax shot up and stood. "You will not treat my staff with such disrespect. You are a guest in this building, and you will do well to remember it." Sparks and the barest hint of blue flames flashed in his eyes.

Everyone at the table where Ragnar and his band sat leaned away from Dax, the power of his ire pushing them back. Normally he'd be more disciplined, even in his anger, but the tale the cards told had frayed the edges of his control. The sudden intruder only served to push him over the line.

Gunnar opened his mouth but closed it with a clack of teeth, swallowed, and took a deep breath. He turned his head to address Suzie. "My apologies. I'm not interested in a drink."

Dax caught his bartender's eye. "It's OK, Suzie. I've got this."

She cast one last annoyed look at Gunnar, then backed away.

"Now please enter and return the door to the closed position in which you found it." Dax strode around the table. "And in the future, I would appreciate it if you would not come into my business and yell like an asshole."

Gunnar's nostrils flared. "And I'd appreciate you respecting my wishes and not pulling my son into whatever mess you've got yourself into. I can't protect my community if you drag them into your fight."

"I haven't dragged anyone into anything."

"What the fuck do you call what happened at the Honky Tonk Woman? Bar fights with Nazi bikers?"

"Dad, sit down," Ragnar said firmly. "He didn't 'drag' me into anything. I invited him out to talk. The bikers showed up. They're the ones who started the fight."

"Dammit, Ragnar, I told you to keep away from him. Sound asleep, I get woken by loud pounding on the door. Nearly gave your mother and me heart attacks. Then I hear you're picking fights with some of the worst scum this city has to offer. The same people who killed my father, your grandfather. You've endangered everything I've worked for. You could have been killed!"

Dax ground his teeth. Gunnar had started at a reasonable volume but finished at a shout. On the other side of the door, the sound of music increased in volume as Suzie turned up the jukebox to try to drown them out.

Sitting at the end of the table, Ragnar breathed heavily, his arms crossed over his chest. "Worked hard for? We hide meekly." Ragnar stood up, bracing his hands on the edge of the table as he leaned over it, glaring at his father. "We let everyone who wants to tread all over us. How can you protect the community if you don't stand up? I didn't start the fight, but I won't let them walk all over me. There has to be a point where we no longer run away from everything. I'm tired of hiding. I'm tired of pretending to be weak."

"You can't fight these kind of people. They left us alone as long as we didn't antagonize them. Now look what's happened." He jabbed a shaky finger at Dax. "He stirred the hornet's nest, and now they're getting nasty. Before he ruined the peace, they never would have done something like this to Tallulah. She kept neut—"

Tallulah stepped up next to Dax. "Gunnar Magnusson, I'll thank you to keep my name from your lips. You do not speak for me in this matter, and I'm not part of your community."

Gunnar's mouth hung open for a moment before he snapped it closed and nodded at her, lowering his eyes.

He took in a slow breath, then exhaled noisily through his nostrils. "Ragnar, you're going to get yourself killed. These are nasty, nasty people. Your mother will be devastated."

Ragnar narrowed his eyes. "Don't throw mother in my face. She raised me to be myself. I'm not afraid to stand up to bullies. I'm not afraid of these thugs."

"You should be. If half of what I've heard they get up to is true, they're some of the scariest people in this city, and that's saying a lot." Pleading slipped into Gunnar's eyes. "Don't be a hothead, son. You're all we have, you're all that matters to your mother and me."

Ragnar looked like he wanted to snap at his father, but Constance reached over and set a hand on his forearm. Taking a moment, he physically regained his control. "Dad, I'm not a kid anymore. I'm a grown man and have been for a while now. You're going to have to let me make my own decisions."

"I know, son. I know you're an adult, but you've got to think of the people I have to look out for. They may be *your* decisions, but the people you're messing with won't respect that distinction. The bikers'll come after you and everyone you love and everyone they love. The decisions will be yours, but the consequences will be shared." Gunnar sighed and looked down. "I can respect your choices, but I can't support them. Not if I'm going to protect what we've built here."

Ragnar's eyes narrowed, and he nodded once, slowly. "I understand."

TWENTY-EIGHT

JAMIE

Jamie stared into the mirror. She didn't recognize herself. The short, artfully mussed hair looked Hollywood-red-carpet ready. She still wasn't sure if she liked how the black leather pants felt, but she did have to admit they made her legs look awesome. The black rubber-soled boots felt stiff, and she hoped they wouldn't take too long to break in.

For her supply of T-shirts, Suzie had taken her to a vintage threads store. The worn, old rock-band shirts were ripe for having the collars and hems artfully cut and ripped. Jamie had argued that she only needed one for the supply, but Suzie had declared it wasn't a disguise but the young woman's new look, and she was rocking it. So she'd acquiesced.

Yesterday had been a full day between hitting shops and a salon, but it would all be worth it if she could pull this plan off. Taking a deep breath, she exhaled and nodded at herself. Time to go.

Popping on the lightweight black leather jacket that stopped a couple inches above her hips, she exited the bathroom and strode purposefully through Dax's apartment.

"Where do you think you're going dressed like that?" Sharon barked as Jamie passed in front of the couch where she sat.

"Out."

"Am I the only one thinking about this family's safety?" The bitterness in her tone was unmistakable.

"No, you're not. But I'm glad you finally are." With deft fingers, Jamie unlocked Dax's door and left before her mother could say anything else.

She took the stairwell and waited by the side of the building, as had become her habit so she could check for anything unusual, such as unwanted observers. She heard Suzie's black Honda Civic nearing before she saw it. When she'd asked about the car's deeper and louder than unusual sound, Suzie had only winked in response.

Pulling the door closed behind her, she buckled in.

"Damn, girl, you're looking hot!" Suzie said, putting the car in gear.

Jamie felt uncomfortable with the compliment, but appreciated it nonetheless. Linda had always said she was a good-looking girl, and Cory had agreed. But mostly she'd just wanted to go unnoticed in high school and get through it.

"Are you sure it's not too much?"

Suzie shrugged. "It's as good of a disguise as anything, plus the gris-gris will take care of the rest, hopefully."

"Are you sure? Will it actually work?" She knew nothing about voodoo, or really about any kind of magic other than her own kind as a wolf shifter.

"Yeah. Manman Delphine is trè powerful. If anyone can make you a magic item that'll work, she's the one."

Jamie had only known Suzie for a little while, but the outgoing young woman didn't seem able to hide her expressions. Jamie was a master at observing moods and emotions. It was a useful survival tool. Before they'd gone to meet the manbo, Suzie had seemed nervous about meeting someone who seemed like a larger-than-life figure in her family's lore. Now the anxiety she'd displayed had shifted to a wariness that also felt self-reflective.

Jamie hadn't understood the manbo's interest in Suzie, but the multiple requests to speak privately in the near future couldn't be missed. Though she liked Suzie—she'd been very kind, friendly, and open with Jamie—Jamie didn't feel comfortable enough to ask something that could be a deeply probing question.

"So, where do we want to start our search?" Suzie asked.

She'd insisted on helping out, saying that Jamie would need a driver and car if things couldn't be handled on foot. Jamie'd been forced to agree that it was a distinct possibility she might need assistance. She'd grown used to having access to Cory and his car, but now she had neither.

"There's an old-school arcade Travis used to hang out at after school. That might be the best place."

"Gotcha." Suzie unlocked her phone and handed it over. "When you're done putting the address in, send a message to Manman Delphine to cast the spell."

Jamie typed in the name of the arcade into the map app and sent the manbo the message, then handed the phone back. Soon, they zipped through the streets of Red City, occasionally dipping down to the speed limit while treating stop signs as suggestions as opposed to hard and fast rules. She was already nervous about being discovered by the biker flunky she'd nearly killed, and the casual disregard for traffic laws only served to heighten her anxiety. Red City cops loved pulling people over for traffic violations, then seeing what they could find on a person. And if they couldn't find something, they'd often plant it if they were in the mood.

Finally, she couldn't stand it anymore and had to speak up. "Um, I don't know how long you've lived in Red City, but the cops are crooked as fuck and love pulling people over and creating crimes to charge them with."

"Honey, I'm from New Orleans. I know crooked cops. But it doesn't matter where you are, cops are cops. I've never been pulled over yet, and I've been driving like this for years." She looked over to her passenger. "But I'll slow down, since it's making you uncomfortable."

Jamie nodded, a weak smile sliding across her lips.

They arrived at the arcade, only a couple minutes later than they would have if Suzie hadn't respected Jamie's request. Driving around the parking lot, Suzie selected a spot that would be easy to get to from the door and wouldn't place them too deep in the lot, blocking a quick exit.

Jamie gripped the door handle, her knuckles white and red. She tried to calm her heart rate but wasn't having any luck. Instead of stepping out, she patted herself down to make sure the gris-gris was around her neck and the backup oil was in her pocket.

"You don't have to go through with this, you know," Suzie said, squeezing Jamie's knee. "It's dangerous at best. These bikers sound like nasty pieces of work."

"But that's just it, I do have to. If I don't do this, I'll never stop running, and I'm tired of hiding and being afraid all the time."

"But you're clearly afraid now."

Jamie nodded. "I am." She inhaled, then sped ahead with her next words. "But it's a different kind of afraid. I don't know how to explain it."

"I think I understand. You ready?"

Jamie answered by opening the door and stepping out. Suzie joined her. Jamie had about half a foot on Suzie, who made up for some of it with some extra-thick platform Doc Martens. They looked like a matched pair in leather and ripped band T-shirts.

Watching her new friend, Jamie tried to match Suzie's casual level of bravado and grace as she strode across the parking lot. Once the door closed behind them, they were assaulted by a din of flashing lights and electronic sounds. Finding a coin change machine, they got some quarters and headed into the arcade to see if they could locate their mark.

After a spin around the winding aisles of overstimulation, they picked a game that looked interesting and was within sight of the front doors. Pulling out her phone, Jamie checked the time. If it was in session, school would just about be ending for the day. But it was now summer... He could be here any time of day, or not at all. This had been a mistake.

Too nervous to perform well at the game, she died quickly and let Suzie have her go at the machine. The Black woman got into it, so Jamie let her keep going. As Suzie played, Jamie flicked nervous eyes toward the door while also pretending to watch her friend kick ass on her turn.

"Hey," Suzie hissed between her teeth. "Calm down. You look like you're casing the joint or something."

Jamie shook her head lightly and looked around her. A few people kept tossing her nervous glances. One girl finished her game and moved down a few spots, checking over her shoulder to make sure the weird woman didn't follow her.

"Right." Jamie closed her eyes and took a deep breath. "Let me have a go."

When Suzie died, she popped another quarter into the game and stepped back to make room for Jamie. Focusing on the screen, Jamie blocked out everything else around her and dove into the game when it beeped for her to start. With her effort applied to the game, it didn't take long to settle in, and her nerves calmed.

"That's better," Suzie whispered. "Oh, nice move."

Eventually, she turned the game back over to Suzie for her turn, and she kept her calm, at least on the surface. She still felt like a cement mixer. Her outside rotated smoothly, but inside was all kinds of stuff, churning, churning, churning away violently.

As she watched Suzie, the door binged, announcing someone entering or leaving. Nonchalantly, she kept her face pointed toward the movements on the screen but allowed her eyes to swing to the door after a moment. She spotted greasy hair and a black leather coat, but little else as the person wearing it slipped behind a bank of arcade games.

She waited, pretending to be looking at a nearby machine and the game being played on it by another person. When the figure emerged into her line of sight, she sucked in a gasp of air.

Placing her hand on the small of Suzie's back, Jamie leaned in until her lips were only a few inches from Suzie's ear. "It's him. He's here."

"Where?" Suzie pitched her voice just enough that Jamie's wolf hearing picked it up.

"From your position, eight o'clock."

Suzie nodded and intentionally lost. "Your turn."

Grabbing a quarter, Jamie stepped up to take her turn so Suzie could check him out.

She turned back and leaned in, standing on her tip toes to whisper into Jamie's ear. "Greasy looking pipsqueak with a leather jacket?"

Nodding, Jamie tried to focus on the game so she looked like she cared about what she was doing and belonged there too.

Suzie snorted lightly. "Can he be anymore cliche?"

Jamie chuckled, missing her move, and died. "Your turn."

Once Suzie took over, Jamie reacquired her target and tried to follow his movements as he wandered around the arcade. Periodically, he would stop and check out a game. Other times, he stopped and stared crudely at one of the girls or women playing a game of their own. Some of them ignored him while others found somewhere else to be. Management really should have been watching who they let in, but the patches on his jacket no doubt granted him more leeway than other customers might get.

She tried to suppress a shudder and looked away. She didn't want him to see her watching him. When Suzie lost her last turn, Jamie stepped up and focused on her game.

Despite having a good run, she felt the hairs on the back of her neck stand up as a psychic shiver ran through her. He must be watching her. She wished she hadn't thought of this idea. He repulsed her after he'd tried to seduce her using his place in the biker gang as leverage. A not small part of her wished she'd actually finished him, but a larger part of her cringed away from killing a person with her own teeth and strength and rage.

"Damn, baby, that's a good run you're having," he said, his voice pouring into her right ear like acid.

It distracted her, and she died.

"Want me to show you how it's done?" he asked. "I'm Travis, by the way."

"I think we're doing pretty good, thank you very much," Suzie said, a bit of bite to her tone.

"I wasn't talking to you." He managed to say it with both venom and a poorly practiced nonchalance that he couldn't quite pull off.

Jamie turned to Travis and gave him a cursory once over, as if he were indeed a stranger. "I'm Danika, and this is my friend Debbie."

His eyes narrowed, and he tilted his head to the side slightly. "Do I know you?"

"I don't think so." She struggled to force the words out of her mouth.

"You're probably right, because I'd remember a fine woman like you." He looked down, running his gross eyes over her leather-clad legs. "Damn, those pants look like they were painted on by Picasso!"

Stopping her eyes from rolling might have been the hardest thing she'd ever done in her life. Her stomach stirred with nausea.

Suzie, who'd already been dismissed by the dick, snorted and suppressed a giggle. "It's a nice ass, but I'm not sure it exemplifies the cubist movement..."

Travis glared at her, though he couldn't quite cover up the confused look that took the edge from his attempt to mean-mug her. He probably had no idea who Picasso actually was, the extent of his knowledge most likely being that he knew Picasso was a painter.

As subtly as Jamie could, she took in a deep breath and plunged ahead. "It might be fun to see a master at work." She stepped back and gestured toward the joystick.

Travis deployed what he must have thought was a sexy smirk that just made him look more weaselly and slid a quarter from the small pile they'd been using. The twerp couldn't even use his own money.

Trying to show off, he hit the joystick too hard, making all kinds of racket, and died quicker than either of them had on their most mediocre runs.

Suzie winked at Jamie so Travis couldn't see the gesture. "After that, there's no debate about his mastery."

Clamping her lips shut to keep from laughing, she glared play-fully at Suzie to stop before she did end up laughing at Travis. "Why don't you take another spin? I want to see that again."

She tried to inject a bit of flirtation in her voice, but thought she sounded a bit nauseous.

"OK, baby, if you insist." He grabbed another quarter and went at it again, rattling the machine. Good thing it wasn't pinball, or he'd have tilted. He didn't do any better that time. "You know what? I'm getting tired of kids' games. Do you want to get out of here?"

Suzie lifted an eyebrow and took half a step back.

"What did you have in mind?" Jamie asked.

"I'm feeling thirsty."

"I could go for a soda."

Travis scoffed. "I'm not talking about kiddy drinks. If I wanted that, I could stay here. I'm talking alcohol."

"I can't get booze. I'm not twenty-one yet." She tried her best to play it cool. He didn't look anywhere near twenty-one either and would likely be bounced from just about any bar that gave half a shit about not getting busted for serving minors.

"I know a place where they won't care. You look like you'll fit in perfectly."

"Are you sure? I don't want to get busted."

"Don't worry, they know me and any friend of mine is welcome."

"Really? That sounds cool. Can my friend come too?"

Travis looked Suzie over, a sneer twitching his lip. "No. Your *friend* isn't welcome."

"Can I discuss it with my friend?" Jamie asked.

"Don't take too long, baby. It's a limited-time offer." He turned and walked about fifteen feet away. He was still within wolf hearing range, so they needed to be careful.

She leaned in quickly before Suzie could say anything. "Only whisper directly into my ear. He'll be able to hear otherwise."

"Jamie, this feels like a bad idea. He could take you anywhere."

Jamie swallowed. "I know, but this could be my chance to discover where they're hiding out."

"Damn it. Dax and Tomi told me to keep an eye on you." She sighed. "Are you sure this is the best method? We could just try to follow him. We can keep a safe distance in my car and report back to the guys once he arrives."

"That's a possibility, but he could change his mind about going to the bar. This is the option that has him taking me somewhere to impress me and get me drunk so he can get in my pants."

Suzie scowled. "That's the problem. You're going without backup to an unknown place that'll be full of people far worse than that little pipsqueak."

"Follow along. I'll slip away, and we can get out of there as fast as your Honda can carry us."

"Ugh. Dax and Tomi are going to kill me." She tapped her foot nervously as she thought. "OK. Let's do it." Suzie's eyes drifted to Travis to make sure he was staying back, then she recited her phone number to Jamie. "Memorize that in case something happens to your phone. Got it?"

"Got it. Thanks, Su—Debbie."

Suzie reached out and clasped Jamie's hand, forcing a small plastic disk into it. "Take this and put it into your pocket. It's a GPS tag."

Jamie nodded. "This will work out." She wasn't sure she believed herself, but saying it helped some.

"I sure the fuck hope so. Alright. We better get on with this." Suzie backed up. "Don't let me cramp your style." Suzie cast her voice enough that it would be overheard. "I came here to play video games."

"Have fun. I'll talk to you later." Jamie made eye contact with Travis and gestured toward the exit with her head.

Travis, a victorious smirk spreading across his face, sauntered after. He reached out as he passed Suzie and grabbed a handful of quarters from the stack, knocking a bunch onto the ground.

What a tool, Jamie thought as she plastered a fake smile on her face. "Where's your car, Travis?"

"Car? Baby, we're going by motorcycle." He led her to the only motorcycle in the lot. It might have generously been described as the entry-level-model motorcycle for the aspiring dirtbag. He climbed on and reached into a leather saddlebag, pulling out a half helmet.

She was glad she hadn't gone with the miniskirt. At no point did she want to hike it up near Travis to get her leg over the bike. She just hoped he didn't offer to "let her ride bitch." She wasn't sure if she could stop herself from punching his teeth in if he did.

"Wear this." He tossed her the helmet.

"Don't you need one too?"

He scoffed. "You can use mine, baby. I'll be good." Turning on the motorcycle, he revved it. The engine roared, popped, then died.

She did her best to hold in a laugh as he fired it up again, though he didn't try to rev it this time. Sighing, she pulled on the helmet, adjusted the strap, and climbed on behind him. The feeling of her arms wrapped around his stomach made her want to gag, but soon a refreshing *whoosh* of fresh air hit her face as he tore out of the parking lot and ramped off the curb to land roughly on the pavement. Clenching her eyes shut, she held on tightly as the bike wobbled. Fortunately, he got it under control.

She forced her eyes open; it was time to see where they were going.

TWENTY-NINE
DAX

Dax pulled another card off the top of the deck and set it down. He still didn't really understand the meanings of the cards or what they portended beyond the simple explanations he'd looked up.

He'd been skeptical about Delphine's suggestion to find someone to read his cards, but when Tallulah had offered, he hadn't seen any harm in assuaging his curiosity. But with each card flipped, it was like the they cut him deep inside. Tallulah hadn't given much of an explanation beyond her initial reading—thanks to Gunnar's interruption— but her body language while performing his reading and directly afterward spoke volumes. But those volumes were inaccessible to him.

Perhaps Delphine could tell him more. Though he wasn't sure he wanted to spread his vulnerability beyond what Tallulah had briefly seen. He was becoming friends with the manbo, but he wasn't ready to be stripped quite that bare in front of her. He wasn't sure if he was ready to be that deeply entangled with her.

However, he couldn't disentangle himself from the bikers. Now Ragnar, along with his bandmates, seemed to have been drawn into his orbit. Tallulah had paid a steep price just because he'd walked into her bar. He'd created a solar system of problems, all orbiting around him like he was a sun. Sorting out who were planets and who were moons would take some work. Finding the rogue planets or planet-killing asteroids would also take some detective work.

He snorted and chuckled, scooping up the tarot cards and sliding them to the bottom of the deck. "Perhaps Delphine knows an astrologer who could help me out too."

After shuffling the deck, he set it aside and stood up, then walked behind the bar to make some tea. Perhaps with something special in his cup he could try another spread. Selecting one of his small, ancient Yixing clay teapots, he sorted through a few discs of Pu-erh, settling on a recent raw version he'd acquired.

With all his accouterment set up on the long table, he took himself through the gongfu ceremony. He rarely made the time to go through all the steps when he just wanted to make himself a good cup of tea, but right now, he wanted the comfort of the process. The elegance of making tea in this fashion allowed his mind to open as he sorted out all the pieces of mystery revolving who wanted him dead. The bikers were just a tool, not the hand wielding it.

Once he filled his little cup from the small pot, he sat down. Cradling the cup in both hands, he let the fragrant steam flirt with his senses. He still couldn't quite find the patterns in his problems. It felt like someone had taken his deck of tarot cards and just smeared them face up across a surface and told him to make sense of it without recognizing he didn't have the knowledge and experience to draw reason from the seemingly random pieces.

He wasn't a tarot reader or a detective.

Perhaps another cup would help. "It couldn't hurt."

Turning on the kettle, he waited until the water was the correct temperature and poured it into the teapot for another steeping.

"You can't go back there," Tomi's said, his voice drifting down the hallway.

"Oh, don't worry, Dax and I are old friends."

With the music in the bar and the voice pitched back toward Tomi, Dax couldn't quite make out who it was. It was time; he transferred the tea into his teacup as the door to his tearoom slid open.

"Dax! So good to see you." Detective Randall Ryan didn't wait for an invitation before stalking into the room and taking a seat on the other side of the table.

Tomi poked his head into the tearoom. "Sorry, Dax. He *insisted.*"

"It's not your fault, Tomi. Some people just aren't good at picking up context clues."

"You want me to hang out here? Fred can manage the bar for a while." The new hire was still in his "training" phase, such as it was, but Tomi thought he'd be ready to fly solo soon. They'd lucked out with Tomi's rash decision to hire him on the spot.

"No. I'm sure the detective and I will be fine."

"OK… Holler if you need me."

Ryan turned to Tomi. "I'd take one of those fancy whiskeys you have on the shelf."

"Are you here on business?" Dax asked.

"I don't hang out in shitholes like this on my personal time," Ryan replied.

"No whiskey, Tomi. We can't contribute to the delinquency of a member of the Redemption City Police Department while they're on duty."

Before Ryan could protest and demand the drink, Tomi slid the door shut, returning to his duties at the front of the bar.

"Since this isn't a personal visit among old *friends*, what brings you to my shithole, Detective Ryan?" Dax took a sip of his tea, looking through half-lidded eyes at the man who'd beaten him a few days ago.

"Just checking in on you. Wanted to make sure you'd recovered from your little accident at the station."

"If you wish to enquire about my health, you may do so through my lawyer."

Ryan leaned across the table and rested on his elbows. "Going to hide behind your lawyer, eh?"

Dax ignored him, taking another sip of tea.

"Going to play it that way, eh?" Ryan pushed back, trying to shift onto one elbow and slouch to the side, but slipped, just catching himself before he slid off the table.

Dax did everything in his power to keep even the faintest of smiles from creeping onto his face, though he'd save that image for later. Instead, he finished his last sip of tea and got up to turn on the water for another steep. He wasn't going to let the pissant detective ruin his tea.

"Word is"—the detective righted himself, pretending nothing had happened—"a car matching yours was seen driving recklessly while leaving a bar out on Highway 77. There was a bar fight reported as well from that location. And oddly enough, a person matching your description was involved in it. What do you have to say to that?"

"If you wish to ask me any questions, you may do so through my lawyer." Dax refilled his teapot and set the time for the steep.

The detective's eyes drifted to the teapot. As soon as the timer dinged, Dax snatched it up and filled his cup, setting the pot on the table next to him where Ryan couldn't reach it. The last teapot the corrupt cop had broken in a pique of ire had been annoying, but nothing of sentimental value. This one... This one was an irreplaceable antique with years of patina on it.

"I could arrest you right now and drag you back down to lockup for impeding an investigation."

Blowing over his tea, Dax looked straight ahead, staring at a fixed point just above the detective's shoulder. When his tea was cool enough, he took another sip and smiled faintly. A moment later, Tomi stepped in without knocking, walked over to Dax's side of the table, and set down his cellphone.

"Speakerphone is on," Tomi said quietly.

"Dax, this is Frank Abernathy. Is everything alright there?"

"Everything is fine," Detective Ryan said hastily. "I was just asking your client some friendly questions."

"You will not question my client without me or one of my associates present. If you do not cease and desist from harassing my client, we will have to file a restraining order and add harassment charges to the suit against Redemption City Police Department we're preparing. Are we clear, Detective Randall Ryan?"

The cop steamed, his jaw grinding as his lips formed a sneer. Hatred burned in his eyes as they moved back and forth between the phone and Dax. After a few moments of awkward silence, he mastered himself, pressing the palms of both hands flat onto the table.

"If your client has nothing to fear, then there's no reason he shouldn't answer my questions," Detective Ryan said.

"That's not how this works in our system with a presumption of innocence. Dax, would you like me to send an associate to your place of business to speak with Detective Ryan?"

Dax caught Ryan's eye and smirked. "I would, since the detective is threatening to arrest me without charges again."

The bench scraped abruptly across the floor and tipped over as Ryan stood up, hands still pressed flat the wood tabletop. He looked like he wanted to dive across the table at Dax or the phone, probably both. Tomi, standing just behind Dax, spread his legs and folded his arms across his chest.

"What was that noise?" Frank asked.

"Yeah, would you like to explain that noise, Detective Ryan?" Tomi asked.

Shoving himself up, Ryan sighed and stood straight. "There's no reason to send your lawyers. I'll be leaving now."

But instead of walking toward the door, he walked away from it and around the table so he could approach Dax, away from where Tomi stood. Leaning forward and bracing one hand on the table, Ryan brought his lips next to Dax's ear. "You won't get away with this."

When he stood up, he swung his arm back, flinging the deck of tarot cards all over the floor. Tomi reached down and snatched up the teapot before anything could happen to it. Ryan didn't say anything more as he strode around Tomi on his way to the door.

Ryan stopped and looked over his shoulder. "We'll be watching you, Dax."

Tomi waited a few seconds before running to the door and peeking down the hall. He gave a thumbs up to Dax, then shut the door. "He's gone. Exited out the front."

"Are you alright, Dax?" Frank asked.

"Yes. He only threatened and sputtered. He did tell me I

wouldn't get away with this, whatever this is. Then he flung my deck of cards on the floor before leaving."

"Has he done anything petty like this before?"

"He 'accidentally' destroyed… Sorry, you couldn't see the finger quotes. But on a previous visit, he knocked one of my teapots onto the floor and it shattered."

"Was it of significant monetary or personal value?" Frank sounded interested in case he could find new charges to add to the suit.

"It was neither, fortunately. We managed to save the one I was using today, which holds value in both ways. That's probably why the cards suffered."

"OK. Unless there's anything else you need to tell me, I'll talk to you later."

"I think we're all good. Thanks for handling it," Dax replied.

"You two stay out of trouble and call me if Ryan shows up again." He hung up, not waiting for an answer.

"Good thinking calling the lawyer," Dax said.

"We have one, might as well use him. Plus, it all goes toward building our case against that corrupt little piece of shit." Tomi walked behind the bar and prepared a small teapot of his own.

Dax turned on the water. "The detective did bring up an interesting point, though."

"Oh?"

"He said my car was seen fleeing a fight at a bar and that a person matching my description was seen participating in a fight at the aforementioned bar." Dax raised an eyebrow and looked at his friend. "Makes you wonder how the bikers knew exactly where I was going to be and when."

"That's true. You got the message from Ragnar asking for the meet, then left. Unless this place is…" He looked around and held up a hand to stop Dax from saying anything else and made a zipped-lip motion.

Nodding, Dax stood up and picked up the cards, but stopped when he noticed the pattern of cards that lay in the center of the mess the detective had made. Curious but unsure about what it meant, he took out his phone and snapped a quick picture. He'd look it up later when he wasn't busy.

When the kettle boiled, they each made their tea, then took their teacups with them into the alley.

"You sure it's safe out here?" Dax asked.

"Hmm. Let's walk around and see what Mama has for today's special."

Once they were situated at a table in Mama Adele's Soul Food, they resumed their conversation.

"We should probably avoid having detailed talks at the bar until we have a chance to sweep it for bugs," Tomi said, rolling his eyes. "Again."

"Yeah. It might be the entire reason Ryan stopped in today. The harassment was just a bonus. Can you find one of those wands like Frank had? It would be more convenient than just looking in every nook and cranny and hoping we find it. We got lucky last time."

"I'll see what I can do. But back to your earlier point. We need to sweep your car too. Arresting you could have been a pretext to get some alone time with your ride and plant all kinds of surveillance junk in it."

"I hope not." Dax thought back to the conversation he, Ragnar, Melinda, and Tallulah had had as they fled from Tallulah's bar. "Otherwise, things might get a lot more interesting."

"Looks like I'm going to be your chauffer again. I wish you still had your motorcycle—at least until we can make sure the car is clean." Tomi swirled his cup, then tossed the last of it back.

Dax liked his newish car, but he did miss the enjoyment of riding his motorcycle. "I miss my bike."

THIRTY

JAMIE

Jamie expected them to head to the south side of town, since that was where she, Tomi, and Dax had lost the trail when tracking Travis and the wolf who'd rescued him. Instead, now they headed east on Highway 77 until they were out in farm country.

They had to be a good thirty minutes outside of town. She didn't trust her hands to reach for her phone, not while hanging on tight behind the inexperienced rider. Many times she'd contemplated bailing off when they'd stopped at a stop sign, but she couldn't let everyone down. She couldn't let herself down.

It wasn't until they rounded a corner on the country highway that she saw something other than trees, fields, and the occasional farmhouse.

Travis slowed down as they approached a shabby, single-story wood building with beer neons glowing on the outside. Motorcycles filled the parking lot. This had to be it. Slipping her hand into her pocket, she pulled out the GPS tag and surreptitiously slid it into the saddlebag on the side of the bike. It would still report her location to Suzie, who she hoped was close, and in the future, it could allow them to find any other places where the bikers might be hiding out.

When he pulled up at the end of a line of bikes and turned his off, she couldn't get off the motorcycle fast enough. Her legs felt unsteady, but she did her best to look calm and collected. Travis winked at her, then stepped onto the wood porch and strode confidently to the door, where a big burly biker stood sentinel.

Travis chucked his chin at the doorman. "Hey, Shank. She's with me."

Shank raised an eyebrow as he checked out Jamie, then shrugged. Travis shoved the door in, remembering to hold it just before it slammed into her face.

"Thanks," she said.

He didn't seem to pick up the sarcasm dripping from the word. Moving far enough from the door not to be in the way of anyone coming in, he stopped and surveyed the scene. The room was darkly lit, with no visible light coming from windows. There didn't even appear to be any windows. A jukebox played loudly. The bar was filled with mostly men, but a few leather-clad women sat at tables with the bikers or fetched drinks for them. Another burly biker stood behind the bar, functioning as the bartender.

In the corner, a biker straddled a chair as another one sat behind him, a tattoo gun in his hand. When she processed what the tattooist was shading in with a bright-red ink, the air whooshed from her stomach. When the design was finished, the red circle and black swastika would cover most of the biker's back.

She hoped Suzie would keep well back from this place. It would be very dangerous for a Black woman caught spying on them. Looking around, she tried to find the restrooms.

She leaned over to Travis. "I need to use the bathroom."

Nodding, he pointed to the back corner. "There you go, baby. I'll get us drinks. What would you like?"

"I don't know… You pick for me."

He grinned. "Sure thing, baby."

She hustled her way across the bar floor. Occasionally, eyes would drift to her. She ensured she kept far enough away that no one could reach out and grab her ass. But she couldn't stop them from groping her with their gazes as she walked by. Once she pushed into the bathroom, she heaved a sigh of relief.

But when she saw a woman looking at her with curious glance, she tensed up again. "It was a long ride."

The woman chuckled and returned to the sink, turning on the water to wash her hands. Jamie darted into a stall and quietly pulled out her phone.

"I'm here. Do you have my location? I'm at a roadhouse. The sign says, Honky Tonk Woman."

Suzie replied, *"I'm close. We know where you're at. Get out of there."*

"They're Nazi bikers, stay hidden."

"I know. Just worry about yourself."

Jamie didn't reply, returning the phone to her purse. She was glad she'd gone with the long cross-chest strap purse. It had been a lot more secure on the ride. Since she was here, and her nerves were on high alert, she availed herself of the toilet. Being a nervous pee-er sucked. After she washed her hands, she looked around. A single window was situated above the sink, but it was too narrow for her to slip through, even if she could stand on the sink and get it open. She'd have to risk going through the bar.

Pushing open the door, she stopped abruptly.

Travis, two glasses in his hands, waited for her. "Hey, baby. Didn't want you getting lost." He held up the drinks. "I hope you like whiskey."

She forced a smile on her face, though she was sure the corners of her lips quivered from the effort. He turned and led her back through the place to a table near the bar on the opposite wall from the bathrooms. He sat down and kicked out a chair for her, setting their glasses down. She sat, not having an excuse to move away from him.

Picking up the glass, she sniffed it, then took a sip. She refused to cringe. This definitely wasn't as good as the shot she'd shared with Dax and Tomi. Triumph bloomed in her heart when Travis took a sip and nearly gagged, then covered it with a lusty sigh of satisfaction. He clearly didn't like whiskey, but he thought it was a tough man's drink. He was out of his league, as always.

She relaxed into her seat, taking another sip of whiskey. "Not bad."

"Glad you like it." He took another drink, cringing again.

Containing the laugh she wanted throw in his face, she took another sip without any sign of her distaste for the drink or the company. She adjusted her seat so she could keep an eye on the door out of the corner of her eye.

"So...how come they're letting us drink here? Aren't they worried about getting in trouble?"

He snorted. "No liquor official is going to come here."

"But what if the cops come in?" She leaned closer, a look of genuine interest on her face. Maybe she could get him to say more than he should and give her some insider information she could relay to Dax.

"The cops don't mess with us. Not here. Not anywhere." He looked smug, as if it were his doing.

Plastering a semi-vapid expression on her face, she moved even closer. "Why?"

"Nobody messes with Black Suns, but especially the cops." He looked around conspiratorially and leaned into to her. "Especially since we help them out with stuff occasionally."

She couldn't keep the look of pure shock off her face, but did her best to force it into some semblance of something Travis would think was her being impressed by the news. "Really? That's so cool."

A tall biker stopped behind Travis and dropped a hand onto his shoulder, squeezing it hard enough the teen winced. "I see you've brought a guest with you, Travis. Let's be sure to show her a good time, but there's no need to tell fanciful stories."

Travis shrank back a little, first from the grip on his shoulder, then at the words. Travis had been showing off, saying more than should be said to an outsider. Jamie let her gaze drift up to the man. She didn't recognize him from when she'd been kidnapped, though Dax had taken care of that by killing most of those who had been there.

He stood about six feet tall with broad shoulders, dirty blond hair, and an appearance that might be considered ruggedly handsome if the cruelty in his eyes hadn't tainted his face. He had the letters *H-A-T-E* tattooed on the knuckles of the hand gripping Travis's shoulder. It seemed a bit too on the nose, but she doubted this man was into irony.

"Are you going to introduce me to your friend, Travis?"

"Sorry, sir. Um, this is Danika. Danika, this is the president of the club."

"You can call me Sigur." He smiled, but the expression only made him look colder. He extended his hand to her.

Reaching up, she shook it, catching the letters on his other hand —*D-E-T-H*. "Pleased to meet you."

"Don't mind Travis. He's a good kid, but sometimes he tells stories that are best kept to himself." He intensified his gaze at her. "Understand?"

Under his scrutiny, all she could do was nod, wide eyed and slack jawed.

"Good girl," he said, squeezing Travis's shoulder hard enough he winced in pain again. Sigur let go and headed off to talk with some other people.

Once he wasn't looking at them anymore, Jamie shivered. She didn't like his presence at all. Something about it touched her deep inside, warning her. She picked up her glass of whiskey, her hand shaking. Forcing it to steady, she tossed back the rest of the shot, letting the burn of cheap alcohol warm up the coldness Sigur had left.

Out of the corner of her eye, she caught Sigur looking at her as he talked to a bearded man with an excess of body hair put on full display—he only wore a black leather vest that he'd left open. The hairy man looked her direction and leered at her. Once she saw his body shift, indicating he was about to climb off his stool, she stood up.

"Where you going, baby?" Travis tried to inject some confidence into his voice but still sounded shaky after the unspoken warning from Sigur.

"I...I need some fresh air. I'll be right back." Slipping her hand into her purse, she pulled out her phone and hit send on the message she'd typed in for Suzie. *"Coming out. Pick me up now!"*

Trying to play it cool, she strode through the bar confidently and let her hips sway a bit more than she normally would, hoping it would provide a distraction. She made it halfway.

"Stop her," Sigur called.

A hand reached out to grab her, but she knocked it away and darted for the door. Her quickness and the time it took people to process that something was going on gave her the edge. The one thing she hadn't worked into her equation was the bouncer. He'd been paying attention.

Standing in the doorway, he held out a hand, palm up. "Stop right there, girlie."

Behind her, chairs scraped against the floor as people moved to intercept her. Instead of trying to juke around him, she dropped and spun a vicious kick around, catching him perfectly on the side of knee. His knee joint popped, and he screamed and fell to the side. Leaping up, she dodged toward his feet, hopped over his writhing legs, and yanked the door open, praying Suzie awaited her.

THIRTY-ONE

JAMIE

The sudden blast of sunlight nearly blinded her after being inside the dark interior of the bar, but she didn't stop to let her eyes adjust. She couldn't afford to lose her head start. When she hit the end of the porch, she stumbled but caught herself and kept running in a graceless shamble until she fully righted herself.

As her eyes adjusted, her heart sank into her gut. She didn't see the little black Honda Civic. But she kept running, anyway, hoping against hope that by the time she crossed the parking lot, her escape ride would be there.

She couldn't afford to look for her friend's approach since she needed to focus on making it through the maze of bikes.

"Get her!" Someone shouted from behind her as a bunch of feet pounded against the wood of the porch.

The bikes… She stopped in the middle of a row of motorcycles, brought up her knee, and mule kicked behind her. The impact of the bottom of her boot hitting the motorcycle felt profoundly satisfying. The crunch of the bike flopping into the bike next to it, sending them cascading to the ground like dominoes, felt even better.

Pushing off hard, she slammed her hip into the bike on her other side, sending up another din of crashing metal. Hopefully, that would slow them down.

Off in the distance, she heard a high-pitched whine growing closer. Suzie!

Jamie dashed forward, shoving out with all her arm strength as she passed through the next line of motorcycles. If they tangled up, it would be even harder for the bikers to chase her and Suzie down, though it probably wouldn't take much to keep up with Suzie in her Civic.

The black Civic flew toward the parking lot, then screeched to a stop just as Jamie leapt off the curb into the highway. She yanked the door open and jumped in. Her butt was barely in the seat before Suzie took off, tires screaming as they found their grip on the road.

Suzie cranked the wheel around, pulling a whiplash U-turn. In the process of reaching out to shut the door, Jamie snatched her hand back as the momentum of the acceleration and turn slammed the door closed.

"Get your belt on, girl!" Suzie yelled, an excited grin raising her round cheeks.

Jamie fumbled around until she found the seatbelt and snapped it home. Suzie, staring straight ahead, worked the clutch and the gear shifter like a pro, accelerating quickly and smoothly. The small car practically rocketed down the road. Like the car, there was obviously more to Suzie than was obvious on the outside.

Risking a look over her shoulder, Jamie smirked as the bikers tried to get their bikes off the ground. Some of them, pissed off about everything that had happened, shoved each other.

"They following?" Suzie asked.

"They're working on it, but some of them are having trouble untangling their bikes. Crap. A few of them are pulling onto the highway." Fear churned in her stomach. Maybe Sigur had seen through her disguise. Did they have her image from the last time? Had it been circulated through the other chapters of the club?

"Don't worry, we'll lose them." Suzie sounded confident.

They rounded a long curve, and Jamie lost sight of the bikers. "Why are you slowing?"

Reaching down, Suzie pulled the emergency brake and cranked the steering wheel as they approached a road that disappeared into the trees. The car drifted around the corner smoothly. Releasing the brake and straightening the wheel, she pushed the gas pedal down, and they zipped down the road.

Jamie turned around and faced forward. Looking out the back window as Suzie took the car through fast maneuvers was making her nauseous. Gripping the handle with one hand and the edge of her seat with the other, she clung on for dear life as Suzie drifted around another right turn, essentially sending them back the way they'd been going, though they still hadn't cleared the trees. Jamie hoped the greenery muffled the sound of the car as it raced ahead.

When Suzie drifted around a left turn, Jamie couldn't contain the tense yell that came from her throat. She'd never driven this fast or wildly. Cory's old Hyundai would have fallen apart if they'd tried any of this. The only thing that had saved them when Dax was chasing them had been a dangerous and lucky hop across some train tracks as a train came by, cutting Dax off. Still, she'd thought the engine on Cory's car was going to explode; it had sounded so bad as they'd tried to press it.

At no point did Suzie's car sound anything other than smooth as she raced through hard turns, curves, and straightaways. Her Civic definitely didn't have a stock engine or probably any of the standard version of the other important parts. This was a car built for speed and maneuverability, and her new friend was letting it out to play.

Another drifted left turn and they were once again heading in the vague direction of Red City. As they emerged from the trees, they had a bit of a straightaway, so Suzie picked up more speed. Risking a quick look back, Jamie sighed in relief when she didn't see any bikes behind them. She hoped she and Suzie had managed to escape around the first corner and throw the bikers for a loop with the bit of a backtrack.

Settling back in her seat, she forced her shoulders down and took in a deep breath. "That was amazing driving."

"Thanks!" Suzie clicked her tongue and gave Jamie a quick

finger gun. "But we're not done yet." She punctuated her statement by flying around another right turn.

"How did you know where to go?"

"I checked out the local roads on my map app while I waited. I figured you might need to come out running, and we'd need to get away from some dirtbag bikers. Now hush and let me concentrate."

Jamie saved her question about how Suzie had learned to drive like this for later. At that point, Jamie decided to try to relax and enjoy the display of her friend's skills as they zipped through the country.

"Oh, fuck!" Suzie checked her mirrors quickly and locked up the brakes.

Staring straight ahead, Jamie nearly passed out. Several motorcycles blocked the road where they'd planned to rejoin the highway. Suzie hadn't gone far enough out of the way.

The car screeched to a stop. Ahead, the bikers fired up their bikes. Suzie slammed the gear shifter into reverse and threw an arm over Jamie's head to grab the back of the passenger seat as she looked over her shoulder. The car threw up smoke from the spinning tires.

"Hang on," Suzie called, cranking the wheel around as she turned the car. Soon had the car speeding away.

Jamie found an angle from which she could look at the right wing mirror and keep an eye on the bikers without turning around. The speed of Suzie's maneuvers had allowed them to open up some space.

If Jamie thought Suzie had been driving fast before, Suzie proved her wrong as they desperately tried to get away from the bikers. Holding on for dear life, Jamie silently encouraged her.

"I've got an idea," Suzie said, then slowed enough to take a turn onto a gravel road. Behind them, a massive dust cloud rose to highlight where they were.

Suzie kept the car at a slower pace as they zipped down the gravel road, the car bouncing and shaking from the ruts and shallow dips. They were headed toward what looked like a farmhouse screened by a line of trees. Slowing down as they neared the house,

Suzie pulled into the large gravel parking area behind the trees and stopped, leaving the engine running.

A minute later, the bikers joined them in the lot, shooting past the parked car. One of the bikers noticed them and slowed enough to take a wide sweeping curve, narrowly missing the picket fence that separated the gravel lot from the grassy front yard of the house.

As the biker neared the back of their car, Suzie slammed the car into gear and took off, sending up two giant rooster tails of gravel. The biker didn't have any sort of wind screen and took a bunch of small rocks to the face. Swerving and trying to keep control, he slammed into a tree. Jamie couldn't see very well through the dust and gravel, but she didn't see much—if any—movement from him.

Instead of leaving the farm's gravel lot, Suzie aimed for the bikers as they brought their bikes around to chase her. They weren't expecting her to come after them, so they sped up, trying to come around and get on her tail. Suzie, who seemed to be holding back, let them. About to ask why, Jamie clamped her lips shut when she figured it out.

As soon as the bikes got within range, Suzie did something with the clutch and gas pedal to cause the car to spin out, throwing up more gravel. These bikes were no better equipped than their buddy's. One wiped out and slid into a ditch on his side while the other tried to pull away, only to ramp over the berm of the ditch and fly into the field to land in soft soil. The bike slowed down much faster than the biker did and he flew over the handlebars, using his face as landing gear. On the next spin around the yard, Suzie turned onto the road they'd just come down and headed back toward a paved road.

"Suzie!" Jamie cried, seeing a fourth biker coming at them.

"I see him."

Instead of braking, she revved the engine a couple times on the fly, then smashed the gas pedal down to zip forward. Jamie wasn't sure whose eyes were wider—hers or the biker's once he realized Suzie wasn't slowing down or trying to turn around. The biker stared slack jawed at them in a moment of indecision before shoving his handlebars over, aiming his bike for the field. But what he didn't calculate right was the angle.

His front wheel flopped into the ditch next to the road and caught in the dirt, turning the back of the motorcycle into a dirtbag catapult. Jamie wasn't sure if he was screaming so loud she could hear him as they zipped past him, or if her brain supplied the sound effects for her.

She held her breath as they drove through the dust the biker had raised, but there was no one there to greet them as they turned right onto the paved road to keep driving away from the highway. The road appeared to be straight and long as it shot through farm country. Suzie opened up and the let the engine propel them down the long straightaway at breakneck speed.

As Jamie's stomach settled, she tried to unclench her muscles. "Damn, that was fucking amazing. I thought I was going to throw up for a second there when we saw those bikers."

"Don't you dare puke in my car!" Suzie pursed her lips. "I just hope I didn't take any gravel dings to my paint job. I don't know anyone here who can fix it."

"Huh." Jamie didn't know what else to say, so she returned to her default mode of being quiet and watching. Besides, Suzie—who didn't show any signs of wanting to slow down—needed to concentrate on her driving. Jamie was glad she'd met Suzie. Maybe she'd want to hang out sometime when bikers and racing weren't on the agenda…

THIRTY-TWO

DAX

"What were they thinking, going off like that?" Dax asked for the hundredth time.

Tomi slid a new can of beer to him. "Dude, keep it down. You're agitated, and it's making the customers nervous."

Dax looked into the back bar mirror. A few eyes kept flicking toward him. Nodding his understanding to his friend, he took a drink of the cold beer and held his breath and counted to ten. Behind the bar, Tomi's phone vibrated. Dax tried to keep cool as he waited for his bar manager to serve a couple customers who'd bellied up to the bar to order their next round.

Once they returned to their seats, Tomi grabbed his phone. "Just got a text from Suzie. Says they're on their way back here. Thirty-minute ETA."

Dax sighed in relief, slumping a little on his barstool. "Good."

With the news that the two young women were accounted for, he was able to relax enough to enjoy his beer while watching the early evening crowd. A man in a gray business suit sat at a stool a couple spots down from Dax.

"Hey, Geoffrey," Tomi said, "What'll it be?"

"Got any new whiskeys?" Geoffrey asked, leaning on his elbows.

"We just got a new Highland Scotch in." Tomi reached up and grabbed an unopened bottle from one of the higher shelves. Pulling the foil and removing the cork, he poured a small splash into the bottom of a dram glass and handed it to Geoffrey.

Geoffrey had been coming in regularly since his first foray into the bar a few weeks ago. Offering a free sample of an expensive whiskey was usually something they only did for valued regulars.

The man in the suit took a sniff then a sip. "Damn, that's smooth as fuck. I'll do that." He set the glass down and let Tomi add a full pour to the splash he'd received. "Thanks, Tomi."

"No prob."

While Geoffrey quietly enjoyed his whisky, Dax brooded some more, though he tried to keep it to himself this time. The thirty minutes seemed to take forever. Before becoming a human, thirty minutes would have been less than a blink of an eye for him, but *time* was as weird as a human. It never ceased to amaze him how long or short the same time period could seem.

And just like that, after being distracted by thinking about the human conception of time, it passed, and Suzie and Jamie walked through the front door. Little Suzie had a huge grin plastered on her face. Jamie looked a bit shaky, her forehead glistening with sweat.

He stood up and waved for Suzie and Jamie to follow him, only stopping to unlock the door to the tearoom. Once inside his safe space, he shut the door. After Ryan had left and he and Tomi had talked about it, they swept the room, finding a clumsily planted listening device. They documented it for the lawyer, then deactivated it carefully so they could save it as evidence of an illegal search since the detective probably didn't have a warrant from a judge to plant the bug. Even though the detective hadn't spent much time in the room or wandered too far, they still swept the entire room and the rest of the bar during a break in customers. Fortunately, the bug in the tearoom had been the only one found.

Even though he was eager to hear what the two women had to say, he couldn't spend time in the room without tea, so he set the water to boil and prepared the leaves. Once he was ready, he poured three cups of tea and sat down.

"So, tell me what happened," he said without preamble.

Suzie and Jamie looked at each other, then Suzie gently nudged Jamie with her elbow, prompting her to start her tale. Starting off haltingly, Jamie warmed up as she got deeper into her story.

Suzie held up a hand to interrupt. "Wait. You stuck my GPS tag in his saddlebag?"

"Yeah, I forgot to tell you in the heat of the chase."

Suzie chuckled. "I guess that's understandable." She pulled out her phone and opened an app. "Yup. It's working. I have the tag's location."

"That was smart of you, Jamie," Dax said. "Is it just a live feed, or can you save the locations, so you don't have to stare at it constantly?"

"I think it has a playback mode. Let me play with it and get back to you."

"Before you do, can you send me the coordinates of its current location?"

"Sure." Suzie tapped away at the screen and a moment later, his phone vibrated.

Pulling it out, he found the coordinates—The Honky Tonk Woman. Either the bike was still there, or they'd returned to the bar after the failed chase. He already knew that was where some of the bikers were, but it was good to have a potential location, though he had no idea what he was going to do if he found the biker's new base. But having information was always better than not having it.

While Jamie continued her story and described the car chase, Dax raised an eyebrow, his gaze occasionally slipping over to Suzie. Not only was Suzie "punk as fuck," based on her own admission, but a bit of a drift car racer too. Interesting.

"Let's go back to this Sigur. You're sure it wasn't one of the bikers from last time?" Dax asked, leaning closer.

"Yeah. When they had me tied up in their clubhouse, I saw most of them, at least those who were present. I mean, he might not have been there that day, but I don't know for sure."

"Can you go into more detail about how he made you feel? Do you think it was just the situation and him being an intimidating presence, or was there more?" If nothing else, Sigur was a dangerous leader, but if he was more…

"It's hard to say. I don't know much about magic. But it felt a lot like when I met Manman Delphine."

"Like voodoo?" Dax's gut tightened. If this Sigur was as powerful as he suspected Delphine was, they might be in for a rough fight.

"No, I don't know. It didn't feel exactly like being in her shop or being in contact with her. It felt like her but different. Like I could feel her power, her aura, maybe? He felt like that, but like the opposite—dark, unwholesome, sinister. It could be his demeanor coloring my impression, but the same unique undercurrent was there."

"And he's also a wolf shifter?"

She nodded firmly. "That I'm more confident about. The whole gang is, at least those who I've come in contact with."

"Can shifters use magic?"

"I…I don't know." She looked down, her cheeks flushing. "I've been one all my life, but I don't know anything real about who or what I am or about my heritage as a shifter."

"I'll have to ask Ragnar. He might know more." Ragnar had said he was a shifter, and his father worked with runes that actually contained power. Hell, he could ask Delphine. She seemed to know everyone and everything worth knowing about the magical community. He sat thinking while Suzie and Jamie sat quietly, watching him.

Finally, he looked up. "Oh, we hired a new guy, Suzie. His name is Fred. He should be here by now to train with Tomi. Would you go take over and send your cousin back for a minute? I want to get his thoughts on what Jamie just told us."

Suzie stood up and headed for the door, mumbling, "I better get a bonus for all this extra shit."

"Don't worry, I'll make sure you're taken care of." Dax picked up his cup of tea and took a sip.

Suzie grinned and winked at him. "Damn, your hearing is good."

Jamie snickered quietly. Tomi joined them a few minutes later and listened to a truncated version of Jamie's story.

"What have you gotten us into, Dax?" Tomi crossed his arms.

"I'm sorry," Jamie said. "It's my fault for shooting you."

"No, you didn't choose to shoot me and frame the bikers, did you?"

Jamie shook her head.

"Someone wants me dead. You were just one of the weapons they used to try to accomplish it." He snorted. "You weren't even the only person to shoot me during that episode."

"Or the only person to be shot because of it," Tomi added. "The question you have to ask is, is this new situation specifically an extension of the previous contract on your head, or a personal vendetta?"

Dax sighed and ran both hands through his hair. "Probably both, at this point. Biker gangs aren't known for their forgive-and-forget ethos. Also, if what Ragnar said about the cops using the bikers as hired muscle is true, then they have to honor the contract they took from whoever paid them if they want to keep getting jobs." He turned his attention back to Jamie. "You said he looked at you weirdly. Do you think he saw through Delphine's magic?"

"I don't know. I didn't stick around long enough to find out. But he clearly wanted me stopped."

Tom shifted in his seat to face Jamie. "You be sure to keep that gris-gris bag on you at all times. And be sure to feed it. Dax has whiskey in his apartment you can use, or we can send some home with you."

Jamie chuckled nervously, shaking her head and rolling her eyes. "I doubt my mom would understand if I dug into Dax's liquor and poured it on a voodoo pouch."

Dax was impressed she could combine so much sarcasm into a few gestures, but then again, she was a teen, and he'd heard sarcasm was their favorite form of communication. "Bring it into the bar when the gris-gris is due for its drink, and we can take care of it when I feed mine."

Tomi laughed. "We should get a protection gris-gris for Suzie. Then we can set up a gris-gris feeding station."

A vibration in his pocket alerted Dax to a text, but it sounded different than normal. Reaching in, his fingers bumped into something cold and metallic that definitely wasn't his phone. He pulled it out. It was the knife the goon had tried to stab him with the other night. He thought he'd felt something weird in his pocket when he pulled out his keys but had forgotten about it in all the chaos afterward.

Pushing the button on the handle, the blade popped out of the top. On it were carved what looked like Norse runes. A couple looked vaguely familiar, like those that had been carved on the bullets meant to kill him.

Carefully, he gripped the flat of the blade between his thumb and forefinger and tried to force the blade back into its housing, but it didn't budge. Standing up, he walked around the bar and grabbed a cutting board and set it on the bar top. He pushed the blade into it, but it didn't retreat into the handle.

He pulled the gris-gris out from under his T-shirt and stared down at it.

"What's up, Dax?" Tomi stood up and walked up to the bar to check out the knife.

"One of the bikers used this knife to threaten me, but when he tried to stab me for real, the blade sank back into the handle."

Tomi picked it up to play with it but couldn't get the blade to budge either, not without pushing the button. "Looks like the manbo saved you from getting an unscheduled new orifice. Good thing she fed the gris-gris and renewed it."

"Indeed."

THIRTY-THREE

DAX

Ragnar turned the blade over in his hands, looking at it from every angle, and retracted and extended the blade multiple times. "You're lucky the blade failed. It has some nasty runes on it."

"I thought some of them looked familiar. Like from the bullets," Dax said, readying tea for his guest.

"Yeah. There are a couple of those here. There are some binding properties and something else nasty. Maybe something that'll stop healing, or perhaps exacerbate bleeding. It's hard to tell."

"Can't you read the runes?" Tomi asked.

"Sure, but they can mean different things and hold different intents. A lot depends on the person who carved and empowered the runes." He closed the blade and handed it back to Dax. "If this was taken off some goon, I hate to think what else they've got enchanted."

"I had the same thought. Have you heard of this Sigur?"

Ragnar shook his head. "No. Sounds like a nasty piece of work though. Oh"—he reached into his pocket and pulled out a metal bracelet and handed it to Dax—"this is why I called you out to the Honky Tonk in the first place. Well, one of the reasons."

"Thanks," Dax said, unsure about the gift. It looked like a nice piece of metalwork, but he had no idea why Ragnar would give it to him.

"It's a little something I'm experimenting with." Ragnar pointed to the runes the covered it on both the inside and outside. "I'm hoping these will counteract the ones they've been using on their bullets."

"You mean it'll protect him from getting shot?"

Ragnar chuckled. "No. I wish. But it will return them being regular bullets, nullifying their magic. If it works…"

"You made this yourself?" Dax held up the bracelet.

"Yeah. I do a bit of smithing as a hobby. Makes for a good way to carve runes."

"And you empowered them?"

Ragnar nodded.

"Do you mind if I ask you some questions about magic and… wolf shifters?"

A red eyebrow slid up Ragnar's forehead. "Depends. You can ask, I just may not answer."

"Fair enough." Dax thought about his first question, wondering how deep he could go with Ragnar. "How does magic work with wolf shifters?"

Ragnar chuckled. "Going for a big one right out of the gate?"

Dax held up the switchblade. "Seems like a pertinent one, all things considered."

"It's hard to say"—he held up a hand to stop Dax from interrupting when he opened his mouth—"for lots of reasons. There's no repository of wolf shifter knowledge, at least not in Red City. Our generational knowledge hasn't always survived this city and its corruption on both the mundane and supernatural side. So, what I'm about to say is a mix of legend, hearsay, and personal experience."

"Alright. That I can understand," Dax said.

"In general, most shifters don't have magical abilities other than their inherent genetic abilities to change into a wolf."

"Most?"

Ragnar nodded. "Some, like myself and my… Some, like myself, can work with magic. I can empower runes. I don't know if this is an inherited gift or something unique to me. I don't know if I can do other forms of magic, but that bracelet is an example of my work. Among the few people who do rune magic, I'm considered one of the most powerful."

Dax slipped on the bracelet absentmindedly as he listened to Ragnar. "Can magic be used on a wolf shifter?"

"In general, it's hard to use magic against a wolf shifter. This is all legend and hearsay though. I've never personally had magic used on me by a witch or caster or whatever there may be." He shrugged. "I don't know many people who use magic, save for Tallulah and Delphine."

Dax wanted to know what Tallulah's deal was. She'd used some interesting magic in her bar, but he'd been too busy escaping to get a chance to examine it. Perhaps he'd have an opportunity to get to know her better and find out.

He held up his wrist with the bracelet on it. "Would something like this work on a wolf shifter?"

Ragnar nodded but didn't elaborate.

Dax held up the knife. "What about something like this?"

Ragnar held up a hand and wobbled it side to side. "It's hard to say without testing it. It seems unlikely they'd have weapons that could be turned against them, but then again, you never know. Without knowing the caster's intent and their power levels, it's all guessing games until you try the item."

Dax knew the gris-gris Jamie wore worked on a wolf shifter, both on the wearer and on other shifters. It would be interesting to see if it worked on Ragnar. He thought about calling Jamie and having her stop in to introduce herself so they could give it a go.

"Interesting." Dax set the knife down. "Not sure I know anyone willing to be the guinea pig."

Ragnar chuckled. "No, I don't imagine anyone would be too interested. I've answered some of your questions. I'd like to ask a few of my own."

Dax nodded. "Sure, under the same caveat you offered. I may choose not to answer or may not be able to."

"Agreed." Ragnar folded his arms. "Why are you asking all these questions?"

"Well, to put it bluntly, those bikers have taken a particular interest in my life."

Tomi snorted. "An interest in your death may be a more accurate way to put it."

Dax acknowledged the point with a wave of his hand.

Ragnar raised an eyebrow, tilting his head slightly. "And you intend to go up against them?"

"I don't have much of a choice. After our previous encounters, they seem even more focused on me."

"Why haven't they tried to take you out here?" Ragnar asked. "If they're so intent, why wait until you're out of your territory? I don't think it was a coincidence the bikers showed up at Tallulah's right after you did."

"I don't know why they haven't made a run at me here lately." Dax didn't know how well the wards around the bar were crafted and how many holes, intentional or otherwise, might be in them. Baron Samedi had no issues entering his home, which theoretically had the same wards. "This place isn't without its own defenses, though I can't gauge how good they are. Much like your earlier comment about not knowing without testing."

"Could be they wanted to get you alone." Tomi drew Ragnar's attention. "How well do you know those bikers? The old ones and the news ones?"

Ragnar scoffed. "I don't hang out with their sort. Those warped fucks misuse and abuse Norse heritage and twist it for their racism and white supremacy. I'm not interested in finding out more about them."

"Sorry, I meant, did you have at least enough passing knowledge of faces and names to know the difference between the locals and out of towners," Tomi clarified.

"No. I've maybe seen a few of the locals in passing. They always seem to turn up often enough to remind you still they exist, but I didn't recognize any of the ones who hassled Dax at the Honky Tonk. Why?"

"Dax cleared out a lot of the old ones…permanently. We think these new ones may be from out of town and are here to retake their club's territory."

"And to get vengeance?"

"Yeah. Definitely that." Dax reached for his tea but scowled when an empty cup stared back at him.

"But why the Honky Tonk?" Ragnar scratched at his beard. "I feel terrible about what happened. The bikers seem to be making themselves at home in Tallulah's bar, and there's no way to dislodge them easily." He'd been less than happy when Dax filled him in on Jamie's report. "Tallulah has been a friend for years and gave my band a shot when no one else would. I owe her."

Tomi chuckled. "I'm not sure Dax's brand of help would put you in much better shape."

"That's enough, Tomi," Dax said.

"What? You removed the bikers from their clubhouse. Quite effectively too."

Ragnar spun to look at Tomi. "The place burned to the ground."

"But there were no bikers left inside!" He grinned, wagging his eyebrows.

Dax leaned forward, looking back and forth between Tomi and Ragnar. "But Tomi's probably right. I'm not a special operative or anything. Last time I helped people out, the results were somewhat calamitous."

"And now here we are with bikers in our business because of it." Ragnar shook his head. "How did you manage to burn the whole place to the ground?"

Dax shrugged. "I walked in, asked them to let some people go, and they chose to fight. I defeated them. In the process, some high-proof liquor bottles were broken. They caught on fire, and it spread."

Ragnar scoffed. "Who all helped you beat a bunch of bikers? A division of marines?"

"He did it by himself." Tomi stood up. "You know what this discussion needs? Whiskey. I'll be right back." Tomi disappeared.

Dax sighed, pursing his lips. "I'm not sure I'm the right person to help you and Tallulah out."

Ragnar shook his head and held up a hand to stop him. "I believe your friend is right. Let's wait for the whiskey before you tell me you can't help solve the problem you helped create." He took a deep breath and exhaled as if to cleanse himself from the response. "What's going on with your Lincoln? Saw it up on blocks in the alley when I walked in."

"Oh. A friend is doing a little work on it, but that can also wait until the whiskey arrives."

Instead of finding some neutral topic of conversation, they let the room fill with awkward silence until Tomi returned with a bottle and three dram glasses. He set them down and filled them with a smoky scotch.

Dax smirked. Tomi liked to break out the more esoteric scotches when he wanted to mess with someone he didn't know.

Ragnar picked up his glass, sniffed it, then tossed the whole thing back. "Nice whisky."

Dax lifted an eyebrow and took a more measured drink. Tomi winked at Dax as he refilled Ragnar's glass.

"I'll start with your last question," Dax said. "Our friends are tearing through my car. Several days ago, I was arrested by the distinguished members of Red City PD and spent a night in lockup courtesy of Detective Randall Ryan, who has been a thorn in my side since I opened this place. We suspect he may have bugged the car. He tried to slip one on me when we left the jail."

Ragnar, about to take a drink, set his glass down with a *thud*. "Red City cops. The fucking worst. I guess this proves the rumors true enough. I'm surprised they're extending cooperation to out-of-towners, though." He ran both hands over his hair again. "Shit."

Dax nodded. "He showed up yesterday and claimed a witness saw my car fleeing the Honky Tonk."

Ragnar scoffed. "What witnesses?"

"Exactly. By then, it was just us and the bikers. I know I didn't call the cops."

"I sure as fuck didn't." Ragnar sounded as if the very idea was poisonous.

Dax leaned a little closer to Ragnar, an intensity filling his eyes.

"Then that leaves the bikers. But how did they know I was going to be there at that time? The only thing that makes sense is that they were tipped off. And unless you're a fairly good actor, I'm pretty safe saying it wasn't you."

"So the cops, using a bug they planted on you, tipped off the bikers you were going to be there. And since you were by yourself and far from your…power base—for lack of a better word—they took advantage of the situation and pounced, making my friend and her bar collateral damage." Ragnar bowled on before Dax could speak up. "Which brings me back to the earlier point, when you said you're not exactly the right person to help us get Tallulah's bar back. Seems like you're *exactly* the right person to help."

"I get that they followed me there, but it's not my fault the Nazi bikers were let into the bar in the first place." Never letting Nazis or other white supremacists in had been one of the big rules he'd established for the bar after opening it. You could never let one in, even a nice polite one. Soon more of them showed up, including not nice ones, and then you were a Nazi bar.

"That's a bullshit argument." Ragnar folded his arms across his chest. "You saw how many there were. There's no way Tallulah could have stopped them."

Ragnar had a point, but Dax had enough trouble taking care of his own issues. He wasn't sure he needed to make others' issues his as well, even if they did overlap with some of his.

"Look. I can sympathize with Tallulah, but—"

Someone shoved the door open and it rebounded in its pocket. "Damn it, Ragnar. Why aren't you answering your phone?"

"This is a private meeting," Tomi said, standing up.

Dax held up his hand to stop Tomi. "It's OK, Tomi. Apparently Melinda has something she needs to say to Ragnar."

Melinda rounded on Dax. "The message isn't just for him, *Slim*."

"Slim?" Tomi asked, an eyebrow raised humorously.

Rolling his eyes, he waved his friend off.

"While you three are in here talking…and drinking whiskey." She huffed, pacing back and forth.

Tomi slipped around her and shut the door.

Melinda stopped and planted her hands on her hips, staring between Dax and Ragnar. "The fuckers got Sippi and Connie, and I haven't heard anything from Jose."

"What?" Ragnar said.

"The bikers kidnapped your band." She shoved her finger through the air in Dax's direction. "They want him."

THIRTY-FOUR

DAX

Silence thickened in the room as Melinda's forefinger hung in the air, pointing accusingly at Dax.

"Fuck," Dax said quietly, lowering his head into his hands to rub his eyes. Abandoning Ragnar's bandmates to the bikers would be a bridge too far. The bikers were pulling his strings. Again. After he'd showed up to rescue Jamie, a person who'd shot him, and her family, they'd guessed rightly that he wouldn't abandon Ragnar's friends. "Sit down, Melinda. Tomi, get her a glass, please."

They waited until Tomi returned. Melinda cringed when she took the first drink of whisky but went in for a second one anyway.

"Melinda, start at the beginning." Ragnar slid onto the bench next to her.

"The beginning. Right. Let's see. I was supposed to meet Sippi and Connie at Sippi's place to hang out. But I was running late. When I showed up, his door was swinging in the wind. I didn't see or sense anyone around, so I slipped into his house. The living room looked like someone had tossed it." She took another drink and cringed, then reached into her jacket and pulled out an opened envelope from an inner pocket, tossing it onto the table. "I found that on the table."

Ragnar took the envelope and pulled out a folded piece of paper and read it aloud. "If you want to see your friends alive and intact, turn over the one named Dax. Call this number to confirm drop details."

"It's probably a burner," Tomi said.

"Can I see it?" Dax held out his hand.

Ragnar shrugged and thrust the note toward Dax. "It doesn't say anything else, except the number."

"It's not the words I want." Dax took the letter.

Tomi, careful to keep his hand covered, slid the empty envelope toward Dax. He picked it up.

Holding them so he could touch both pieces of paper at the same time, he closed his eyes and looked for the threads. The strongest and freshest belonged to Ragnar and the next to Melinda. He brushed them aside and looked deeper. A little farther back, he found some others who'd briefly touched it. When he found the strongest of those, he followed it backward.

Dax hoped the thin thread attaching the letter to the carrier would hold. Insignificant things touched briefly only collected the barest of psychic connections to those who handled them. He'd hoped the one who'd penned it had carried it the longest, but this string felt too tenuous.

"There," he whispered in triumph.

He leapt off the thread near its origin and found the letter writer, who'd poured his anger and hate into it. Dax backed off. A dark, roiling entity waited, and he feared drawing its attention. Whoever or whatever it was had power—dark power, blood power. He couldn't dive in and find out more, or he might leave a thread of his own that could be followed back.

Flinging the papers away, he gasped in a deep breath. Once he calmed a little and opened his eyes, he was shocked to see Melinda and Ragnar leaning away from the table as far as they could without actually standing up and running away. Fear was etched on their faces.

"Um, your skin slipped a bit there, dude." Tomi picked up his glass and tipped it at Dax, clicking his tongue, before taking a drink.

"How much?" Dax said, his voice raspy and hollow.

"Just enough."

"What are you?" Ragnar whispered, holding onto Melinda's hand.

Making sure his human skin was firmly in place, he sat up straighter but shrugged. "For the moment, an ally."

THIRTY-FIVE

JAMIE

As Jamie strode across Dax's apartment dressed in one of her new outfits, her mother didn't even bother asking where she was going, ignoring her instead. When she pulled the door shut behind her, she sighed and leaned against the wall for a moment. Though she'd never had the best relationship with her parents, she had been closer with her mom. They'd started drifting apart once Jamie turned into a teenager and became more aware of what was going on around her.

Her growing awareness answered the question of why she'd never been close to her father, but the ties to her mother had grown more brittle as she saw what her dad's gambling did to the family and how her mother enabled it. Now that her father was dead and Jamie had become more independent through no fault of her own, her mother seemed to resent her for what had happened.

She pushed the heel of her palm into her eyes and growled quietly.

Now wasn't the time to get maudlin. Suzie waited. This was the first time she'd been invited to do something involving her new circle of acquaintances. Previously, she'd injected herself because of the links forced on them by the bikers and whoever wanted Dax dead.

Pushing off the wall, she left the building and climbed into Suzie's car.

"Why so nervous?" Suzie asked, startling Jamie.

"What? What makes you say that?"

"Your finger is tapping quite the beat on the oh-shit bar." She tipped her head toward the fold-up handle on the roof just above the door.

"Ah." Jamie exhaled. "I don't know. Dax has never invited me to anything before. What's going on?"

"I'm not sure, but something happened with some of his new friends, and they're having a meeting and wanted you there too. And me, I guess." Suzie chuckled. "I guess we're both in the same boat. At least you're a cool wolf shifter."

"Come on, Suzie. You're an awesome getaway driver. And I would know. I've been in a couple car chases. You're the best driver I've ever seen." She didn't elaborate about Cory, who was a mediocre driver with a mediocre car. Well, mediocre would have been a big step up when it came to his car. Suzie needed the confidence boost as much as she did. And Suzie was indeed a kick-ass driver.

A few minutes later, they pulled up to the bar and parked around back. As they passed by the soul food place, Jamie inhaled deeply, remembering the meal Dax and Tomi had hooked her up with.

"Suzie girl, is that you?" a voice hollered from the pickup window.

"Hey, Auntie Adele. This is my friend Jamie. Jamie, this is my aunt Adele Chenevert—Tomi's mama."

"Ah, Jamie. Good to meet you officially. You both have either great or bad timing, depending on your opinion."

"Why?" Suzie asked suspiciously.

"Don't worry, Suz. Just need you two to take the food Tomi ordered."

When Adele finished stacking up the food, they both could barely see over the boxes loaded with tinfoil pans and trays. The smell was outstanding since the hot boxes sat under Jamie's nose.

"We going around the side?" she asked.

"Nah. Standing order is to always carry food through the bar to stimulate interest in ordering food." Suzie backed into the front door of the bar, pushed it open, and held it with an elbow as Jamie passed through, heading straight to the back.

"Oh, that smells good!" Becky said.

"There'll be plenty. One of us will spell ya so you can grab a bite," Suzie said as they passed. Once they reached the closed tearoom door, Suzie gave it a light kick. "Tomi, open up. We've got food."

The door slid open a moment later and people crowded around, licking their lips and making grabby hands.

"Back up, y'all! I'll drop everything if you're not careful," Suzie scolded.

Tomi waved from the back. "Suzie, put everything on the bar. We'll dish up buffet style."

Backing away, everybody made a clear path to the bar. Tomi met Suzie and Jamie there and helped them unload the boxes and lay out the food along the tea bar. As soon as the lids were peeled off, a line formed and people served themselves, then found a spot among the tables.

A diffident knock on the door drew everyone's attention. Tomi answered it, poking his head out.

"There's a real sketchy guy here asking to speak with Dax," the blonde bartender said. "He's waiting by the bar."

Tomi nodded and left the tearoom, closing the door. He reappeared a minute later with The Rat, who looked more houseless than sketchy. His mismatched clothes didn't seem to fit him well, though they were clean. Unlike usual, his long, shaggy hair was slicked back and parted at the side. His beard, though scraggly, had been recently trimmed, but not well, and looked lopsided. He held a knit hat in his hands and he twisted it nervously. Spotting the large Black man with the shaved head Jamie hadn't met yet, he chucked his chin toward him.

Tomi directed him into the room, shut the door, then sent the man to get some food. When The Rat finished, he looked around, spotting Jamie. "Jamie! Friend of rats."

Jamie smiled and waved, her mouth full of food. She'd have

beckon him over to join them, except she and Suzie sat at one of the tearoom's two-person tables. After smiling back with his awkward grin, he spotted a place near the tall, bald, Black man and took it.

Jamie looked around the room as she ate. It was a disparate group of people, of which she only knew a couple of members. Periodically, her eyes would flick back to The Rat as he opened his coat and shoved a piece of food into an inside pocket. Chuckling to herself, she shook her head. He'd brought a rat friend with him, no doubt to bolster his confidence in the world above his tunnels.

Dax, who'd been watching The Rat, sighed, rubbing his temples. "Your friend can come out. Just be sure he minds his manners and doesn't invite any of his siblings or cousins. I have enough trouble with the city's officials without the health inspectors becoming involved."

The Rat nodded and reached into his pocket to pull out a large brown rat and set it down gently on the table. Instead of waiting to receive crumbs, the rat tucked into the man's plate, exploring the offerings.

While Jamie was familiar with The Rat and his friends, she'd never witnessed them sharing a plate together. Choosing to ignore it, she focused on her food instead of letting the rat ruin her appetite. Either the rest of people knew the man and his oddities, or the quality of the food didn't prevent anyone from losing their appetite.

It was the best meal she'd eaten in ages, and she couldn't help but go back for seconds. Wolf shifters could always use extra calories, and she was a teen, though probably done growing.

As people finished eating, the tension in the room rose. Jamie wasn't sure how the last few people eating could bear to keep going with everyone waiting on them, though they too finished shortly. Once the tables were cleared, everyone sat around looking at each other, waiting for something to happen.

Clearing his throat, Tomi stood up. "Thanks everyone for coming. I guess to cut to the chase...some friends have been kidnapped by the asshole Nazi bikers, who want to exchange them for Dax. We've assembled everyone here so we can figure how to get them back. Let's go around the room and introduce ourselves, for those who don't know each other. I'm Tomi. I run the bar for Dax." He gestured to his slim friend in the leather jacket.

Dax stood up, looking like a vulture about to dive. "I'm Dax. I called you all here since I'm the subject of the current problem."

A tall, handsome, muscular red-haired man stood up. "I'm Ragnar Gunnarsson. Those who were kidnapped—Sippi, Connie, and Jose—are my friends and bandmates. I'd like to free them."

Suzie leaned over and covered her lips as she whispered into Jamie's ear. "I'd like to climb him."

Jamie snorted and covered it up with a fake cough.

A muscular blonde woman stood up next to Ragnar. "I'm Melinda. I'm in Ragnar's band, and the victims are also my dear friends."

Tomi gestured toward Jamie and Suzie.

Looking at each other to see who would go first, Jamie took the initiative. "I'm Jamie. I've dealt with these bikers before when they made the last few attempts at…killing Dax."

Suzie stood up next to her. "I'm Little Suzie—Tomi's cousin."

The tall Black man stood up. "I'm Boudreaux. I do a bit of this and a bit of that, and me and my crew have helped Dax with these bikers before." He had a thick New Orleans accent.

A white woman with curly light-brown hair and wearing a pearl snap western shirt stood up. "I'm Tallulah. The bikers are currently squatting in my bar, and I'd like to kick them out."

The Rat seemed to have withdrawn into himself, looking around the room furtively.

"That just leaves you, Mr. The Rat" Dax said. "I wasn't sure you'd be interested in getting mixed up with these guys again since they're not in your tunnels this time."

The Rat stood, looking down at the floor. "Sippi helped me out of some trouble a couple times." He finally raised his head, looking around the room. "He's my friend."

Dax nodded. "Whatever reason brings you here, we're glad to have you." He paused to catch everyone's gaze. "So, the problem, as raised by my associates here, is we have some missing friends and a bunch of bikers in a bar that doesn't belong to them. I could try what

I did last time, but that runs the risk of causing a lot of damage, up to and including the whole fucker burning down."

Tomi snickered, bumping elbows with Boudreaux.

Tallulah cleared her throat. "I'd prefer it if we didn't burn down my livelihood. I'm not sure my insurance covers Nazi wolf shifter bikers or other magical catastrophes."

Dax gave her a subtle closed-mouth smile. "Agreed. Since the bar I burned down belonged to the bikers, I wasn't as delicate as I could have been. The problem is, with that many bikers hanging out at Tallulah's, there's bound to be at least some damage, probably a lot. They might not be in the mood to leave the bar in one piece after what happened to their clubhouse."

"What we need is a distraction to get the bikers out of Tallulah's bar," Ragnar said, folding his bulgy arms over his muscular chest.

Catching her staring, Suzie elbowed Jamie in the ribs and laughed quietly.

"Thanks to Jamie and Suzie, I think we can provide that." Dax gestured toward Jamie.

"What?" Jamie looked like a deer caught in headlights.

Suzie snickered and nudged her again. "Tell them about the tracker."

"Oh. Yeah. Um, I, uh, in disguise, got in contact with someone I knew from high school who is a member of the biker gang."

"Why were you in disguise?" Tallulah asked.

Jamie shifted her attention to the attractive woman. She couldn't quite tell how old she looked. "Well, I was there when Dax burned down their biker bar. They probably want me dead too."

Tallulah's eyes widened. "What are you, honey, twenty? Isn't that a little young to have a biker gang out to kill you?"

Jamie shrugged. "It wasn't exactly my choice. Anyway, this guy took me back to a bar—I guess your bar—so he could ply me with booze and show off. Suzie gave me a GPS tag so she could track in case I needed to run away, which I did. But before I went into the bar, I dropped the tag in his saddlebag. And I'm almost nineteen."

Suzie stood up, raising her hand. "I've been recording his movements for a couple days now. There are a two other places besides the bar he's gone to several times. We suspect one of them might be their new base."

"Where is it?" Ragnar asked.

"South of town." Jamie turned to Dax. "We need like a projector and a screen or something."

Dax scoffed. "In my tearoom? No."

"Anyway"—Tomi stood up—"it looks like some old fenced lot just outside of town. We haven't had a chance to do a drive-by on it yet and check it out."

The Rat stood up. "If you give The Rat the address, scouting can be done."

"But where are our friends being held?" Melinda asked.

"I would guess in that compound," Dax said.

"How do we know they're not at the Honky Tonk?" Melinda looked between Dax and Ragnar. "Can she"—she pointed to Jamie—"go back to bar and visit her little friend?"

"No." Jamie shook her head. "I think my disguise failed. They chased me out and I wrecked a bunch of their bikes. If I have to go back there, you'll have to rescue me too." She gulped nervously. "Or arrange my funeral."

"So that's out," Suzie said firmly.

"Right." Dax gave Jamie a faint smile. "Jamie has already done a lot. Otherwise we wouldn't have this information. So, to help Tallulah get her bar back, we need to distract the bikers and draw them out. And to do that, we're going to attack their compound and rescue the hostages."

Melinda snorted. "We're going to do all of that"—she gestured around the room—"with only these people here? I'll give you this, Slim. You got a pair on ya."

THIRTY-SIX

DAX

"God damn it, Dax. Why do I let you talk me into this shit?" Tomi pulled rain pants on and then some rubber Wellington boots. "This is going to be nasty."

The Rat gave a high-pitched ratty little laugh as several rats skittered about around him. "Next time, make friends with someone called 'The Bird' if you want to keep your feet dry."

Dax chuckled, pulling on his own rubber boots. "He's got you there. Besides, who expects someone to come through the sewers?"

"People who used to be your friend, that's who." Tomi scowled.

Dax knew Tomi didn't mean it; he was just nervous and grousing about it. The bond they'd formed over the years had grown strong beyond merely casual friendship or bar owner and bar manager. They were family.

"Do we need some welding torches or something?" Tomi asked. "I know Boudreaux can get some."

Dax rocked on his feet to settle in the boots. "I don't want to drag that kind of shit through the sewers. I can handle the grates without one."

"No, why take shit to the sewers. There's already plenty there." Tomi shook his head, grumbling and cursing quietly to himself. "And it's Nazi biker shit too. I bet that's extra stinky. I don't get why I can't go with Boudreaux and his crew."

"Because I need someone to watch my back." Dax rose and laid a hand on Tomi's shoulder "Thank you. There is no one I'd trust more than you to do that."

Tomi sighed. "Damn it. You always have to say shit like that. So are we going or what? If I have to think about this anymore, I'm going to go home."

The rats orbiting around The Rat surged forward and disappeared into the darkness of the tunnel. Dax pulled on a headlamp and turned it on, then handed a second one to Tomi.

With their beams fixed on The Rat's back, they followed him into the narrower tunnel. Secretly, Dax agreed with Tomi. He'd seen the worst sides of humans, and while he realized sewers were practical and ultimately a good thing for public health and cleanliness, they were still tubes filled with waste. In the distance, the squeaking of rats echoed back to them.

"They wonder why we're so slow." The Rat chuckled, and the high-pitched, squeaky sound joined that of his minions. "There are tunnels to explore and new places to find food. New nests to build."

Beside him, Tomi shook his head and grumbled some more. "Better not get the fucking plague…"

Dax shivered involuntarily. The Black Death had been a particularly dark time and a busy time for one whose trade was dealing with the dead. So many people dead. The psychopomps who ferried them to their promised lands only grew weaker from a paucity of worship in already tight times. Though the realms of the Christian hell and heaven did gangbusters business.

"My little friends will not harm you, Tomi Chenevert. As long as you don't harm them…" The Rat replied in a sing-song voice.

"You have good ears," Dax said.

The Rat squeaked a laugh, rubbing a hand around his ear like he was an animal grooming. "Very good ears."

Tomi dropped the volume of his complaints.

"Don't worry, Tomi, you'll get to frolic in the sewers with my little friends soon. Don't you worry none." The Rat's confidence and comfort had returned as soon as they'd stepped into his underground kingdom.

Dax could understand why his friend was so unsettled. The Rat was a unique individual who'd earned his name in more ways than having a connection to the little rodents. Tomi and The Rat had gotten off to a mildly acrimonious start, though it had become more friendly as they continued to work together to keep each other alive.

Tomi's prediction proved true as the stench of sewage intensified the farther they walked. Next to him, Tomi coughed a few times, grumbling even more. Finally, he stopped and pulled the respirator mask out of his pocket and yanked it down over his head, dislodging his lamp. Once the mask was securely seated over his mouth and nose, he rearranged the lamp.

His friend still complained inside his mask, though the thick rubber and plastic served as a better muffler, rendering everything he said indistinguishable. Dax could solve the same problem of the horrible smell by slipping into his skeletal form, but he still didn't trust The Rat well enough to reveal any more about himself than the man already knew. The Rat had seen Dax's form, but he had no idea what all Dax could do in it. They might be allies, or at the least enemies of each other's enemies, but he wasn't sure he could count the little man as a friend yet.

He could stand the smell no more. His human senses were sometimes a severe inconvenience. He took a second to pull on his mask, though he removed the lamp before doing it. He did have a certain dignity to maintain.

The Rat had stopped to wait for them, laughing and shaking his head at those much more squeamish. Then he turned and led them deeper still. Twenty minutes later, he stopped. Dax looked over the shorter man's shoulder. They'd reached the junction with the sewage "pipe."

In fact, it was running open a few feet below them. The city had passed a levy several years ago to update the entire sewer system, but like most public projects in Red City, the money had gone into the pockets of corrupt politicians and crooked businessmen. A few places—the wealthier neighborhoods—indeed did get new sewer systems and the appropriate property value bumps while everywhere else got the shitty end of the deal. Literally, and all while paying for the rich to get richer.

"And now we get to know our fellow humans much better." The Rat cackled and jumped into the sewage trench, sending up a splash. The rats found purchase and climbed up onto some pipes running along the wall near the ceiling.

Dax looked at Tomi and said loudly through his mask, "Well, here goes…" But instead of jumping in with gusto as The Rat had, he sat down on the edge and slid down. Fortunately, the floor was flat and solid, made of either brick or concrete.

On the ledge, Tomi looked down, turned around, and took a few steps back down the tunnel, then returned, sitting on the ledge like Dax had. He flipped Dax double birds and slid into the muck. Dax would have to make it up to his friend. He didn't like it any more than Tomi did, but he'd seen much worse than this place. Death didn't have a delicate constitution when it came time to collect the souls of the deceased or to help those on the brink of crossover.

He tried not to think about the before times, before his exile. He wasn't fond of his human shell or the requirements involved in taking care of it. But if he focused on the here and now, it was mildly bearable. Being friends with Tomi also helped.

Ahead of them, The Rat hummed a tune, though Dax didn't know it or care right now. He was used to walking through water, but the extra viscosity of the sewage made his skin crawl under his protective gear. He should have had Ragnar do this mission so he could've helped Tallulah liberate her bar instead. Alas, Ragnar was better suited to that part of their mission.

When he stumbled on a ledge, he had to give up hiding from the current situation in his head and concentrate on what he was doing. He did *not* want to fall all the way in. Fortunately, they didn't have to go much farther. The Rat stopped and waited. His army of rats, marching along the pipes, streamed through the bars blocking the bigger creatures from advancing.

Dax wasn't looking forward to this part, but he stepped forward so he was within reach of the iron bars running vertically to block the tunnel. It wouldn't be an arduous task, but he would have to take off a glove.

Sighing, he reached over and removed his right glove. At least he wouldn't have to use his flesh. He shifted his hand from meat and skin into bleached white bone.

Death didn't just revolve around living beings, but all things. He thrust his hand forward and pinched the central bar between the bones of his forefinger and thumb and concentrated.

The bars, made of a cheap steel alloy—thank you, corrupt contractors—began to rust on the surface. He gave the bar a little shake and red chunks flaked off, revealing untouched steel. After touching the steel and shaking off the rust a few more times, the bar snapped where he'd been working at it, but the bottom of the bar was still solid below the sewage.

He grabbed ahold of the bar and shoved it forward. It held for a couple seconds, then it bent. Dax adjusted his grip and pulled back. The bar groaned and bent back toward him. He'd hoped the cheap materials would mean the portion under the sewage would be weak and break. What he hadn't expected was to be *that* right. Before the bar came back to level with its compatriots, it snapped. If it weren't for the proximity of Tomi and his quick thinking, Dax would have back flopped into the muck.

When he attempted the same thing on the next one, he was prepared. After that, he worked his way down the line until there was enough space for them to step through sideways without risk of damaging their safety gear; even the bigger Tomi had no trouble.

When they were through, Dax stopped and stared at his bony hand. The bones were clean. He couldn't get infected while in his Grim Reaper form, but they felt dirty. Tomi seemed to understand and pulled out a bottle of antibacterial gel from a pouch in his coat, shaking it in Dax's face. He nodded, and Tomi squirted some onto his bones, most of it dripping between the long white fingers. He rubbed it in with his gloved hand, then let his skin slip over the bones and returned the glove to his hand. It was a ridiculous thing to do, but sometimes the human brain controlling his meat sack demanded such things.

Catching The Rat's attention, he tapped his wrist even though there wasn't an actual watch there.

The Rat understood the gesture. "Almost there. Another ten minutes. Then their compound."

Dax nodded and pointed down the tunnel. The Rat turned around and advanced.

Wading through a river of shit… This was one of those times when his human brain seemed to stretch time out interminably. Ten minutes was nothing, but down here when he wanted to be absolutely anywhere else, especially knowing how much his friend hated being here, ten minutes felt like the time from the sun's birth to the universe's heat death.

Finally, The Rat held up a hand and pointed up. A shaft rose above them into the darkness. Conveniently, a ladder rose up the wall to disappear into the shaft. But after seeing how easily the steel bars broke, Dax looked down at the surface of the sewage, knowing that underneath, the ladder was probably nearly rotted through with rust. He hoped the rest of the steel ladder was firmly fixed into the concrete wall. This was not a high dive he was interested in performing.

"Are you ready? This is it," The Rat said.

To punctuate the point, his rat friends shimmied their way up the ladder, finding enough purchase on the patches of rough rust that they could climb to the next rung.

Dax wasn't sure he'd been any more ready for anything in his life. Until he thought about what waited for him up above.

THIRTY-SEVEN

JAMIE

The last time Jamie had "fought" the bikers, it hadn't been a choice. She'd been kidnapped by them and used as bait. The little bit of fighting she'd participated in had resulted in her shooting the president of the gang. She wasn't ready to get more blood on her hands. But as long as she labored under the weight of the problems her father had created, she'd have to keep fighting for her own future. At least now she wasn't fighting alone.

"You're awfully quiet," Suzie said.

"Just thinking."

Suzie laughed, though it sounded nervous. "Stop that. It'll only get you in trouble."

"Have you ever done something like this before?"

"Drive my car? I've done that tons."

"No. This whole thing."

"Jamie, there's nothing about this whole thing I've done before other than drive my car recklessly. And if I think about it too much, I might just fuck even that up."

Jamie reached over and patted Suzie's leg. "After seeing what you can do behind the wheel, I doubt you can fuck it up."

"Here's hoping." Suzie looked over at her briefly before returning her eyes to the road. "How are you feeling 'bout all this?"

She sighed. "I'd rather be somewhere else, but it doesn't feel like I have any choice."

"Are Dax and Tomi forcing you to help?" Heat tainted her voice. "Because I'll thump them something good if they are."

"No. They aren't forcing me to do anything. It's something else. Let's just say, unlike Dax, I know exactly why the bikers have it out for me. And until they go away, I'm going to have to do what I can to keep myself out of trouble."

Suzie raised an eyebrow. "Let me get this straight, you're trying to keep yourself out of trouble by helping a bunch of virtual strangers assault a gang of white-supremacist bikers?"

Jamie chuckled weakly. "Yeah. That sounds stupid, but it doesn't mean it's not correct."

Suzie laughed. "I like you, Jamie. I think you're a little cracked in the head, but hell, seems like the rest of us are too."

Jamie couldn't resist Suzie's infectious laugh. "Yeah, I guess so." She looked down at her phone and the map app. "Ten minutes and we're there."

"Yeah. Ten minutes to dumbshitmageddon."

"Us or them?"

"I can't help but thinking everyone involved in this is a dumb shit." Suzie sighed. "You be careful. Don't take any unnecessary risks. I kind of like you, and I'd hate to lose a new friend."

Warmth spread through Jamie's heart. She needed a friend, and so far, Suzie had been more ride or die than her last friend had been when it came down to it. Or in this case, drive or die. "I like you, too, Suzie. I could use a friend, and you're pretty awesome. I'll try my best to be careful."

"Good."

Jamie's phone buzzed. "Ragnar says they're in position."

"That man is too pretty to be fighting bikers. Mmm, mmm, mmm."

Jaime laughed, the comment helping to lighten the tension. "Maybe he's single."

"Oh, I'll just admire from afar. He's really not my type."

She nodded, not sure exactly what Suzie had meant by *not her type,* and what about him didn't qualify. White? A redhead? Muscular? Bearded? A man? It didn't matter. Suzie was right. He was a nice man to look at.

"I just hope he knows what he's getting into with these bikers. They're nasty."

Suzie laughed loudly. "Yet here we are, about to tangle with them —a short, chubby Black woman and a skinny eighteen-year-old brown girl."

It was ridiculous. The more she thought about it, the more absurd it sounded. She laughed along with Suzie. "Yeah. That's about the straight of it." The laughter died on her lips.

They'd just come around the long curve leading up to Tallulah's bar, and the parking lot was packed with motorcycles. Suzie slowed, pulled into the dirt parking lot, and stopped. Jamie grabbed the sledgehammer from the backseat and grunted at the weight. Ragnar had said it was one of his smaller sledges. Who knew there were light and heavy sledgehammers and that a person would need more than one.

Jaime took a deep breath. She could do this. She'd survived before, she could do it again. "I'll pop out, you get ready to go."

"Right. Good luck."

"You too." Jamie rolled down the window, then stepped out of the car.

Resting the sledgehammer on her shoulder, she strutted across the parking lot toward the first line of motorcycles, hoping she looked like a bad ass. As soon as she was within range of the nearest motorcycle, she stopped and cupped her other hand near her mouth. "Hey, fuckers! Remember us?"

Several bikers who'd been sitting at table on the porch stood up and looked her way to see what the commotion was.

Gripping the handle of the sledge with both hands, she drew it back, twisted her body, and brought it around with all her strength, punctuating it with a shout. The hammer smashed into the frame of the motorcycle. But instead of tipping it over and shifting it, the motorcycle exploded off the hammer's head and slammed into the bike next to it, starting a chain reaction of twisting steel.

She stared at the chaos, dumbfounded and jaw hanging open. Ragnar said he'd placed a rune on the sledgehammer to increase the force of its hits, but she hadn't expected that. Behind her, Suzie honked her horn. Jamie had been caught gawking at her unexpected handiwork. She ran back to Suzie's car and jumped into the seat, stowing the hammer on the floor. By the time she'd shut the door, a bunch more bikers had come out to see what the commotion was about.

Suzie took off immediately, carving a tight donut in the dirt parking lot, flinging rocks and dust in the air as she spun her car in circles. Jamie shoved her arms out the open window and deployed the double birds. Suzie continued with the donuts, laughing wildly in the driver's seat as she concentrated on her craft.

The racket of the motorcycles crashing over, the souped-up Civic's noisy racing muffler, and the gravel pyrotechnics had done the job of drawing out everyone inside the bar. Once a few of the bikers figured out what the hell was going on, they started jogging toward the Civic.

"Suzie, go! Now!" Jamie yelled.

Straightening out the steering wheel, Suzie aimed the car at the road. It also pointed the back of the car in the direction of those running after them. The shower of gravel and dirt the car flung at the bikers discouraged them somewhat as the tires worked to grain traction.

As soon as they did, the car rocketed out of the parking lot. It dropped off the curb and bounced hard, the tires squealing to grab the pavement. Jamie stuck her head out the window to look behind them. A few bikers were still trying to run after them. The smarter ones were getting on their bikes and firing them up. Someone stood on the porch shouting orders, trying to tame the chaos and regain order.

Tucking back into the car, she whooped and situated herself in the seat. "They're coming! And they're big mad."

"That's what we wanted." Suzie didn't say any more, focusing on the task at hand.

They flew around the curve they'd just come around a few minutes ago. Twisting to look out the back window, Jamie checked on their progress.

"How we looking?" Suzie asked. "Enough space?"

"I think so."

"Good. Get ready."

Jamie sat down and buckled herself in. Suzie didn't quite slam the brakes, but the deceleration was jarring. The car had barely stopped before Jamie had the door open, grabbed the hammer, and ran into the bushes, diving into a tall bank of grass. Suzie squealed away, and the door slammed shut with the momentum.

About a half minute later, the first of the motorcycles roared by. A few seconds after that, a bigger cluster followed. Then it was a steady parade of assholes chasing after the black Honda Civic.

Jamie hated waiting so close to the edge of the road, but it was the best she could do right now. If she tried to hide farther into the tree line, any movement might draw unfriendly eyes, so she watched through the vegetation and listened as the noisy motorcycles joined the chase. After the last one went by and quiet descended, she waited a full five minutes more just to make sure.

Even when no more motorcycles followed, she kept low, crouching and darting from bush to bush and tree trunk to tree trunk until she was well back in the woods. Only then did she stand up and jog toward the rendezvous point.

When she arrived, she wiped the sweat off her forehead and dropped the hammer. It might be one of Ragnar's "lighter" hammers, but it was still heavy as fuck, especially when you had to carry it while running.

"Did everything go as planned?" Ragnar asked by way of greeting.

"Yeah. Though you didn't tell me this thing was Mjolnir." She prodded the handle with her foot.

Ragnar bent over and scooped it up, inspected it, then gave her a dirty look. "What do you mean?"

"I hit the motorcycle, and it was like I launched it from a catapult."

"I guess the force rune worked." He set the hammer on his shoulder.

"Yeah, it did. That bike is probably now scrap."

Melinda walked up wearing tight black workout clothes. "I'll text Slim and let him know the bikers are on their way."

"Thanks, Melinda." Ragnar turned back to Jamie. "Are you sure you want to go through with this? You've now doubly pissed off the bikers. Triply, I guess. You can hang out back here while we go in."

Jamie folded her arms across her chest. "Don't worry about me, I can handle myself."

Melinda laughed. "She's a fierce little pup. Slim said they'll start their end of the party now."

Jamie scowled at Melinda, choosing to ignore the pup comment. "Why do you call him Slim?"

She shrugged. "Because he's skinny."

Jamie rolled her eyes.

Tallulah stepped up next to Melinda. Unlike the other woman, she wore a diaphanous dress that looked like it came straight from a Stevie Nicks yard sale. "Careful, honey, you don't want to sprain your eyes before we go retake my bar."

Jamie wished they'd stop treating her like a child. She was eighteen, and she'd had to do a lot of growing up way too fast to survive her parents and the bikers.

Tallulah was a mystery to her. Jamie knew Ragnar and Melinda were wolf shifters like her. Though she couldn't communicate with them. The trio of shifters weren't pack or family—she could identify a fellow shifter at first sight. Tallulah wasn't a wolf shifter, but didn't seem uncomfortable or surprised about discussions of the supernatural. Jamie figured she'd just have to wait and see if Tallulah was something other than a mundane human.

"So when do we go in?" Jamie asked.

"Let's give it a little more time. We need to make sure Dax has started his part of the deal and captured the interest of the bikers," Tallulah said.

"She's right." Ragnar rubbed a smudge off the head of his hammer. "We don't want them to come back and find something going on. We need them to commit to defending their headquarters and abandoning Tallulah's bar."

"Slim's going to get himself killed is what he's going to do. Sneaking in there with nothing but his human bartender and some of his buddies and The Rat."

"The Rat," Jamie said. "Do any of you know what his real name might be?" He'd never told her, nor had she asked when he was hosting her in his tunnels.

Ragnar shrugged. "That's all everyone's ever known him as. I've only met him a time or two because of Sippi."

"What about you, Tallulah?" Jamie asked.

"No idea. Red City attracts odd ones, and he's one of the oddest. I'd heard of a 'rat whisperer;' tonight was the first time I've ever met him. Dax seems to think he'll be useful."

"Oh, he can be very useful. As can his rats…" Jamie flashed back to the screams of the assassin as the rats descended on her. Shivering, Jamie drew in a clean breath of forest air to purge the memory of the tunnels.

"Yeah, but who's gonna watch Slim's skinny ass?" Melinda shook her head.

Jamie chuckled. "Don't worry about Dax. He's more than a match for these dirtbags."

Goosebumps rose on her arms, remembering him in his true form, when he'd decimated the bikers as flames leapt around him. She'd had a few nightmares after that. She couldn't imagine how badly he'd haunted the dreams of the few bikers who'd survived his inferno.

Tallulah raised an eyebrow. "Do you know what he really is?"

"I don't know exactly." She had her suspicions. He looked like a grim reaper, maybe *the* Grim Reaper, but she didn't know if that was actually a thing. What he was was scary as fuck. "But I've seen him in his other form, and there's a reason the bikers aren't challenging him directly. It was…scary watching what he did to them last time."

"And you won't venture a guess at what he is?" Melinda leaned closer, her eyebrows raised in curiosity.

Jamie folded her arms across her chest, a little annoyed at Melinda's persistence. "Like I said, I'm not too sure, and it's not my place to guess or reveal things he isn't willing to tell you directly. Let's just say, don't get on his bad side."

"Huh." Melinda walked off, probably contemplating what she'd heard.

"Ugh. I hate waiting," Jamie said, tapping her foot on the soft forest floor.

"It won't be long," Ragnar said reassuringly. "Soon it'll be our turn. And then you'll feel like it's too soon."

THIRTY-EIGHT

DAX

They'd reached the top of the steel ladder and now waited for the signal. The Rat had sent his minions ahead to infiltrate the compound using other methods than the ladder, though several still waited with their master.

When Dax's phone vibrated in his pocket, he reached down to get it but couldn't manage it through the safety gear he wore. That was an oversight he'd have to account for in the future. But the only person who usually texted him was standing on the ladder just below him. With the exception of Becky, who texted Tomi with work-related questions, the few other people who had his number were participating in this mission against the bikers.

"Alright," he whispered. "Let's go."

The Rat nodded but held up a hand indicating to wait. A rat sitting on his shoulder squeaked faintly. "OK. We should be clear now."

Dax took his glove off again and shook off his flesh, setting his skeletal hand against the giant steel plate above them. He rubbed along the edge until he found the bolts attaching the hinge to the lock.

One by one, he hastened the death of each of the bolts until he could snap off the bottom of each one. Poking a finger at each broken-off end, he rusted out the bolts. The hinge was no longer attached to the plate covering the hole.

Climbing up another rung, Dax awkwardly propped his shoulder under the plate and pushed up. The metal above him groaned but didn't give. Taking another breath through his mask, he pushed harder until he heard the snap and scrape of metal. He stopped once there was a crack he could see through. Despite the odd angle, he looked through the crack but didn't see anything moving.

He pushed the lid the rest of the way off, reaching up to catch it before it slammed backward. Slowly, he lowered the lid until it rested securely, then climbed out and moved out of the way. Once Tomi made it to the top, Dax helped him out and waited to help The Rat, though the man didn't need it. He nimbly emerged with his rats climbing up him to skitter off into the darkness.

They tucked into the darkness and shucked their protective gear, then Dax closed the lid quietly. Reaching into his jacket, Tomi pulled out the Beretta 9mm Boudreaux had lent him.

The compound was surrounded by a tall chain-link fence covered with tin sheeting on the outside. Razor wire capped the fence. A few small buildings were scattered around the lot, near a single larger building in the center of the compound. It looked to be a single-story structure, though there could be a basement. Nothing about any of the buildings looked well maintained. There were plenty of broken windows to go around.

As Dax's eyes became used to the lighting of the dark night without their headlamps—they'd turned them off once they reached the top of the ladder so they wouldn't give themselves away—he noticed movement along the ground, as if it writhed. But when a bit of light reflected brown fur, he understood. The yard literally crawled with The Rat's furry minions.

"What's the situation?" Dax whispered.

The Rat held up a finger and concentrated. As one, the rats stopped and turned around to look at their master. The dim moonlight and a bit of light drifting in from the sparse streetlamps reflected in their eyes. Hundreds of little red patches gleamed and stared at them. Dax shivered at their focus.

The Rat pointed. "Those three small buildings are empty. Everyone is in the big structure. Give me a few minutes. They're going in now."

Dax was glad Sippi had done some favors for The Rat, otherwise they'd be flying without any sort of intelligence. The Rat might not have accepted Dax's request for help for a stranger. Having hundreds of sneaky little spies might just save them a lot of grief. He had no idea who or what The Rat was and how he controlled or communicated with the rats, but he was turning into a handy fellow to know.

"Yes. The hostages are in the center of the room. It's a large, open space. They're tied to chairs. Um, there are…many in with them. Armed."

"Can you get a better idea on the numbers?" Tomi asked.

"Rats…not precise. To them, few or many." The Rat shrugged. "Sorry."

"Can they tell us where they're standing?" Dax asked.

The Rat cleared a patch of dirt with his palm to create a blank space and drew a rough map of the building's interior and where the people inside were located.

Dax looked over the crude dirt drawing. "Good. So, we have a pair at the gate and maybe a dozen inside?"

"I think so."

A bright light burst to life, slapping them in the faces. "Hey, you! Don't move." A silhouette pointed something metallic and shiny at them.

Fear and frustration coursed through Dax's veins, but he raised his hands as did his two companions.

"What… What the fuck?" The man let out a gasp as rats swarmed up his leg, some stopping to bite him while others kept climbing. He dropped the light, and it rolled away, highlighting the corroded tin covering the fence.

Reaching into the aether, Dax grabbed his scythe and strode

forward, cutting the man's life thread before he could scream and alert the other bikers. "Tell them to move."

The rats scattered.

"Quick, stand next to me. We need to get the gate taken care of before things go any more wrong." Dax waved them over. "I can shield us, but I don't know how big of an area I can affect."

Tomi jogged over and stood just behind him and to the side. The Rat eyed the giant scythe and his ratty eyes—the light struck them just right to reflect the same red glow of his rat companions—darted around nervously.

"Hurry up, dude." Tomi waved to emphasize his point. "You'll be fine."

"Much better than if the bikers find you by yourself," Dax added.

That seemed to tip the scale for The Rat. He ran up and stood behind Dax's other shoulder.

"OK…" Dax said it more to steady himself than to speak to his companions. He closed his eyes and searched for the feeling of darkness and occlusion he'd used when he'd been hiding from the bikers and the police the last go-around, though he'd only shielded himself then. Tomi and The Rat didn't really need to know he was uncertain if it would work on them as well.

Opening his eyes, he pushed the sensation out and a shadowy curtain descended, turning everything a misty, diaphanous dark gray.

"What's happening? Where are we? I can't see anything…" Panic saturated The Rat's voice.

"Don't worry. Dax won't let any harm come to us," Tomi said.

"We're still here, just in a shadow," Dax whispered.

Dax appreciated his friend's confidence and the attempt to reassure The Rat. He'd have to check in with Tomi later to see what it was like for him, as a human, to be shrouded in shadows. It definitely reduced his own ability to see distance and detail, but he wondered if it was a blackout situation for those inside the curtain with him. He'd also have to experiment with Tomi to see what it looked like from the outside. Were they completely invisible? Was the shadow visible? Could someone see through it? If tonight didn't end the situation with the bikers, he might have to really rely on his skills to save his bacon and his friends' someday. And if he didn't know what the limits and functionality of his powers were, he might misuse them at a critical point.

"Guys, keep quiet. I'm not sure if this blocks sound."

"You don't know?" The panic in The Rat's voice spiked.

That was a mistake. He should have just asked for quiet to concentrate.

"I haven't always been a human, and I don't know what powers are left to me and how exactly they function, so just relax and let me work. Please." The Rat didn't say anything else. "Tomi, let Boudreaux know we're moving to the gate. Now, put a hand on my shoulder and radio silence for all."

He felt Tomi's large hand on his right shoulder and The Rat's smaller hand on his left. At first, he took tentative steps to ensure they kept close and slowly picked up the pace until they shuffled along at a decent enough speed to get them where they wanted without raising a din. Steering toward the fence and away from the floodlight on the front of the building, he skirted around the pool of light created by a tall light pole in the center of compound until he needed to turn toward the gate, where two guards stood keeping watch. Once he made it to the halfway point between the corner of the fenced compound and its gate, he was forced to leave the embrace of the shadows.

He stopped and turned to address Tomi. The Rat's superior hearing would be able to pick up what he said. "Stand directly behind me. When I give you the signal, stop and give me room to work," he whispered.

Once they'd stepped behind him, he continued toward the gate, hoping the two men guarding it were bored and not paying attention. A scuff in the gravel would certainly be enough to attract their wolf-shifter-enhanced hearing. The three of them had made it almost to the light when a pebble shot out from under someone's foot, skittering across the gravel.

Clenching his teeth, Dax stopped, and Tomi bumped into his back. The nearest guard perked up and looked around.

"What is it?" the other guard asked.

"I don't know. I thought I heard something." The guard took a step forward, slowly scanning the yard, though he didn't quite swing his head around to look down the fence line. He swept the other way, then stuck his nose up, sniffing.

Dax became too aware of the sewage stench clinging to The Rat's clothes. He really wished the rat had agreed to wear the safety gear they'd offered him. What way was the breeze blowing? He couldn't feel it inside their shroud of darkness. He tried to spot a flag or a tree or a scrap of paper fluttering around, or anything else that might indicate which way it was blowing.

The other guard added his nose to the sniff fest. "Ugh, fucking sewer must be venting again. I can't wait until we're done here." He snorted a laugh. "Maybe we'll dump that fucker's dumb ass down the sewer pipe when we're done with him."

"I don't know if it'll be that easy… He's got to be tough if half of what they said happened is true." The first guard backed up and rested his back against the pole holding the gate up.

The other guard scoffed. "These local pussies couldn't even handle one man. We should have taken them to the vet years ago and had them neutered."

The other guard chuckled, then the pair returned to their silent boredom. Dax gave them a couple more minutes to settle in, then decided he and his entourage had gone far enough. Shaking Tomi's hand off his shoulder, he took a step forward. As his human skin and flesh sloughed off into the aether, he stretched his bones until he stood over seven feet tall.

He let the front of his shadow shroud drift way as he stepped out of it, wafts of dark clouds curling around him like smoke. With a thought, he closed up the shroud, hoping it would stay over Tomi and The Rat while he dealt with the guards.

"Fucking hell…" The nearest guard had noticed him.

With another step, Dax drew within range and slashed with his scythe, shearing the man in half from the junction of his shoulder and neck down and out under the other side of his rib cage. The second guard stared in horror, the blood draining from his face. Dax stepped over the bloody mess of the first guard.

The second guard's hand shook as he fumbled to raise his gun. Swiping at the charging lever on the automatic rifle, his hand slipped over it. Dax was tempted to let the guard shoot at him to add to the horror of what was about to happen, but two people with vulnerable flesh were only a few yards behind him.

"Valhalla awaits me… Valhalla awaits me…" the guard mumbled as he brought his gun up.

Behind the guard, the giant form of Hel stepped out of the shadows. Dax groaned internally. She'd shown up after he was done with the bikers before, but now she seemed overly eager to capture their souls as soon as Dax killed their bodies. He hadn't calculated for her presence and had to hope she'd not fuck up their plans. Not that he could do anything about it either way.

Like the previous times he'd seen her, Hel had arrived in her true form. Half and rotten while the other part looked like it belonged to a beautiful Scandinavian woman. She stepped forward and caressed the guard from behind with her skeletal and putrid flesh-covered hand. "Valhalla isn't for you. You are not of the noble dead."

Raising her head, she made eye contact with Dax and nodded. He brought his scythe around in a backhanded arch that moved forward and up and plunged into the groin of the guard. With a yank, he pulled out and split the guard from legs to chest. Behind Dax, someone retched.

Hel graced him with a wicked grin as she drew the souls from the two dead men. Dax took a certain pleasure from the dead men's writhing horror as they realized they'd spend their eternity as tortured and ignoble souls under the power of Hel. As soon as she had her harvest, she returned to wherever it was she waited when she knew more souls would be available to take.

He'd have to spend more time with the thought later, but she'd arrived in anticipation of the carnage this time. Last time, she'd only showed up to do her work after he'd finished. Baron Samedi said Dax was being watched, but it appeared it was by multiple entities and likely for a wide variety of reasons. He just wished they'd leave him alone like they'd promised.

At least he'd dealt with the guards quickly before they could raise an alarm. Wrapping his flesh around himself, he turned around. The shadow was gone, and Tomi rested on his hands and knees, dry heaving. Tomi had never seen him use his scythe in such a gruesome manner before. He'd been guarding their rear when Dax had gutted the assassin. The few other times he'd killed with Tomi there as a witness, it'd been done with the clean simplicity of reaching into the aether to sever the living creature's life thread.

Dax helped Tomi up. "Why don't you go wait around the corner of the building. In case they come out front, you can be behind them."

Tomi nodded and jogged off, sticking to the shadows.

Dax turned to The Rat. "I'm going to reform the shadow around us. You take care of the gate, and I'll watch the front of the building. Also, send your rats to watch the street and to keep an eye on things inside the main building."

The Rat kicked some dirt over Tomi's mess and stepped around it, nodding. He unslung his backpack and pulled out a pipe bomb they'd taken from Sippi's stash in his garage. Dax moved them to the center of the gate, where the two sides were locked together.

"Are you sure you know what you're doing?" Dax asked, glancing over his shoulder to watch The Rat attach the bomb to the chain and padlock holding the gate shut.

"Oh, yes. Sippi has helped me open up tunnels. The most interesting things are down tunnels with locked gates." He chuckled quietly and returned to his work. A minute later, he stepped back, bumping into Dax. "Ready."

"And the fuse is long enough?" Dax didn't want to test what his body—either version—could withstand.

"We'll see." The Rat cackled loudly, then shut it down after remembering where they were.

Dax exhaled and collected his patience. "Light it."

A lighter flicked to life. A moment later, the fuse hissed as it caught and started burning.

"Now, good time to run away," The Rat said, walking briskly toward the corner of the building near where they'd emerged from the sewer.

Dax jogged after him, picking up speed. When he passed the Rat, the small man broke into a run to keep up. Rats streamed after them, clearing out from where they figured the blast zone was. He and The Rat tucked behind the concrete that protected the entrance to the sewers. Dax hoped Tomi had found a good place to hide.

Peeking over the edge, Dax watched the fire sizzle up the fuse. Tension curled through his muscles as all the things that could go wrong presented themselves at that moment. Number one—no one knew how powerful the bomb was because Sippi didn't label them in a method that was easily decipherable. As the fuse neared the bomb, Dax ducked and waited. Nothing happened.

"Shouldn't it have blown up by now?" Dax whispered.

The Rat shrugged. Dax was about ready to poke his head up and check when they heard an explosion with a cacophonous detonation that shook the building and sent a high-pitched whine through Dax's ears. A deafening silence descended for a split second before twisting metal groaned and shrieked.

Shaking his head a couple times to try to clear it, Dax popped up. The gate was gone and had taken a good chunk of both sides of the fencing with it, blown out of sight by the explosion. A sizable crater had been carved in the gravel where the gate had been.

"Holy shit," The Rat said.

Dax could only nod with his jaw hanging open.

THIRTY-NINE

JAMIE

Jamie wished they'd get on with it already. The waiting was the worst part. She'd been terrified on the ride out to the biker bar, but once she had to get out of the car and do her thing, she'd been fine. Nervous and a bit scared, but not knee-knocking terrified. Now she had to wait while Tallulah and Ragnar checked out the bar and decided when the right time to strike was.

"Quit pacing, kid. You're starting to get on my nerves." Melinda sat up and tipped her hat back to reveal her eyes.

Jamie stopped, her brow furrowing in a scowl. "How can you be so calm right now?"

Melinda shrugged. "Beats wearing out my boots on fruitless pacing." Her head perked up. "Quiet. I think they're coming back."

Jamie looked in the direction Ragnar and Tallulah had gone. A shadow emerged and took the form of Ragnar.

"Where's Tallulah?" Jamie asked.

Ragnar stopped at the edge of the small clearing they waited in. "She's, uh, working on something. You two ready?"

Melinda stood up and stretched up. "Yup."

Jamie nodded. "Yeah. Guess so."

"You don't have to do this. Our plan doesn't require numbers."

"Damn it." She folded her arms and glared at Ragnar. "I can handle myself. I've survived these bikers before. I can do it again."

Melinda walked up next to Ragnar. "Shouldn't you be worried more about school dances and makeup? Rather than fighting Nazi bikers?"

"Shouldn't you be worrying about minding your own business?"

"Kid, when it's my life on the line"—she thrust her thumb at her chest—"it is my business."

Ragnar held up his arms. "Hey, save it for the bikers. We're supposed to be on the same side here. Jamie, I won't ask anymore and neither will Melinda. Melinda, wolf?"

Melinda scraped the scowl off her face and sighed. "Let's walk in. I can shuck these clothes quick enough."

Jamie had worn one of her new shirts with the collar and hem cut off. She could pull it off fast and shift, then slip out of her pants. "I'll stick to this form too."

"OK. Get walking. There's a deer path just over there that goes around and lets you out at a place just past the Honky Tonk. You should be able to sneak across the road and get to the back door. We'll wait until you get across to head up front."

Jamie nodded and jogged toward the path Ragnar had pointed out. She wasn't sure what exactly they had planned, but she hoped it was big enough to distract the bikers while she snuck around back. As she neared the highway, she slowed down, crouching and ducking through the shadows until she stood behind the last tree before the open strip next to pavement.

The lights in the parking lot and the neons under the porch glared brightly in the dark night. She watched the door, waiting to see if any movement marked a doorman, but saw nothing. Checking left and right, she took a deep breath and exhaled before dashing across the two lanes of country highway.

Her shoes slapped hard and noisily on the pavement, sounding thunderous in the quiet night. Maybe sneakers would have been a better option than her new boots. Once she made it across road, she slid to a stop in the dirt and crouched behind a stack of old tires filled with concrete and holding a pole that marked the boundary of the bar's parking lot.

So far it appeared she'd gone unnoticed. Looking back to where she guessed Rangar, Melinda, and Tallulah were, she saw nothing but trees, until light shone off something metallic. Shadows moved around just behind the last line of trees. Squinting, she leaned forward as a green glow pulsed weakly then grew steadily stronger until it resolved into a churning green maelstrom.

She yelped but stifled it quickly when the report of cracking wood shot through the silence. The trees rustled and groaned as if a heavy wind wished to challenge them for supremacy over their domain. Then, illuminated by the green glow, something moved.

"Ents?" she whispered before catching herself. *No. Ents are pure fiction. I hope...*

The trees remained where they were even though they shivered and shimmied, but something broke the steady dull black expanse of the pavement. It looked like a massive python slithering across. Squinting, she focused on whatever it was. She could pick up the woody patterns and smaller offshoots from the massive root growing across the road at a vastly accelerated rate.

When it reached the curb, it climbed over, reared up, and plunged into the ground. Out of the corner of her eye, she watched the green glow shift, breaking the plane of the tree line and floating out of the woods, following the line of the massive root. In the center of the glow, a figured hovered.

Jamie's jaw dropped in wonder. It was Tallulah, her diaphanous dress floating around her in undulating waves. Her arms were outstretched with her palms down, and her legs hung below her with her toes pointed rigidly toward the ground.

Flanking on her both sides, Ragnar and Melinda walked along the ground. Ragnar had stripped off his shirt. In the glow of Tallulah's power, sweat glistened off his bare chest. He carried a large sledgehammer, bigger than the one he'd loaned her. Melinda was unarmed, and she stalked across the road as gracefully as a big cat on the hunt.

When they reached the parking lot of Tallulah's bar, they stopped and spread out a little bit. Ragnar walked over to the handful of bikes huddled in a mangled pile of twisted steel—the bikes she'd knocked over with the hammer—and reared the hammer back and swung it down onto the nearest bike.

The bike folded in half like a tissue, metal tearing and screaming in pain. He shook the scraps off the end of his hammer and swung it around in another huge arc before bringing it down on the next bike, turning it into scrap.

He stopped for a moment, resting his hammer on his shoulder, and drew in a chest-expanding breath. "Come out here, you parasites!" To punctuate his request, he smashed another bike. "Before I start destroying the working motorcycles."

Finally responding to the noise of destruction, a dozen bikers streamed out onto the porch. One of them stepped out into the lot. "Do you know who you're threatening?"

"The scum of the earth. Parasites. Fascist trash. Sound about right?" Ragnar called back. He twirled the handle of the hammer and spun the head around to catch the light and draw their attention.

"You have violated the sanctity of the guest," Tallulah said, but her voice came out in a weird, beautifully eerie harmony. It was freaky as fuck but still warm, like music generated from instruments made of wood. "You will vacate this place or suffer my wrath."

"It's our bar now, witch," the biker said. He drew out his gun and aimed it at her. "Get the fuck out of here, or we'll take your life along with your property."

Tallulah threw her head back and laughed. The sound raised the hairs on Jamie's neck and arms. "You have been warned."

She floated toward the biker and raised her hands, palms now up, green light crackling around her fingers. As she moved forward, two bikes were shoved out of her way on each side by an unseen force and clattered to the ground.

Shaking, the biker squeezed the trigger and missed. He squeezed it a second time, but it fired off into the air. What Jamie didn't see, and neither did the bikers as Tallulah floated across the lot in a green ball of fury, was the root snaking underground. As the biker pulled the trigger a third time, the root rocketed out of the dirt under him, impaling him and lifting his body in the air. The gun fell from his hand.

As one, the bikers broke and ran back into the bar, slamming the door behind them. Shit! She'd gotten distracted from her mission by Tallulah's and Ragnar's displays of power.

Breaking from cover, she sprinted along the side of the bar, skidded around the corner, and made for the far side and the back door. She hoped it was unlocked. The screen door was propped open. Stepping up to it, she tucked in against the wall and carefully reached out, grabbing the doorknob. It twisted.

She crouched down and pushed the door open a crack and poked her nose in. Seeing nothing, she slipped in and quietly closed the door behind her. Surrounded by stainless steel, she kept below the counter line of the kitchen. Looking up, she found what she was looking for. The ten-inch chef's knife felt good in her hand—balanced and light. She didn't test the edge, guessing it would be sharp enough to do the job.

"Hey, go check the back door," someone yelled.

Jamie looked around desperately and tried to find a nook to shove herself into. She wasn't there to fight the bikers. All she could do was shuffle over to the darkest corner and hunker down and make herself as small as possible. A big shadow cast darkness over the kitchen as it moved toward the kitchen door. He twisted the deadbolt, locking the door, and turned around, taking a step. But he stopped.

Backing up, he looked into the kitchen. "I thought I smelled something… Oh, it's you. Sigur is going to be happy to see you."

It was the goon that Sigur had tried to send after her when she'd been here with Travis. She still wore her gris-gris bag, but he was looking and smelling for that person, not who she actually was.

Scrambling up to a crouched fighting position, she kept her hand with the knife well hidden.

"Don't do nothing stupid, girlie. I don't want to hurt you. Well, that's not true. But Sigur wants to be the one to order it after he's had a little word with you."

"What are you doing back there, Buck?" someone called out.

"Having a little fun. Don't worry, I'll be back in a minute."

She didn't have much trouble plastering a scared expression on her face. She was scared, bordering on terrified. If the goon got ahold of her, she'd be in real trouble. So when he reached for her with a nasty sneer on his face, he didn't suspect she had claws.

Shifting her weight, she rotated and swung the knife brutally at knee height. The cutting edge caught him just below his kneecap. At first his jeans split, then blood welled up. Finally his ligaments snapped, and he collapsed with a scream of pain. He writhed around on the ground, grasping at his knee. She danced back, keeping low.

She stared at him. She should probably finish the job and kill him, but he was still dangerous even if wounded. If he got her in his grasp, he wouldn't be waiting for Sigur's word. He'd choke the life out of her... If she was lucky.

"Will someone go see what that idiot is yowling about..."

Skirting around him, she crouch-walked to the exit. As boots thudded into creaky floorboards, she waited just out of sight. The kitchen was U-shaped. The goon was wounded in the back part. She just needed the guy coming toward her to take one step past the front part of the U.

She ducked as low as she could. Jeans-clad legs moved into view and took another step and another...

Rolling forward, she came up in a crouch and slashed hard across the man's hamstrings. He collapsed, shrieking. What she hadn't anticipated was him falling backward onto her. Raising her hands to protect her head, the knife plunged into his back and turned him into dead weight, trapping her under his bleeding body.

She clamped her teeth together to keep the scream forming on her lips from escaping. Letting go of the knife, she shoved with all her wolf-enhanced might. Once the man tumbled to the side, she looked up into the baleful stare of another biker.

He snatched her hands before she could do anything and dragged her out of the kitchen.

"Let me go!" She scrambled to get purchase with her feet, but he kept tugging her off balance.

"What the fuck is going on back there?" A bearded man in a black leather vest stepped into view. "Who the fuck is that?"

"This bitch killed Jefferson. And she's probably the reason Spike is howling." He stopped dragging her.

The bearded man squatted next her. She stared back, a blend of terrified and angry. As he lowered himself to get closer a look in the dark bar, she whipped her leg up and caught him in the side of the head with the tip of her boot. He collapsed forward into her arms, breaking the hold the other biker had on her. Yanking her arms, she rolled away from the stunned biker and scrambled back toward the kitchen.

"Get her!"

Several sets of boots thudded after her. She caught sight of the handle of the knife in the back of Jefferson and tried to yank it out, but she couldn't get it to budge. Soon hands reached for her, and she screamed and flailed with her fists. A boot thudded into her ribs, and she yelped and collapsed. Hands grabbed her wrists and ankles and dragged her back into the main part of the bar. Each bump sent stabbing agony through her body. When they stretched her out, she shrieked again as her body protested. Then they slammed her to the ground, and she saw stars.

"Tie her to a chair. Fast. The witch is coming!"

Regaining some control, she thrashed and screamed. "Help!" The pain in her ribs added extra volume to her yelling.

The front door slammed open, and the green glow flooded into the bar. Jamie squinted as Tallulah came into view. Wherever her green glow touched, the chairs and tables creaked and shifted until their legs bent and snapped, forming joints.

Freed from being inanimate objects, the tables and chairs skittered across the floor and slammed into the bikers, knocking them about. The deeper into the bar Tallulah penetrated, the more furniture came to life and attacked the trespassers. Ragnar and Melinda flooded in after her, fanning out. A biker made a run for it, aiming for Ragnar.

The big redhead lunged forward, his hands spread on the handle of his hammer—one near the head and the other near the end. Slamming upward, he cracked the handle into the biker's face, knocking him back, then swung it around in a devastating arc ending at the knee of the biker. Jamie cringed at the sound of the joint popping violently. The biker howled in agony. If the biker survived, his knee would probably never be right again, even with wolf healing.

The bikers forgot about her. She scrambled away from them and the violent furniture and backed up into the corner.

Melinda, still weaponless, darted in, weaving like a boxer. When a biker tried to get past her, judging her the weakest link, she brought him up quick with a left jab to the cheek followed by a brutal, bone-cracking uppercut to the jaw. He collapsed in a heap.

The last couple of bikers fell to their knees, backing away and pleading for their lives. Ragnar walked up to one biker and menaced him with the business end of the sledgehammer. The biker froze. Melinda chose the expedient option of kicking the other one over.

Ragnar, his upper lip curled, had no mercy in his eyes. "What do you say, Melinda? Should we let them live? Or should I collapse their skulls with my hammer?"

"It's Tallulah's bar. If she wants to scrub brains out of the wood floor, that's her business. But you better ask her first."

Tallulah rose higher until her head nearly touched the exposed beams of the ceiling. "They shall have their lives so they may tell their ilk they are not welcome here. Ever." Her voice reverberated through the wood of the bar in the beautiful, eerie harmonic tone.

"What are we going to do about our dead friends?" the one next to Ragnar asked.

The green glow surged and flared. "They. Are. Mine."

The glow spread across the entire bar, and the walls and floor began shifting. Wood creaked, cracked, and groaned. Near the few dead bodies, the floorboards opened to form dark maws, and the other floorboards undulated under the bodies, conveying them into the awaiting holes.

Jamie gagged, scrabbling away from the nearest hole. When her back hit wall, she grunted and sagged to the floor, cradling her ribs.

"Now take your wounded and go, or I will feast upon the living next!" Tallulah flashed iridescently, and the whole building shivered.

Ragnar nudged the nearest biker with the head of his sledgehammer. "You better get going, hoss." The biker scrambled desperately to his feet and looked around, frozen in indecision.

"Grab your hurt Nazi-ass buddies and go!" Melinda lashed out with a weak kick to spur them on.

Despite their wounds, the bikers made surprisingly good time. Soon the roar of their bikes faded into the distance.

Tallulah slowly descended to the floor, and the green glow faded. As soon as her feet touched the ground, the glow disappeared, and she tipped to the side. Ragnar, moving quickly, caught her while Melinda slipped a chair behind her. Tallulah sagged into it and rested her elbow on the nearby table, propping her head up with a hand.

"Thanks," she whispered. "Someone get me a beer."

Ragnar caught Jamie's eyes and gestured toward the bar. Groaning, she got up and walked over gingerly. Her wolf healing had already taken the worst of the pain from her injured ribs, though they still throbbed badly. She grabbed a pint glass and stuck it under one of the beer faucets, not knowing which one to pick, and opened the faucet slowly. Foam spewed into the glass until she opened it all the way. When the foam neared the top, she closed the tap and took the glass out to Tallulah.

Raising herself off her elbow, Tallulah narrowed her eyes at the pint, which was about two-thirds foam, and chuckled weakly. Shaking her head, she sighed. "Will one of you go show her how to pour a proper pint?"

FORTY
DAX

Dax stared at the devastation of the gate and fence, then cringed as bright headlights blared in his face. They bounced hard when they hit the crater and again when they bounced out. The black van came to a skidding halt in the gravel of the compound's yard.

Men in ski masks flooded out of the van, carrying automatic weapons. One of them approached him and peeled up his ski mask.

"What the hell you doing standing around and gawking, Dax?" Boudreaux called. Behind him, gun fire broke out as men streamed out of the building.

"Sorry." Dax jogged to the side of the building and tucked in out of the way. He turned around and The Rat was right behind him. "Send in your minions."

The Rat nodded and concentrated for a second. Rats surged around their feet and poured into the plentiful cracks of the dilapidated building. Inside, men screamed and the exchange of gunfire stopped.

Stuffing his hands in his pockets and whistling a tune, The Rat strolled around to the door and pulled it open. Yelping men beat at the rats swarming over their bodies, biting and scratching. The dead bodies were ignored in favor of the ones still moving. Several rats crawled over the hostages, clustering around their hands, which were bound in thick rope. The rats' sharp teeth made quick work of the bindings. Soon the hostages stood and rubbed their wrists, looking warily at the sea of rats covering almost every inch of the concrete floor.

Between Boudreaux's buddies and the rats, not a single biker lived.

Spotting The Rat, Mississippi Pete laughed and a lop-sided grin spread across his face. "Do I have you to thank for this?"

The Rat shook his head quickly. "No"—he pointed at Dax—"he's our dance master."

Sippi looked over at Dax, his head tilted. "Wait. Aren't you the asshole from the bar who started all this?"

Dax shrugged a single shoulder. "Or you can just call me Dax."

Tomi stepped up by Dax, his arms folded across his broad chest.

"Dax it is. Thanks, pardner." Sippi clicked his tongue and winked.

Dax nodded, studiously keeping his eyes up to avoid the sight of the rats feeding on the corpses. They'd earned it, but he still didn't want to watch. "Are you all OK?"

Sippi looked at Connie and Jose and collected nods from them as they rubbed their wrists.

Off in the distance, the faint rumble of engines grew louder. A man ran into the building, panting heavily.

He skidded to a stop and turned around, facing the wall to avoid the sight of the rats. "Holy shit. What the fuck?"

"What's up?" Boudreaux asked.

"That's fucked up, man. Um…" He shook his head to collect himself. "Those bikers. They're coming."

"Shit," Dax pulled out his phone. Either Suzie had brought them here faster than planned, or it had taken them longer to get out of the sewers. Either way, he and his team were about to be ass deep in pissed-off bikers. "Boudreaux. Get your men loaded up and into position. Tomi, you and The Rat get the hostages moving."

Some of Boudreaux's people brought out loaded bags from their van and tossed them onto the ground.

Tomi grabbed one and opened it up. "This is some safety gear. I highly suggest you put it on."

Boudreaux ran out to the yard. "Someone get this van pulled around. We need to move fast."

Tomi helped everyone put on the boots, respirators, and other safety gear, then ran out to where he'd placed his gear by the opening to the sewer to put his on. The Rat directed his furry friends out of the building. Soon only Dax and the rat-chewed bodies remained inside.

Walking from wall beam to wall beam, he sped up the death of the materials holding up the structure, then went outside to attend to the three outbuildings.

The lid to the sewage entrance was down, a glove sticking out from it. The van fired up and sped out of the yard, sending gravel flying behind it. The tires screeched on the pavement as it blasted away from the compound just as the bikers rolled up.

Dax stepped into the shadows and pulled his shroud of darkness around himself. The bikers stopped outside the gate, some of them taking off after Boudreaux. Dax hoped most of them would follow the van. Boudreaux had surprises for them, though they might be wary after Sippi pipe-bombed their last attempt to chase a van.

Only about half the bikers followed Boudreaux. The other half streamed into the yard. Fortunately, Dax had picked an out-of-the-way spot. The bikers dismounted and spread out. In pairs, they entered the building using military tactics. A minute later, one of them walked out and strolled up to the one in charge standing in the middle of the yard. He was most likely Sigur.

"They're all dead and the hostages are gone."

Sigur clenched his jaw. "What happened?"

"I don't know. Looks like some of them were shot, but the others were chewed up and...eaten."

"Eaten?"

The man nodded.

"Sigur." Another biker ran up. "The sewer lid is busted out and I found this glove." He handed over the rubber glove to Sigur.

"The sewer? Get twenty men and go after them."

"Into the sewer?"

Sigur pulled a pistol out of a shoulder holster and shoved the barrel between the man's eyes. "Did I stutter? Get twenty men. And Go. Get. Them. Back. Or I'll put a bullet in your brain, and the bullets I got loaded… They'll stay, and I'll toss you into the sewer anyway. So take your pick. Alive or dead?"

"OK, OK, OK…" He stalked away and started gathering men.

With twenty going down the pipe, that'd leave about twenty in the yard. Off in the distance, gunfire broke out but faded into the distance. Dax knew he didn't have to worry about Boudreaux and his crew, but he did anyway. These bikers were nasty. Soon the twenty bikers descended into the sewer. Groans and complaints drifted across the yard, but Sigur didn't tell them to shut up. Apparently he didn't care what they said as long as they did what he told them.

The remaining bikers fanned out and looked for more clues, probably trying to get away from their boss, who looked murderously angry. Dax could practically see thunder rolling in Sigur's eyes. Drifting away from the sewage pipe, Dax had to be careful to avoid the bikers milling about, trying to look busy. Since everyone was moving deeper into the compound, Dax headed to where the gate used to be and stopped there.

The ground shook under his feet. Keeping the shroud firmly around him, he crouched low. The bikers all looked up, trying to figure out what was happening, when the lid flew up and flames erupted from the sewage pipe, shredding the concrete collar at the top. Concrete chunks fell from the sky, hitting a couple men. One large piece fell onto one of the outbuildings and, thanks to Dax's earlier handiwork, the structure collapsed into a pile of twisted metal.

When they'd set the pipe bomb booby traps on the way up the sewer pipe, they certainly hadn't anticipated or planned for that level of destruction. The fresh air moving in and mixing with the sewer gases must have made for a potent cocktail. He hoped his friends and the hostages had made it far enough away to avoid the destruction.

The bikers slowly picked themselves up from the ground and stared at the destruction and the likely deaths of twenty of their Nazi brothers. Most of them looked dumbfounded at the smoking ruin of the sewer pipe.

Standing with his hands clasped behind his back, Dax let his shroud of shadows drift away. "I believe you were looking for me." He added in a bit of the spooky harmonics of his otherworldly voice.

The bikers swung around. Sigur took a step forward but stopped. "You did this?"

Dax nodded once. "You didn't learn from your dead brothers from the local chapter?"

It had been while since he'd dug around in the darker recess of the brain of the biker's body he'd stolen when he first appeared in Red City, but the old vocabulary came back to him easily enough.

Sigur snarled at him. "You think we'll ever stop hounding you after this?"

Dax moved closer. Letting his skin disappear from his hands, he held them out wide in an encompassing gesture. "I give you one chance to leave Red City and never come back." Letting a bit of his throat fade out, he'd tapped into the dark, hollow rasp of his other voice, and cranked up the effect.

Sigur laughed. "Or what?"

"Or"—he reached out along the thin tendrils of his awareness he'd left attached to the buildings and selected one of them—"this."

It collapsed.

"Or this." He brought down the last outbuilding. "Or this."

The main building groaned, then folded in on itself. Screams competed against the shrieking of metal. A few bikers were still inside. He felt two lives wink out. Another one held on tenuously.

"Or thisss…"

Dax let his skin and flesh slowly disappear as his tattered black robe drifted into place, billowing out as the breeze caught the hem. He snapped the scythe from the aether and made sure the blade was plenty visible as he charged it with a power he hadn't tapped into in a long time.

A red glow wrapped itself around the long curve of the scythe blade and down to the tip, where it dripped onto the ground, collecting in glowing pools.

Several of the bikers stared, frozen in terror. One fainted. Sigur blinked hard, his jaw hanging open.

Extending a bony finger on his other hand, Dax pointed directly at him. "Flee, or I collect your sssoullll…"

One biker, smarter than the others, sprinted toward the huge gap where the fence had been ripped away. He tripped and fell, crawling on all fours until he got back to his feet. He jumped on a bike and kicked it to life, then tore off. Another one broke for it.

Sigur, seeing his men abandon him, lifted his pistol, swung it toward the one dashing for a motorcycle, and gunned him down, shooting him in the back twice. The man fell to the ground and didn't get up.

The rest of the bikers looked between Dax, the symbol of death, and their leader, who'd just shown he'd cut down any one of them if they betrayed him.

A shrill, hollow, gagging laughter rose from the back of the compound. Hel, twenty feet tall, faded into sight, the wind plucking at her thin hair. Reaching into the remains of the building, she ripped out the souls of the two who'd died. As the building shifted, a brief yelp sounded out and then silence signaled the third death.

The men in her hands still looked like humans, though silvery and transparent. Her laugh rose to a higher pitch as bits of spittle flew out of the rotted hole in her cheek. She crushed the souls and hurled them into the ground, where they disappeared. Holding out an empty hand, she reached toward the man Sigur had shot, but no soul emerged in her grip.

She roared. "What have you done? You think you can deny me my right?"

Dax let his awareness slip over the shot man. Sigur had killed him with bullets similar to what had been used to kill Jason. Working quickly, he found the thread and took the glowing blade of his scythe and ripped it through the body of the man, slicing him in half.

He didn't have to do it that way, but the optics were just as important as severing the tether that imprisoned the man's soul in his body. There was still a last shred of the man's life thread tying him to his corpse, but it should be weak enough for Hel to finish. Dax nodded at her.

A vicious grin spread across her face as she ripped the last tiny, frayed thread. "Who did this?"

Dax leveled his scythe at Sigur. "He has tried to rob you of your due, Mistress of Niflheim."

An angry screech erupted from her mouth as she swiped her hand through the wreckage to claim the soul inside. A huge chunk of flesh flew from the body and killed another man, so she claimed his soul as well, then stared at Sigur and took a step toward him.

Staring furiously between Dax and Hel, Sigur walked backward away from them, tucking the gun into his pocket before turning and running. The rest of his men didn't wait for permission and sprinted after him. Their motorcycles fled into the night.

Hel watched them go, then sniffed, bending over to collect the last soul. Raising it to her head, she saluted Dax and gave him a grotesque smile before fading out.

Looking around at the destruction, Dax removed the power from his scythe and let the glow blink out before stashing it in the aether. He resumed his human form and turned to check out the abandoned motorcycles of the dead. He had a handful to choose from. He pulled out his phone and texted Boudreaux to let him know the rest were available.

Reaching out to the bike he'd selected, he followed the thread back to its dead owner. Dax slumped. Hopefully it wasn't a hard pocket to find. He didn't feel like getting bloody.

A couple minutes later, he fired up the bike and rode into the night.

FORTY-ONE

DAX

Dax swung by the bar and made sure Becky and Fred had locked up properly. Everything looked fine. Checking his texts, he saw several telling him to meet at the Honky Tonk Woman. When he saw the message from Tomi saying he was OK, much of the tension in his shoulders left, and he felt the first bit of relief in a while.

The night was clear and cool. It would be a good night for a ride into the country. Straddling his stolen motorcycle, he turned it on and rumbled down the road, picking the route that would get him to Route 77 the fastest. Once he hit the open road, he relaxed and enjoyed the ride.

He hadn't counted on Hel sticking her half-rotted nose into things, but it had likely saved him a lot of pain, especially if Sigur had managed to shoot him. Being denied her souls had royally pissed her off. He hoped the assist he'd given her would earn him some favor with at least one death deity. And he'd been able to sever the soul without cutting it entirely, which should be enough to keep him off the radar of anyone looking over his shoulder.

There were probably a dozen bikers who might seriously think about finding a new way to spend their time after being chased off by the death goddess of their pantheon. They all thought they deserved places in Valhalla with the honorable dead, but apparently the Valkyries had no interest in white supremacists or criminal motorcycle gangs.

When he arrived at the Honky Tonk Woman, Boudreaux's vans—he must have brought extras to take care of the bikes left here—were parked out front, as was Suzie's car and Sippi's van and a few other cars. Some of Boudreaux's crew were loading up more bikes, so they could do whatever it was they did with vehicles of questionable origin.

"Dax!" Boudreaux waved. "Thanks for the tip. I've got a few fellas already there."

"My pleasure. Glad to make it worth your while. Oh, leave the one I came in on. I think I'm going to keep it. Probably going to need you to do some work on it though. If you know what I mean." Dax tapped a finger by his nose. It was a gesture he'd found amusing, so he used it periodically.

"I gotchu." Boudreaux extended his fist. Recognizing the offer, Dax tapped his friend's knuckles with his own.

Dax walked by a pile of destroyed motorcycles and mounted the porch. As he approached the door, it glowed green and popped open. He stared at it for a moment, wondering what was going on.

"Either out or in, but I'm not going to hold the door for you all night," Tallulah called from inside.

He strode through, careful not to bump up against the frame. Boudreaux followed him in.

Dax smiled when he saw Tomi. He wore fresh clothes, no doubt having stopped to get a shower after escaping from the sewers. The only one conspicuous by his absence was The Rat.

Tomi walked up and pulled Dax into a hug. "Glad you made it out OK."

"Me too. I thought the whole compound was going to go up when you touched off those bombs."

"So did I. We were far enough away. But it was a close thing."

"Where's The Rat?"

Tomi chuckled. "He thanked us for the invitation, but said he didn't want to venture where there were no tunnels for him. He did offer to send a rat as a representative, as long as we bought it back to him when we finished, but I declined."

Ragnar and his bandmates sat around a table, hoisting beers and renewing acquaintances after several of them had spent time as the unwilling guests of the bikers. Jamie sat with Suzie, talking animatedly.

"I know you know how to pour one, so get yourself a beer, Dax," Tallulah said from the chair she sat in.

She looked tired and had dark rings under her eyes.

"I'll grab you one and meet you at Suzie's table," Tomi said, heading toward the bar.

Dax pulled out a chair and sat across from Tallulah. "Well, you got your bar back."

She nodded wearily. "I did. Only cost me the life of a few bikers and a lot of energy."

"Are you alright?" he asked, concern spilling into his eyes.

"I'll recover." She sighed and took a drink of the brown liquid in her glass. "It's my own fault. I got complacent. Otherwise, the assholes would have never been able to kick me out of my bar in the first place. But what's done is done. I take it your end of things went well?"

"We thinned the herd a bit more. I don't know how many Boudreaux managed to take care of, but there's probably only about a dozen left, and I don't think they'll be back for a while." Dax took the beer from Tomi as he passed by to join his cousin and Jamie. "Unfortunately, Sigur got away. He might be one to keep an eye out for—he's the kind that'll hold a grudge."

"Yeah. He's a bad one. There's something dark about him."

"There's definitely something about him, though I didn't get much of a chance to check him out. I'm just hoping the motorcycle club will give up on pouring resources into Red City."

She snorted, lifting her glass to her lips. "This city? There's too much money to be had for those without any kind of morals. They'll be back, but maybe it'll take a while." She looked him over. "So you chased off a bunch of bikers all by yourself? There's definitely something about you that doesn't match the gawky loner look."

Dax shrugged. "I have my ways."

For the moment, they were on the same side, but he was in no hurry to give away all his secrets to strangers. He'd kept his identity under tight wraps for years. Now more people than he was comfortable with knew too much about him.

"Don't we all." She lifted her empty glass. "Mind slipping around the bar and fetching me a glass Macallan 18?"

Dax nodded and took her glass. He dropped it off full on the way to joining his friends. He stopped before reaching the table, wondering when he'd started considering Jamie as a friend. Since their lives had become entwined, he'd gotten used to seeing her about. She was certainly spirited, which was great as long as it didn't get her killed.

Tomi slid out a chair for him. Dax sank into it, groaning happily to take the weight off his feet. He'd had a busy night and would need a good night's...day's sleep. Except Jamie's mother was currently in his apartment. Tomi's couch it would be.

"Boss, you got to hear this." Tomi gestured toward Jamie.

They all leaned in, and she whispered her story. She needed to be extra quiet, since there were wolf shifters in the room, even if they were occupied with laughing and trading stories about their adventures over the last couple days.

Dax listened with interest. Apparently there was more to Tallulah than the tarot reading bar owner. He'd seen some of her power when they'd fled from the bar a couple nights ago but had no idea of what she was capable of. Anyone who could harness the power of the forest and turn the bar into a willing accomplice was someone to stay on the good side of.

When they asked him what had happened once everyone had left him in the compound, he gave only the barest of sketches. He needed more time to think about what Hel's interests were in his doings. Plus, he didn't want to say anything that might invite scrutiny from others in the bar. Those questions would lead to people wondering how he might know a death goddess, particularly one of her ilk.

His friends looked at him oddly, then shrugged and changed the topic of conversation. When Tallulah offered up the bunkhouse for anyone who didn't feel like driving into the city, Dax took her up on the offer. He could ride home in the morning.

He thought he'd lie awake poring over everything, but as soon as his head hit the pillow he was out. Evil bikers and death goddesses could wait for another day.

The Red City Reaper will ride again in **Death On The Rocks**!

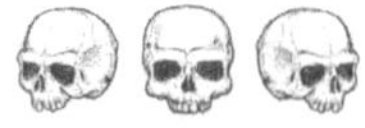

THE RED CITY REAPER RIDES AGAIN IN

DEATH ON THE ROCKS

NOTE: THIS IS AN UNEDITED AND UNPROOFED SAMPLE.

Dax revved the engine of his new motorcycle as he waited at the three-way intersection. Looking down at the map on his cell phone, we watched the dot marking the planted GPS tracker approach from his left. Soon, the hunt would begin.

Though it was just after midnight and dark and he didn't see the light from headlights behind him, he cast a quick glance at the little round mirror on the end of his handlebars. Nothing.

Revving the engine again, he reveled in the vigorous purr and vibration of the freshly tuned engine. He'd just gotten it back from Boudreaux. As usual, his friend had cleaned up the bike, repainted it, and made sure its origins weren't traceable back to the outlaw biker gang it had been stolen from.

"Almost…" Dax could hear the roar of the motorcycle approaching. He tipped his ear towards the sound. No. Motorcycles.

Stuffing the phone into his pocket, he drew a bit of the darkness in and pushed it out in a weak veil of shadow—enough for him to blend into the dark road and surrounding bushes while allowing him to see through the cloak of shadows.

Several headlights burst onto the cross-street as they came around the corner. Ahead of him in a nearby neighborhood, a few fireworks burst into the air. Patting the long, hard lump inside his jacket, he smiled, reassured. The sawed-off shotgun had been Boudreaux's idea. It would do good work in close situations and add another tool into Dax's arsenal. And on a night filled with illegal fireworks, it would be easy to hide a few extra gun shots in night. Not that anyone gave a shit about gunshots in Red City, not if they didn't want to get mixed up in something deadly that is.

He quickly counted five sets of headlights moving around on the two lane road, often crossing over the center line as they pleased. As soon as they passed, Dax set his other hand on the handlebars and waited for a moment, then slowly pulled out onto the road behind them. The veil of darkness came with him.

He gave the bikers time to notice that something had pulled onto the road behind them, but when they didn't a fear grin spread across his face. He let the veil disappear and accelerated.

The cool summer night air whipped through his shoulder length black hair, bringing with it the scent of unpowered and burnt metal. The bike handled beautifully as it ate up the distance between himself and the five wolf shifter bikers.

He didn't know if they from the local chapter of the Black Suns, a white supremacist biker gang he'd been tangling with for a few months when they tried to kill him, or if it was from the back out of out-of-towners who'd come in to reinforce them and help them exact vengeance for the destruction of the local club's bar and headquarters. The one Dax had burned down.

He reached toward the slightly open black leather jacket and the handle of the sawed-off but stopped halfway. Tonight, the first night of their counter-offensive, demanded something different. Something more personal. Something more Dax.

Grinning, he reached into the aether and found his skeletal form. Tattered and hole-filled black robes flapped out behind him, though the hood stayed in place, cover the bleached white bones of his skull. The otherworldly blue light of the flames in his eyes cast a feint glow into the night. Extending his bone hand out to the side, he brought forth his scythe. The dull metal gleamed with the light of a partial moon, occasionally reflecting the bright sparks of another explosion of fireworks.

He laughed, the sound tainted with their hollow disharmonics blew back into his face. Accelerating, he readied his scythe to strike. So far, they hadn't noticed… One of the bikers looked back, his eyes opening revealing the whites of his eyes like two small moons glowing back at Dax.

Dax left the headlights off, instead pushing out and letting the blue flames of perdition sweep up the shaft of the scythe and onto the wicked hooked blade. He tossed back his head and laughed.

Ahead of him, the biker who'd spotted him and couldn't return his eyes forward shivered involuntarily and violently. His hands wobbled on his handlebars, sending the bike swerving back and forth. The biker lost control of his bike and spilled himself into the road.

Having nearly caught up with them, Dax had to swerve into the oncoming lane, but as he swerved by the biker, he lowered his scythe. The biker rolled along the pavement and under the blade of the scythe. Dax had missed him. But with a quick shift in his wrist, he dragged the blade through the motorcycle as it spit sparks and pavement pebbles into the air around it. The hot blue flames of death cut through the metal of the motorcycle leaving a rusty gash in its wake.

After the drag of thick frame, the fuel tank felt like tin foil. The tank split, spewing gasoline into the air to turn into vapor and mix with the air. The sparks joined the party and the vapor exploded into a bright fireball.

Dax yanked his scythe free and sped away from the explosion, swerving back into the lane behind the bikers. By now, they'd discovered his presence when their friend had fallen. They cast furtive looks over their shoulders, though none of them let themselves become beguiled by the presence of what by all appearances and many powers was the Grim Reaper.

He didn't know if the bikers had been one of the few that escaped from either of the fights he'd had with them. They might not know who their enemy was, or believed those who'd told them. But they did now.

They rode as if Death himself was on their tales.

Dax continued to gain on them. Boudreaux's guys had done a great job adding more muscle to the bike. And perhaps the fact that a skeleton rode it meant it was lighter than the load being carried by the other bikes with their beefy, wolf shifter riders. Dax wasn't actually sure about his mass in this form. He snorted, chuckling to himself. Maybe he'd have to test it on a bathroom scale. If he owned one...

Stupid thoughts to have while hunting Nazi bikers...

The cluster of four bikers spread out, either by plan or circumstances. It would work better for him this way, so he didn't care why.

As he gained on the biker last in line, the gleam of moonlight glinted off the dark steel of a hand gun.

Dax started swerving side to side to make the shot harder. Though it would likely miss him in this form, he didn't want to risk it. If it hit bone, it would still hurt like the fires of hell. And if it was on of the magic bullets they'd been using, it might fuck with his form, perhaps forcing him back into his mortal shell. He didn't want to risk either possibility.

The biker had to keep looking forward to make sure he wasn't going to crash. Crack and a flash of muzzle fire. The biker missed. Dax was nearly on him. Swerving toward the left into the oncoming lane, Dax readied his scythe to strike. The biker, his gun in his right hand, couldn't twist around enough to keep his pursuer in his gunsights. He righted himself and tried to swap the gun to his left hand. But it was too late.

Dax held the scythe level as he passed the biker, the dark blade bit into the bikers flesh and sliced through his torso like a hot knife through soft butter. The biker's lower half slipped backwards and tumbled off the back of the motorbike as the last death grip of his hands kept his upper half clinging to the handlebars. The bike swerved to left, just passing behind Dax's bike.

The remaining three, using the time Dax had spent in the oncoming lane, had adjusted their grips to their left hands. Two shots flashed at him. Swerving hard, Dax corrected at the last moment as he bounded over the rumble strip on the shoulder.

Unlike the bikers, he didn't have to clumsily juggle his scythe as he balanced a speeding motorcycle. He threw the scythe into the aether, returned his right hand to the handlebars, and pulled the scythe back into this plane with his left hand.

With an angled downward arc, Dax claimed his next prize, splitting the biker in half from the left side where his neck joined his torso and out just above his right hip. Blood and guts splattered out into the wind. A haunting, blood-hungry roar of a laugh erupted from his skeletal jaw.

He was tired of playing. Tired of being their punching bag. Tired of being of visiting the hospital for near death wounds. It felt good to be on the hunt.

The two remaining riders gave up on shooting at him and focused on speed and evasion, swerving wildly around and making sure neither of them moved near the other. He didn't know if it was a coordinated attempt to force him to split his attention or the dirtbags just trying not to be the one chosen.

He chose to split the difference and ride the center line, his robe flapping behind him. He wondered if he looked as cool as the Batman on his weird tank wheel motorcycle. As he ganged slow feet on the trailing biker, he smiled at being a vigilante going after the corrupt scum of Red City.

The Black Sun Motorcycle Club made a huge mistake when they took a contract to kill Dax. At least that was the assumption. The club had been the enforcers for the city's most corrupt power brokers and the cops when wanted the violence strictly off the books.

He'd had enough of being on someone else's books, under the table or above. It was time to find out who was pulling the strings. But first, he needed to work his way through the trash to get to one collecting it.

In annoyance, he clenched his teeth and tried to get more speed from his bike as they approached a three-way intersection. The bikers, seeing their chance, split up. In a split second, Dax went after the one taking a right. He'd lagged behind his fellow biker. Sure enough, he wobbled as he cut the corner too shallowly and nearly went into the ditch on the far side of the road.

His mistake cost him life and Dax sheered through the bike and the dirtbag riding it. Waiting until he was past the rolling wreck he'd just created, he stopped when the sparking heap slid off the pavement and into the ditch next to the road.

The biker who'd taken the left was already making good his fortune, shooting away into the distance. Dax soon lost him as he took another turn into a tree-shrouded lane.

"Fuck." He thought about attempting to track him down, but decided against it. Let him tell the tale to his brothers.

As he turned his head to see if anyone was coming down the dark road he'd just come down, he saw a shadow running along the black-top. The biker who'd fallen from his bike, the one he'd missed, was sprinting down the road away from him.

Kicking his bike into motion, he turned left and gunned it. Once the biker realized that he hadn't gone unnoticed—why he hadn't tried to go through the fields or find a dark hiding place, Dax didn't know. Hell, he could have stripped off his clothes and gone wolf and disappeared where Dax couldn't chase on bike or foot—he picked up his speed, such as it was. Motorcycle boots were not renowned for their versatility as running shoes.

As Dax neared him, he checked ahead and found no cars coming toward him, so he whipped around the biker and slid to a stop, blocking the road. The biker skidded to a halt, losing his footing on the bits of loose pebbles and gravel that accumulated on poorly main-tained roads.

Casually stopping off his bike, he forced more flames into his eyes and slowly advanced on the biker as he tried to regain his foot-ing. The click and clack of his bones on asphalt staccato notes marking the biker's impending doom.

The biker abandoned his attempt to rise onto his feet and turned and tried to crawl off. Reaching out through the aether, Dax grabbed ahold of bikers life thread and tugged on it, halting the biker in place. The biker flipped over and tried to crab walk backwards, but found he couldn't move. With a whimper, he flopped onto his butt, his eyes wide with terror.

"Where is Ivar?" Dax asked, the disharmonics filling his voice.

The biker's teeth chattered as he panted and looked away.

"I. Want. Ivar." He gave a little tug on the life thread and raised his scythe a bit.

"I-I-I d-don't know." He shook his head vigorously. "I'm new to town. P-p-please."

"Give me Sigur's location."

He shook his head again, his mouth working open and closed like beached carp.

"Sigur! Now!"

"I don't know…"

Dax took a step forward, flushing more flames into his eyes and back onto the blade of his scythe.

"I swear! I'm not from their chapters. We just got to town a couple days ago. Please."

He raised his scythe to strike, debating whether to claim the biker's life or let him scurry away to report what had happened. The one who'd escaped could only witness the events. This pile of trash could carry a message.

"You've seen my works. Witnessed my power. This will be the only warning. Red City belongs to me now. The Black Suns—ALL OF THEM," he roared. "Must leave town immediately. You have twenty-four hours. After tomorrow night, I coming for you. Each and every one of you, and I won't stop until you're wiped from the face of the earth." Dax bent over, pushing his face toward the biker's bearded mug. "Do you understand me?"

The biker cringed and whimpered, but nodded aggressively. He couldn't seem to get his tongue to work as he mouth flapped open and closed. The scent of fresh urine filled the air. Standing up, Dax turned and walked back to his motorcycle, mounting it. Without a look back, he fired it to life and rode away. After he disappeared around the corner, he released the biker's life thread. He laughed. There wasn't much length to it.

The Red City Reaper will ride again in **Death On The Rocks**!

GLOSSARY

Adyeu - Goodbye
Bon chans - Good luck
Bonswa - Good afternoon/evening
Bourré - A popular card game played in the New Orleans region of Louisiana
Byenveni lakay, zanmi m - Welcome home, my friend
Cher - dear (a term of endearment)
Lwas - spirit, god, saints
Manbo - female voodoo priest
Manman - mother (a term of respect)
Misye Lanmò - Mr. Death
Mwen, oswa chat ou? - Me or your cat?

YOUR FREE BOOK IS WAITING

Death Uncaged is a Dax adventure novella that takes place between A Shot for Death and Death Orders A Double and is exclusive to the Dispatches from C. Thomas Lafollette newsletter. Please sign up for your free copy and you'll also receive a twice-monthly newsletter with news, book updates, recipes, drinks tips, and other fun stuff. Your email will never be given out, rented, or sold.

Free Copy of Death Uncaged

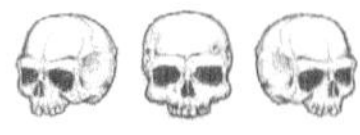

ABOUT THE AUTHOR

C. Thomas Lafollette is a student of history and a world traveler. He's dined with a Prime Minister, read poetry with Yevgeny Yevtushenko, and drank beer with monks. He's the author of the action-adventure urban fantasy series Luke Irontree & The Last Vampire War and the forthcoming Red City Reaper series. Besides reading and writing, he loves a good action movie, be it a Hollywood blockbuster or a classic Samurai flick, as well as the occasional rom-com. He lives in Portland with his partner – the devastatingly talented author Amy Cissell – his stepdaughter, and their two jerk-face cats.

facebook.com/CThomasLafollette

bookbub.com/authors/c-thomas-lafollette

amazon.com/C-Thomas-Lafollette/e/B09JMTR7W7

goodreads.com/cthomaslafollette

tiktok.com/@cthomaslafollette

instagram.com/CThomasLafollette

ALSO BY C. THOMAS LAFOLLETTE

Luke Irontree & The Last Vampire War

Book 0 - The Centurion Immortal

Book 1 - Dark Fangs Rising - March 22, 2022

Book 2 - Dark Fangs Raging - April 19, 2022

Book 3 - Dark Fangs Descending - May 17, 2022

Book 4 - Blood Empire Reborn - August 23, 2022

Book 5 - Blood Empire Avenged - September 20, 2022

Book 6 - Blood Empire Infiltrated - October 18, 2022

Book 7 - Blood Empire Burning - November 15, 2022

Book 8 - Ancient Sword Falling - March 21, 2023

Book 9 - Ancient Sword Unyielding - August 22, 2023

Book 10 - Ancient Sword Shattering - January 4, 2023

The Luke Irontree Historical Adventures

Rise of the Centurio Immortalis - April 5, 2022

Fall of the Centurio Immortalis - May 31, 2022

The Moonlight Centurion*

The Highway Centurion*

Red City Reaper - A Dark Urban Fantasy Adventure

Book 0 - Dead in Red City*

Book 1 - A Shot For Death - March 26, 2024

Book 1.5 - Death Uncaged - March 21, 2024

Book 2 - Death Orders a Double - July 23, 2024

Book 3 - Death With A Twist - November 7, 2024

Book 4 - Death On The Rocks* - February 25, 2025

Book 5 - A Fifth Of Death*

Book 6 - A Dash Of Death*

Book 7 - A Chaser of Death*

Book 8 - A Nightcap of Death *

Red City Runesmith - A Wolf Shifter Urban Fantasy*

Titles To Be Determined

*Forthcoming

Titles and release dates may be subject to change.

9 781960 766182